Advance Praise for Red Rain

"Lara Bernhardt's *Red Rain* is *Eat, Pray, Love* meets *Best Exotic Marigold Hotel*."

—ADELE HOLMES, M.D., AUTHOR OF
WINTER'S RECKONING

"A beautifully woven story of one woman's journey through overcoming grief, and the redemptive value of friendship, love, and forgiving oneself."

—C.H. ARMSTRONG, AUTHOR OF *THE
EDGE OF NOWHERE*

"A tender and touching story of a young woman's chance to rebuild her life, against the colorful backdrop of rural India."

—JULIA THOMAS, AUTHOR OF *THE
ENGLISH BOYS* AND *PENHALE WOOD*

"*Red Rain* shows the indelible power one person can make in circumstances that seem insurmountable. Unbreakable human spirit for the win!"

—SUSY SMITH, AUTHOR OF *ASYLUM*

"Lara Bernhardt delivers empathy for women's dignity when faced with a lack of modern conveniences. *Red Rain* is provocative with a title that pertains to more than the mysterious storm mentioned in the book."

—JULIA BREWER DAILY, AWARD-WINNING AUTHOR OF *NO NAMES TO BE GIVEN*

RED RAIN

A NOVEL

LARA BERNHARDT

WWW.ADMISSIONPRESS.COM

RED RAIN

Copyright © 2022 by Lara Bernhardt

All cover art copyright © 2022

paperback ISBN: 9781955836081

eBook ISBN: 9781955836098

hardcover ISBN: 9781955836104

"Helping others is the way we help ourselves."

OPRAH WINFREY

To the women and men behind the documentary "Period. End of Sentence" and The Pad Project. Thank you for shining a light on this problem and working so hard to improve the lives of our sisters around the world.

And for Arunachalam Muruganantham, the Menstrual Man, who dedicated his life to improving the lives of women and is an inspiration to us all.

Red Rain

LARA BERNHARDT

Chapter One

Olivia Montag questioned her sanity. Anyone she'd shared her plans with had questioned it for months now, some with raised eyebrows, skeptical silence, and shrugs as if to say, "If that's what you want." Some had opted for a more straightforward approach and outright bursts of, "Have you lost your mind?" But she'd brushed them all aside, reassuring them—and herself—that she knew what she was doing. She needed this. She'd read *Eat, Pray, Love*. This was how people found themselves again after their lives fell apart.

Until this moment, she'd remained stubbornly convinced she was right and completely ignored the naysayers. Excitement had buoyed her steps as she'd boarded the plane to leave, Mom giving one last look of concern as she waved goodbye. The thrill of adventure and the certainty she was embarking on a life-empowering trip of a lifetime (and perhaps delirium brought on by lack of sleep) got her through the thirty-six-hour journey, including transfers and layovers, to New Delhi, India.

She'd slept most of several days, enjoying the exotic newness of it all when awake, slowly adjusting her day/night cycle. Watching flocks of green parrots fly overhead as she soaked up tropical sun by the pool of her five-star luxury hotel, she'd breathed deeply and congratulated herself, awash in the knowledge she'd been correct. This was exactly what she'd needed. A fresh start, halfway around the globe, as far from her previous surroundings as she could possibly run.

Now, stepping off the rusted-out, rattletrap bus that brought her from Kochi, Kerala, after a long-delayed, nearly five-hour flight from New Delhi, and clutching her single bag of possessions, she entertained the notion that perhaps she should have listened to the naysayers—at least a little bit.

The crowded bus station, constructed of bare concrete and worn from years of hard use, bustled with people. Most of them appeared to be running hours behind schedule, and the spot she occupied apparently intersected with everyone's trajectories, judging by the way they all jostled and bumped her.

If her ex-husband could see her now. She could picture the look of disgust and the head shake that had become such a familiar sight the last few years. If she'd done something really stupid, he might also roll his eyes. Yes, this adventure probably would've earned an eye roll along with the head shake. And his running commentary about what smart people did and didn't do. "Smart people don't just run off to India," she could hear him say. "Especially with no idea where they're going or how they'll get there. That's just not smart." The longer she stood there, lost and wondering how long she should stand in the bus station watching more competent people en route to their destinations before seeking help, the more she thought she deserved her ex's scorn.

Someone was supposed to meet her. She'd received an email promising a ride. But the taxi drivers and rickshaw operators who pressed in on her in an ever-shrinking circle of offers to help—for a very good price—didn't get that email. *Chai wallahs* and vendors joined the throng, pushing "refreshing lassis" and snacks and handicrafts toward her.

"No," she told them. "I don't need any of this. I have a ride already."

"Yes, ma'am!" one of the taxi drivers said. "I am your ride! Come!"

"You're my ride?"

He grabbed her by the arm and gripped the handle of her bag. "Yes, madam."

She clutched the bag tighter. "I'll keep my suitcase."

"No problem, madam. I will carry." He pulled it from her hands.

"You're my ride?" she asked again as he steered her toward a waiting taxi. "They sent you to pick me up?"

"Yes, madam." He opened the taxi door and moved to take her bag to the back.

"I'll keep that." She managed to get a good grip and wrest it back into her possession, clutching it on her lap.

He closed her door and climbed into the passenger seat. "Where to, madam?"

She threw the door open and jumped out, her ex's derisive scoff of disgust echoing in her mind. *Smart people don't get duped by taxi drivers.*

He followed. "Madam! What is the problem?"

"My ride would know where I'm going. You're not my ride. No one sent you to pick me up." Even as she said it, she wondered if she was correct. What if someone had sent him to pick her up? Was she stupidly walking away from her ride? She shook her head, not sure what to do anymore.

"Yes, madam! I give you good price! Where do you wish to go?"

"I already have a ride, I think. I don't have the address—"

"Olivia?"

She spun at the sound of her name in a familiar American dialect. A man, probably still in his twenties, waved at her from across the street. Yes. She'd been correct to leave the taxi behind. She clutched her bag and waited for a break in the string of cars zipping past.

"Madam, sixty rupees!" the taxi driver insisted as she started toward the American man.

"Sixty rupees?" She raised her voice and noted with some delight that the man cringed.

"Yes, madam. I carried your bag to the taxi."

"I told you not to! I'm not giving you money for lying to me and trying to trick me into paying a fare for a ride I don't need." *Smart people wouldn't have fallen for it and gotten into the taxi.*

The driver held out a hand. "Sixty rupees, madam."

"Hi!" The American man who knew her name joined them, somehow having crossed that endless sea of traffic. "Olivia, I presume?"

"Yes! You're my ride?"

"Sure am. Shall we?"

The taxi driver didn't relent, even as they tried to cross the road.

"Sir! She owes me money."

Embarrassment warmed her cheeks. Why had she been so gullible? She never should have listened to him. "I don't owe him a thing. He's demanding sixty rupees for carrying my bag after I explicitly told him not to when he said he was my ride and tricked me into his taxi."

"Ah." The fellow American thrust a hand into his pocket and palmed the driver some coins.

"Hey!" she objected. "Don't—"

He grabbed her by the elbow and steered her away from the appeased driver, who thanked them profusely. "It's not even a dollar. Those rupees will feed his children."

"But he lied!"

"Surely you're aware of the severe poverty some of the people in this country grapple with. And the number who go hungry every day. Haven't you seen it?"

She squirmed, remembering the squalor she'd seen from the bus windows on the way here. How she'd stared, horror-struck at the bare-chested women scrubbing clothing against rocks in a putrid, gray-brown river. She'd even seen a dead carcass float by at one point. "I've only been here three days. I didn't leave the hotel much."

Still clutching her elbow, he dashed across the street, hopping between oncoming cars, the drivers blowing horns. She sucked in a breath, thinking her ex-husband would love to hear how she'd idiotically dashed in front of on-coming traffic.

But the man guided her safely across. She let out the breath she'd been holding.

"Well, trust me on this. Besides, it's my dollar and I can help feed that man's kids if I want to." He opened the door to an ancient car and gestured her in.

Irritation percolated and a witty barb fought its way to her lips. But seeing the bright smile on his face, she bit the harsh words back. "I don't want his kids to go hungry, obviously." She settled in while he climbed into the driver's seat and maneuvered into traffic.

"The jet lag sucks, doesn't it?" he asked as the rattling car shuddered to a stop at an intersection.

"It's awful. I slept so hard on the bus, I'm lucky I didn't sleep right through my stop."

"I hear that. It's the middle of the night back home. Your body is running on its internal clock. Give it a couple weeks to reset."

He threw another cute little grin at her. She glanced at his left hand. No ring. Hopefully he wasn't getting any ideas. Dating was not on her agenda. At all. Her thumb ran over the ring finger of her left hand, still disturbed by the bare skin no longer covered by a gold band.

"I've been emailing someone named Vanya," she said. "I thought she would pick me up."

"Ms. Vanya, yes! She oversees our housing complex, but she can't drive. She'll be waiting for you there though. And she'll help you settle in."

"Why can't she drive?"

"Not many women drive in India. The housing complex has this car to use but can't afford a staff driver. They operate primarily with volunteers, like us. We're able to borrow it whenever we like." Another grin.

He seemed to be making a serious effort to connect. She didn't come to India to connect with a guy. And if he got to know her, he wouldn't be interested anyway.

"How long did it take you to get used to driving on the wrong side of the road? It seems a little daunting." She hadn't thought about how she would get around here.

He waved a hand. "It's a little weird, but I got it. No worries. You can just hop in a rickshaw once you've learned your way around and feel more comfortable. If you'd prefer."

She stared out the window at the crowds of people, congested streets thick with battered vehicles, air heavy with smog. Doubt formed a hard knot in her stomach, congealing with disappointment and fear. "That might take a while."

"You'll adjust. Trust me. Until then, holler if you need anything at all. I'm glad to help. Although, rule of thumb is you don't want to go out alone anyway. At least take one of the other female teachers with you."

Whoa. That didn't sound good. Everything she'd read indicated India was safe. "Why?"

"Women are better off together or accompanied by a man. Didn't anyone tell you that?"

"I thought India was safe."

"It is safe. But you want to take certain precautions. Just like you would anywhere. Even back home, ya know?"

She remembered her mom asking repeatedly, though gently, *"Are you sure this is a good idea, sweetie?"* She'd been so sure it was, but maybe she hadn't thought through it well enough. Maybe she hadn't done enough research. *Smart people would know what they were getting themselves into.* She wanted to tell her ex-husband's residual presence, still lodged firmly in her brain, to shut it. The divorce was finalized, but even halfway around the world she couldn't leave him behind.

The car wound through the streets. Outside the massive, congested cities of India, the countryside unfurled into open fields, stretching to the horizon, dotted with smaller communities. They turned down several more streets, each narrower and bumpier than the last, until they pulled off the road and parked in front of a crumbling concrete wall.

"Here we are," he said.

"Here we are?" she asked, scrutinizing his face for signs of a joke.

He hopped out and opened her door. "This is it."

Ignoring his offered hand, she stepped out, clutching her bag, searching for signs of a guest house.

He led the way to a rusted gate, which allowed passage through the concrete wall, opened it, and gestured her through.

The concrete walls enclosed a rather large compound. What she presumed to be the school buildings formed a U directly in front of her and to the sides. The center courtyard sat quiet and empty. She tried to envision it full of squealing, playing children, but saw only dirt and dismally worn buildings. Though the buildings had been painted white, gray streaks dripped down the concrete structures and mud splatters ringed the bases. She hovered in the gateway, not sure she wanted to go inside.

The man—had he shared his name?—latched the gate and encouraged her. "That's the school. The housing is back this way. Come on. Ms. Vanya will be excited to meet you."

She followed him along a worn dirt path. What choice did she have? This would be her home for the next six months. Tropical trees surrounded the school on all sides, fronds and leaves waving above the roofline as if greeting her. "Welcome to the Jungle" ran through her mind. Better than her ex-husband's contempt.

The path wound to another, smaller compound with another smaller courtyard. These buildings had been painted a pale yellow, though the blistering heat of the summer and the annual monsoons appeared to have taken their toll. Faded, streaked, and dingy, the watery color struck her as an ironic mockery. Nothing bright or sunny anywhere. Her mood diminished another notch.

Rock and concrete planters dotted the courtyard. But pieces had chipped off and fallen away and no flowers burst forth with frothy petals to cheer passersby. Nothing but bare dirt greeted her, mutely witnessing her somber march to her new home.

"So that building"—he pointed to the right—"is the women's housing. And this one is the guys' housing plus the dining hall. We all share meals together, which is nice. We'll see each other every day. Come on. Ms. Vanya is always in the kitchen."

The door seemed ready to fall off its hinges when he pulled the handle. It scraped along a well-worn rut in the concrete. Stairs rose up directly in front of the entryway. A large room with tables and chairs sat to her left.

"The stairs lead up to the guys' rooms. And no girls allowed so don't get any ideas."

She knew severe jet lag and shock currently skewed her emotions, but this guy really knew how to push her buttons. Who said things like that? And at their age? They may have logged a similar number of years, but she felt ages older than he acted. She forced her facial features into a bland countenance, willing her eyebrows to relax and her mouth to smile. "What was your name?"

"Oh, sorry!" He held out a hand. "I'm Chris."

She shook to be polite. "Thank you for the ride, Chris. I promise I will not attempt to sneak into the men's housing." *Especially not into your room.*

"I'm just kiddin' ya. You probably have a boyfriend back home anyway."

She ignored the blatant fishing and looked around the dining hall. Peeling paint, worn table and chairs. Decaying, like the exterior of the buildings. Like so much of the country she'd seen so far. Her research had not prepared her for this. She doubted any amount of research could have.

Remembering the taxi driver desperate for a dollar's worth of rupees, she wished she'd handed him something. And was glad Chris had.

An older, heavyset woman bustled from a door on the opposite side of the dining hall. "Hello, dear! Is this her, Chris?"

"Yes, ma'am. Olivia, this is Ms. Vanya."

The woman wiped the flour from her hands on an apron and pushed gray strands of hair that had escaped the long braid hanging down her back behind an ear. "So happy to meet you! I will take you to your room."

"See you tonight at dinner!" Chris called after them.

"Yes, you will take your meals here every day," Ms. Vanya told her as she trundled out the door.

Olivia adjusted the grip on her suitcase and fell in step beside her. The glaring sun blinded her as they crossed the dry, cooked dirt and cracked concrete of the courtyard to the women's housing. A plume of smoke twisted skyward from a pile of smoldering garbage on the side of the building, joining hundreds of similar plumes and the exhaust from millions of vehicles to form a perpetual haze of grimy pollution that blanketed the country. Ms. Vanya opened the outer door of the building and waddled down the hall.

Oppressive heat slammed against her before her eyes could adjust to the dim lighting. She opened her eyes wide and blinked rapidly, trying to expedite pupil dilation.

Dilation. The word stopped her where she stood.

Nine centimeters dilated! Almost there. Push! Push!

In the vivid memory—were daymares a thing?—a hand squeezed hers and she squeezed back as she labored through the most intense, excruciating pain she'd ever experienced. Physically. Worse pain had awaited her, but she didn't know it then and remained blissfully unaware, focused on the impending birth. The coming pain had not been physical, but it had torn her apart and left her scarred as nothing else could.

"Miss Olivia?" Ms. Vanya's voice pulled her back to the present.

Olivia shook off her stupor and rubbed at her eyes, drying the tears before they could wet her cheeks. "Sorry. My eyes are slow to adjust," she lied.

"Not to worry. This is your room." Ms. Vanya's brilliant smile couldn't be missed, regardless of dim light and watery eyes.

She stepped into the doorway and swept her eyes over the room, fighting to keep the shock trembling through her from showing on her face. "This is great," she lied again.

Ms. Vanya crossed the room to the window, where an air conditioning unit perched, and pressed a button. The unit whirred to life, and Ms. Vanya raised her voice to be heard over the noise. "It is easy to use. This switch turns it on, and this dial controls the temperature. Here is your key. I will let you settle. I will prepare dinner. See you then."

She nodded, murmured thanks, and closed the door before turning to face the room she would call home for the next six months. A sagging twin mattress rested on a rudimentary metal frame in one corner, its counterpart against the opposite wall. Would she share this room with someone else? No one had mentioned the possibility of a roommate.

She dropped her lone bag on the bed farthest from the door and nearest the air conditioning unit. Standing directly in front of the vents, she lifted her limp ponytail and allowed the cool air to blow across the rivulets of sweat dripping from her neck. That was such a welcome relief, she shed her shirt to expose her damp back. Her skin prickled at the sudden change.

Faded, threadbare carpet sort of cushioned her feet as she crossed the room to see the bathroom. She passed a rod to hang clothes on inside an indention in the wall—a makeshift closet with no door. A little dresser sat against the wall, presumably to store clothing.

In the tiny bare-concrete bathroom, she discovered a toilet (blessedly Western style), a sink, and a showerhead above an open drain in the cement floor. A green bucket rested in one corner. That was it. Not a single cabinet or shelf. Nothing to store toiletries on.

She turned and plodded across the room. She sat on the bed, shoved her bag to the floor, and flopped onto her back.

The heavy whir of the window unit fighting to overcome the heat outside wasn't enough noise to drown out the tiny, high-pitched buzzing of a mosquito in her ear.

Mosquito. Hadn't she read something about malaria somewhere? Was it rampant here? This time of year? She couldn't remember the specifics.

She slapped the side of her head. Crumpled legs and wings along with a smear of blood confirmed she'd killed the potentially diseased little beast.

She fell backward again. She wasn't a diva. God knew she'd grown up with only the barest basics. Mom had kept the roof over their heads and food on the table—it wasn't a huge house in the best neighborhood and the food was simple and minimal. But they had a home and never went hungry. She never had name-brand clothes and often what she did have was acquired at a second-hand store or discovered on clearance. No gadgets or devices or vacations or game systems. She was accustomed to going without.

Her ex hadn't been one for lavish purchases either. He always asked her, "Do we really need that?" whenever she felt tempted to buy something. If she'd spotted a pair of shoes she adored and the soles weren't falling off her current shoes, she really couldn't justify the expense. Her mom called him a miser, and coming from the self-dubbed Clearance Queen, that was saying something. "Skimping and stretching due to necessity is one thing," Mom told her. "Making you do without so he can pad his bank account for no apparent reason is completely different." Still, they'd lived comfortably, their salaries affording a perfectly fine life.

She didn't need much. She'd learned to manage on a shoestring budget, selecting "gently worn" furniture and clothing at second-hand shops. She hadn't expected anything lavish or extravagant from India. But she hadn't expected this either. What exactly had she expected? Looking back, she realized she really hadn't thought much at all once she'd seen the opportunity to volunteer and applied for the program. The notice she'd been accepted had been so exciting—distracting, a welcome diversion. Preparing to leave on her adventure had likewise kept her mind occupied. And she'd been in dire need of something else to focus her attention on. Otherwise, she feared she would have sunk into a debilitating depression and never recovered. She'd been well on her way. Friends had tried to reach out. Mom encouraged her to find a new normal. Instead, she'd flown to India.

What had she gotten herself into?

Chapter Two

Olivia heard the buzz of conversation from the dining room even before she opened the door leading into the building. She stopped, hand on the door. Maybe she should just go back to her room. She'd almost stayed there, unsure she could handle meeting new people in her current state. But she remembered reading advice somewhere to adapt as quickly as possible, forcing yourself to try to stay awake during the day and stay in bed at night, even when you found yourself lying in the dark unable to sleep. It also meant eating meals on this side of the Earth's schedule.

She took a deep breath and opened the door. Turning the corner into the dining room, she marveled at the change several exuberant personalities could bring to a space.

"Hey!" Chris called, waving her in to join them. "I saved a seat for you."

Besides Chris, four young women sat at the table, which was only half full. She didn't need a saved seat but welcomed his familiar face in the roomful of strangers.

The four women stood, all of them smiling.

"Hey!"

"Welcome!"

"Nice to meet you."

"Another woman! Five to one, Chris."

Chris laughed. "I'm strangely okay with this." He pulled back a chair and motioned for her to sit.

Once they all situated in their places, the woman directly beside her held out a hand. "I'm Watisha. But everyone calls me Tisha. Please do."

Chris introduced her rapid-fire to the three women sitting across the table from them. "That's Melanie, Aubra, and Delilah."

They all greeted her with a wave. She was pretty sure she heard a British accent from one of them when she walked in.

"And then there were six," one of the women said in a deep south drawl.

Which one was she?

Chris laughed. He seemed to do that a lot. "Delilah was a lit major, so get used to it now. She always has some book quote ready for any situation. Although, I'll point out in *Ten Little Indians*, the count decreased, not increased. Six out of ten."

Delilah pulled a face at him. Delilah. The bookworm with a southern twang. Not the British one. They all stared at her.

"I'm not very quick with names. I hope there won't be a test later."

The table erupted in laughter. At least everyone seemed easygoing and friendly. She felt her nerves calm a bit. Working with a nice group of like-minded people would help the six months pass more quickly than working with a group of jerks.

One of the girls—the one with the British accent!—replied, "No, we give you a week to study before we make you sit the exam."

"That's Aubra for you," Chris said. "Always gives plenty of time to study."

Aubra. The British one. Aubra. She'd get these names down yet.

"The kids' Indian names will give you more trouble, I bet," Melanie said. "Just hang on and don't get frustrated. Like Aubra said, about a week in, you'll have it down."

"What did you major in?" Tisha asked.

"I have a master's degree in English, actually," she said.

"A Master of English! You'll have a leg up on us. Have you taught before? Certified teacher?"

She shook her head. "I teach English at community colleges, but . . . well, things changed. Life kind of took an unexpected turn and I thought I could use a change of scenery. So here I am." *Unexpected turn.* Understatement of the year. Her mom had pleaded with her to try to maintain normalcy, to apply for the job she'd worked so hard to qualify for. Nothing seemed worth it anymore though. She'd clicked the link to apply for the full-time English faculty position and broke down crying. Nothing felt right. That was her old life, before. Besides, Scott's skeptical voice continued to ask, *"Do you really think you can handle a full-time job?"* even though he was gone from her life.

But these people didn't need to hear her sob story. And the last thing she wanted to do was break down crying in front of a group of strangers. She'd be working with them and didn't need them to file her as a crazy woman right off the bat.

"You've only taught college-level students? Not even high school?"

"That's right."

She saw the glances they shared. New dread settled over her. Scott's residual presence chimed in. *Do you really think you can handle teaching? You don't have any experience.*

"Well, this will be different to say the least."

Concern must have shown on her face. Chris said, "Don't worry. We'll all be there, and the kids are eager to learn. You'll get the hang of it."

The kitchen door swung open, and Ms. Vanya appeared carrying a platter in her hands.

"Ohhh, biryani." Chris grinned at her. "She must be celebrating your arrival. This is one of my favorites."

Cauliflower and potatoes, dotted with cumin seeds and vivid yellow with turmeric, followed. Next came a huge dish of fluorescent-yellow lentil soup, which she'd learned was called *dal*. And finally, a plate stacked with *chapatis*—flat, round breads which resembled tortillas.

Tisha leaned over. "She makes those chapatis herself from scratch every night."

She watched the others scoop servings onto their plates and pass the communal dishes along. Mimicking them, she added a spoonful of everything to her own plate, even when she didn't think she would much care for it, like the cauliflower and potatoes. Not a fan of cauliflower, she started to pass on it but didn't want to be rude. Besides, she didn't see any additional options rounding the table. Her growling stomach prompted her to take two scoops.

"Looks delicious, doesn't it?" Aubra asked. "Well, tuck in."

The others dove into their plates. She stared down at hers—flat bread, thick, fluorescent-yellow soup, a rice dish, and the potatoes with cauliflower. She had eaten at Indian restaurants before. Usually tandoori chicken jumped out at her among all the other meat entrees, though she'd sampled many, particularly at buffets. But no such dish circled the table.

"There's no meat?" she asked.

Chris made a big show of chewing and swallowing his current bite, hand over his mouth. "Very rarely. We can request it, but you'll probably be happier if you just go vegetarian during your stay. Ms. Vanya can get meat, but it's expensive and less readily available."

"And hard to store," Tisha added. "Since electricity is so sporadic and goes out pretty regularly."

"It does?" she asked. She hadn't read anything about that. How had she missed so much important information? Was she so blinded by excitement she hadn't paid any attention?

"Oh, yeah." Melanie wrinkled her nose and shuddered a bit. "Without consistent refrigeration, Ms. Vanya has to buy the chicken alive and slaughter it out back. I accidentally happened onto that once. I'll never eat chicken again."

Delilah nodded. "I've adjusted too. I don't miss it. But you know, Ms. Vanya was surprised when we reacted so squeamishly to her 'preparing the chicken' so I explained how we buy meat back home—how it's butchered in a factory and packaged before going to the grocery store. Ms. Vanya practically turned green she was so repulsed by the idea that we would buy and eat something we hadn't prepared ourselves. Who slaughtered it? How old is it? Is it safe to eat? Completely different opinions on the matter."

"Speaking of the market," Tisha said, "I remember how empty and dismal my room was when I first moved in. We need to take you shopping."

"Yes!" Melanie clapped. "We'll show you all around and get you set up!"

"I need a few things anyway," Aubra agreed, "but I'd go along regardless. Settling in is a challenge. We'll help you. Can you go with us, Chris?"

"Of course. I'm happy to help out. We want you ready and in top shape Monday morning when you meet your kids."

A guy who wanted to go shopping? She found that hard to believe. Scott had always behaved as though she'd suggested they amputate a foot anytime she proposed a shopping excursion. And then he only accompanied her to keep an eye on what she bought and how much she spent. She'd prefer not to have such a stifling presence along. "It's okay. We can handle the shopping. Aubra, you can drive us, right?"

The other girls exchanged glances.

"Of course I can, but it's really much better if Chris drives," Aubra said.

"Girl, didn't you study up at all?" Tisha asked. "You're not in America anymore."

"Well, we won't be going alone. We'll be in a group. A group of women is okay, right?"

"We'd be okay together," Delilah agreed. "But much better with a guy chaperoning us."

"Chaperoning? Are you serious?" The last thing she wanted right now was to rely on any guy for any reason.

"Only when you go outside the school," Chris said. "It's just a safety precaution. You know, better safe than sorry and all that."

Aubra frowned. "It's more than that. A woman driving, particularly in a small town like this, is such an unusual sight, we would attract a lot of unwanted attention. We already stick out like sore thumbs. Trust me. You don't want that."

"What kind of attention? What do you mean?"

"This culture doesn't accept women drivers. People would shout at us. Other drivers would be aggressive and maybe even try to run us off the road. If a woman drives the speed limit, she's assumed to be timid and uncomfortable behind the wheel. If she speeds, she's reckless and doesn't know how to handle a vehicle or follow rules. It's best if Chris takes us."

She stared at them, dumbfounded, waiting for someone to say, "Just kidding!" and the entire group to burst out laughing at the joke. But not a hint of amusement glimmered in a single eye. They were completely serious. She didn't expect to drive during the course of her stay. She'd read how easily one could find a taxi or, even more economically, an autorickshaw (*tuk-tuk*, as they were called in the country—she'd learned that at least). Walking around alone as a single woman was highly discouraged, she got that. But no female drivers? Something about that shocked her, illuminating yet another way how completely unprepared for this trip she'd been.

"I didn't read anything like that. I did research. I *did* try to prepare—"

"We learned the hard way," Aubra said. "I tried to drive us once. Never again. I've never felt so humiliated in my life."

"But I'm here," Chris said. "And I worked hard to learn to drive on the wrong side of the road—"

"You mean you finally learned to drive properly," Aubra corrected him.

"Ummm, we invented the automobile, so we definitely drive the right way," Chris said. "We got to make the rules since we made the first car. Not sure why you Brits 'mucked it up,' as you say."

Aubra's jaw tightened, and her eyes narrowed. Olivia sensed this was no longer all in good fun.

Tisha patted her hand. "It's okay. I promise. The good things here in India totally outweigh the adjustments we need to make."

The others nodded.

"You'll see."

"Wait till you meet the kids! They're amazing."

She nodded, trying hard to quell the anxiety gnawing at her stomach. She'd eaten every bite from her plate. The food sat heavily, hunger replaced by unease.

When the others cleared their dishes, she followed suit. Ms. Vanya took away the communal dishes and platters.

Delilah blew out the candles. "'To bed. To bed. To bed.'"

"Don't quote Lady M!" Aubra looked shocked. "That's bad luck."

"Only in a theatre," Delilah corrected her.

"It's rather early for bed, though," Chris said. "You guys want to hang out? Olivia?"

"No, thank you. I think I'll go back to my room." Although what she would do there, she had no idea.

"At least come to my room for some chocolate," Aubra insisted.

"Oh, yeah!" Tisha said. "Her parents send her Cadbury chocolates from England. Come have some!"

"No fair!" Chris said. "I can't go over to your place."

"You've had plenty!" Aubra said. "I'll bring you some tomorrow. Tonight is all about Olivia."

"Fair enough," he conceded. "I'll see you tomorrow at break-fast before we shop."

Olivia allowed herself to be pulled across the courtyard by the other girls, enveloped by a horrible sense that she'd made a terrible mistake.

Chapter Three

Olivia's eyes ached. Her head pounded. Her exhausted body and psyche cried out for rest. But she couldn't sleep. Her circadian rhythm believed whole-heartedly that it was the middle of the afternoon, not the middle of the night.

She heaved herself to a sitting position and groaned. After extracting a notebook from her suitcase, she rummaged through her purse for a pen. She stared at the blank page, then wrote:

Mom,

I've discovered I hate jet lag. I suspect you would too. So stop feeling so guilty we never went on vacations when I was growing up. Turns out traveling sucks. Haha!

She paused, then added, *But I'm glad I came! Really,* lest her mom worry too much. She would worry anyway. Poor Mom. Maybe she should have taken into consideration that Mom's life had turned upside-down too. She wasn't the only one torn apart. And Mom had been through more than enough, that was for sure. But unlike her, Mom was strong, and she would muddle through. Mom would never upend her life and run away halfway around the world.

What am I doing here? She didn't know anything about

teaching children, hadn't learned enough about the culture, and had no business using this as an excuse to run from her problems instead of facing them. Tears pricked her eyes as a rush of home-sickness sneaked up and pounced on her unexpectedly. Last week she couldn't wait to get away, today she wanted to be home. What a mess she was. Too late. She'd simply have to press on, get through the next six months, and go home. Maybe by then she'd have cleared her head and put enough time and distance between things that she could figure out how to start over.

Her left thumb drifted to her ring finger, attempting to twirl the rings no longer there. The bare finger remained a shock. She'd never realized how much she used to fiddle absently with her wedding rings until they were gone.

She'd struggled with taking them off. The divorce hadn't been her idea. God no, it hadn't remotely crossed her mind. Sure, Scott had been remote and withdrawn, but everyone dealt with tragedy in their own way. When he looked her in the eye and said, "Smart people don't stay together when it just isn't working anymore," the sentence had devastated her. And continued to rip her heart out every time she remembered the moment—the look on his face, the disgust and blame in his eyes, the total defeat in his tone. Smart people didn't ruin their marriages like she had.

She'd nodded and agreed. What else could she do? She couldn't beg him to stay with her. He didn't want her anymore, and she had no interest in making someone miserable. But taking the rings off when it was final—that churned up some difficult emotions. They'd promised—vowed—to stay together forever. And failed. *She* had failed, more precisely. Her bare finger broadcast her failure every time she saw it or rubbed her thumb idly against it, followed by the momentary burst of panic—*Where's my ring?* Wearing it would be a lie. She wasn't married anymore. But not wearing it somehow felt like a lie too. She wasn't the same person she'd been before she married. She didn't feel single and free. She felt lost.

She set aside the notebook and stood, stretching. She paced

the room yet had nowhere to go in the middle of the night. Rummaging through her suitcase, she cursed herself for not bringing a book. She'd gotten rid of nearly all her possessions when she'd moved. In fact, most everything she owned now fit into this suitcase. How had her life come to this?

She and Scott had sold the home they'd bought, lived in, decorated and filled with memories, planned a future in. They got lucky—the neighborhood home values had skyrocketed in the years they'd lived in it. They made money off the sale, a decent amount even after they divided it in half. They'd split their joint savings in half as well. Turned out Scott had a savings account in his name only that she hadn't even known about but her lawyer had discovered. Scott had amassed quite a sum and had been forced to give her half, leaving her with a chunk of money at her disposal for the first time in her life—and no desire to do anything with it. Buy a house? For herself? And rattle around the empty thing listening to it echo her failure and loss with every passing moment?

Her mom had propped her up as much as possible. And when Mom extended the invitation to move back in with her, she'd jumped at it. When she was growing up, they'd lived just the two of them. Falling back into the old routine had sounded easy. Except it wasn't easy. She wasn't the same.

Mom had commented on how changed she was. Gently, but several times. After she'd married, obviously she saw less of her mom. Which was only normal. People change and mature during college and after getting married. Scott didn't get along with his parents at all and didn't want to spend holidays with them or go visit or really even talk to them on the phone. At first, she'd secretly been glad she didn't have to split holidays and could continue planning them to include her mother who would be left all alone without her. But then Scott had started discouraging her from seeing Mom, though he didn't call it that. *"I'm not discouraging you. I'm just pointing out it isn't healthy for a grown woman to see so much of her mother. Smart people don't stay dependent on their parents. But if you feel like you have to see her . . ."*

He always trailed off like that to let her draw her own conclusion and make her own decision. But what did it say about a grown, married woman who remained so close to her mom? That left her conflicted. If she ignored him and continued with her plans, she was needy and dependent. Which she must be. Because she'd missed her mother horribly when she started going months and months without seeing her. How did Scott do it? How did he go without seeing his parents? He never shared stories of abuse or neglect or admitted to any falling out. In fact, he lifted a skeptical eyebrow at her when she'd probed for details. "I'm a normal, healthy adult who doesn't need to be embroiled in my parents' business all the time. And I don't need their constant affirmation to make decisions."

That last comment, of course, was a barb at her struggle to make decisions.

So, yes, she'd moved back in with her mother, feeling slightly guilty, since a stronger person wouldn't need that. Scott would probably roll his eyes and shake his head, and say something like, "I knew it. I could've predicted that." But Mom kept saying she was different, that she'd changed. "You're not my Liv anymore, full of life and ready to take on the world." Olivia frowned at that, utterly confused by the comment. Ready to take on the world? What was Mom talking about? And then Mom gave her examples: how at the age of eight, she had jumped in front of her dad when he was on a bender, fists up, ready to protect her mother if necessary; how she'd stood up to school bullies as a child, protecting other children being picked on during recess; how she'd led a community initiative to raise funds for homeless.

Her mother's reminders sparked memories. She'd all but forgotten those moments in her life. It was like remembering a dream or hearing stories about another person. What had happened to her?

But remembering didn't result in a sudden, miraculous transformation back to the person she'd been before marriage, before tragedy, before divorce. Had she ever really been that person? Or was that simply who Mom wished her daughter to be? Maybe that was why Scott wanted her to spend less time with Mom— Mom filled her head with dreams she could never live up to.

Rudderless, anchorless, no wind in her sails, she merely drifted. Until she packed a bag and flew to India, certain teaching English to impoverished children would be the solution she needed.

What had she done? She would be in the exact same place when she returned home. She'd only delayed facing the truth— she had no idea who she was anymore, what her purpose was, what her future would hold.

She'd known specific things, been absolutely certain that she would get married, earn her master's degree, teach English for a while, have children, live happily ever after with her husband, watching their children flourish too. She got such a good start. And then failed in the most horrific way. Now that things had fallen apart, the needle playing the record of her life hit a scratch —and skipped and skipped and skipped, unable to move on.

Her mom knew how broken she felt, possibly even understood. Except Mom had sought divorce, fought for it, to end the narcissistic, alcoholic, abusive tyranny her father had terrorized them both with. No amount of pleading, cajoling, or crying could appease him, particularly when he'd drunk himself into a good rage. As young as she'd been, she vividly remembered, those moments of sheer terror burned indelibly in her mind.

She saw her mom for the superhero she was—wedging herself between her enraged husband and young daughter, standing up to him, finally working up the courage to demand a divorce, and then never backing down, never once allowing his drunken pleas to sway her into allowing his return or retracting the divorce proceedings. She'd ignored the gossip and whispers at church too, where divorce was considered the ultimate failure. She'd held her head high as mutual friends and acquaintances questioned her choice, wondered how someone who appeared to be such a devoted and kind man in public could be facing divorce. In retrospect, Olivia wondered how none of them recognized the textbook signs of an alcoholic, admittedly one amazingly adept at lying and hiding his problem.

All the while, Mom stood between them, shielding Olivia from her dad—her sperm donor as she thought of him. And once the divorce was final, he disappeared from her life completely, never arranging for visitation, never once checking on her, never contributing more than the bare minimum of child support garnished from his wages—when he resurfaced long enough to actually hold a job.

Mom seemed to have exhausted all her fight getting away from him though, never once attempting to hunt him down and collect back child support. "I would rather work several jobs and barely scrape by than go back to him with my hand out," she'd said.

No matter how Olivia argued it wasn't charity, it was money he owed them and making him pay it wasn't admitting defeat, Mom turned a deaf ear.

"Severing all ties carried a cost," Mom told her finally. "I knew it would. But, sweetie, it also carried a huge reward. The relief of knowing I never have to see that man's face again or depend on him for one blasted cent is worth it. Knowing he can never hurt you again—" She broke off, trying to hide the tears welling in her eyes. "Knowing that would've been enough in and of itself."

She never pushed Mom again, no matter how badly she longed for nicer clothes, brand-name shoes, and the latest trendy gadgets—a cellphone as she got older and all her friends had them.

And no matter how badly she'd wanted to go to the mother-daughter craft each month at a local sewing store. Her best friend Julia went with her mom the second Saturday of every month. Olivia asked Mom if they could go too. Mom thought it sounded like great fun, the two of them sewing the same craft, spending Saturday morning together. But when she called Julia's mom and learned registration cost twenty dollars each, not twenty dollars per mother and daughter, which would've been strain enough, she said she'd think about it and went to her room and cried for twenty minutes, thinking Olivia couldn't hear.

Olivia hated her dad in that moment more than ever before, knowing child support could have eased the constant burden on her mother and allowed them to occasionally afford something fun. His last words to her had echoed in her mind: *"She wants the divorce, she can deal with it. She'll never make it without me. She'll be sorry."*

But Julia's mom called and told Mom she'd found a coupon to The Sewin' Place Saturday craft—one free registration with two paid. Mom looked so relieved and gave permission for them to pick her up and take her. Julia's mom had used the right word —coupon—and Mom never questioned it. After all, coupons almost equated to cash in Mom's world. Back then, she'd diligently clipped coupons anywhere she found them and thrust fistfuls of them to the checker at the grocery store each week, eyes glowing as the total decreased with each scanned scrap of paper.

Olivia hadn't questioned it either, until she watched Julia's mom hand over three twenty-dollar bills and no coupon at The Sewin' Place. Julia's mom had winked at her and said, "Don't tell your mom, okay? There will be a coupon every month." She'd nodded and kept the secret, treasuring the time, the fun, and the matching crafts she and Julia made together and often wore to school the following week to show off—felt scarves embroidered with their initials and later matching hats delighted her mom too, as that meant one less thing she needed to buy for cold weather.

"You guys make great things!" Mom gushed. "Really generous of The Sewin' Place to offer a coupon like that."

She'd held her breath, afraid Mom might catch on, but no. Mom was smart, but also sweet and trusting and never expected anyone would tell her anything that wasn't true. Probably a huge reason she'd fallen victim to an alcoholic like Dad—he'd hidden it well and lied to cover any suspicions before they'd married. After, she'd learned the truth and suffered years of consequences. Once she'd decided to change that, Mom worked hard, went without, and never looked back. Olivia saw her for the fighter she was.

She wished she'd lived up to the Liv that Mom remembered, someone strong, ready to take on the world. Scott had seen through her, seen her failings and weaknesses. Mostly she'd listened to his suggestions and critiques and tried to improve herself. All those years of realizing he was right, of letting him have his way and make the important decisions, had been for nothing. The one time she'd stood up to him and refused to do things his way, look what had happened. She'd destroyed her marriage. Completely. She should have listened to him.

She flopped onto the bed and dropped her head in her hands. She wasn't good enough. She wasn't strong enough.

She wasn't anything.

Chapter Four

Olivia sat in the front seat of the little car, Chris behind the wheel, while Melanie, Delilah, Tisha, and Aubra squeezed into a backseat meant to comfortably seat two.

"Is this legal?" she asked, picturing the six of them pulled over, Chris being chastised and handed a ticket for driving an overloaded vehicle with no passengers wearing seatbelts.

"Oh, yeah," Chris assured her. "It is here. Watch when we're driving. You'll see entire families this size clinging to scooters, half the kids hanging on for dear life."

"The rest of the world expects citizens to monitor their own safety," Aubra said. "Unlike the United States, where your litigious population constantly needs someone to warn them and look out for them."

"Aubra, just scoot!" Melanie said. "We don't need lectures about America. We live there!"

The other women laughed and squealed, smashing butts together an inch at a time and ootching closer until able to slam the doors.

"Okay, Chris, we're good!" Delilah said, voice taut as if she were crushed by a vise. "Go quick before the car bursts open at the seams!"

Chris shook his head, grinning, and pulled the car into traffic.

"You might as well sit on my lap," Melanie told Tisha.

"Girl, no. I'd crush you."

"Please. I've gained ten pounds since I got here. Starting tonight, no more seconds for me at dinner."

"I've gained fifteen," Tisha commiserated. "I need to get some bigger pants while we're shopping today. I'll diet with you. Ms. Vanya's cooking is just too good."

"Would be nice if we could exercise more," Delilah said. "But we can't go jogging alone."

"And Chris refuses to be completely at our beck and call." Aubra punched his arm.

"Hey, now. Easy on the driver." He changed lanes. "I think I manage to help out whenever you ladies need me. Of course, Olivia needs to be the main focus for now. She's new. You guys can get by."

"Never!" Aubra teased. "What would we do without you? We need you too. If you can't choose, we'll all five have to share you."

Olivia glanced back, noting Melanie rolled her eyes. Okay, so she wasn't the only one trying not to gag right now. She was starting to suspect Aubra had a crush on Chris.

"Worse things," Chris said, "than having five women fight over me."

She shook her head. "I'm not—"

"Kidding!" Chris interrupted.

He pulled off the road and parked. The women in the back opened the doors and tumbled out in fits of giggles, gasping for air as though they'd been suffocating.

The market sprawled before them along the street. Vendors sat on blankets beside bags of rice and lentils and other dry goods, or baskets of chilis, peppers, spices, onions, and potatoes. She saw stalls set up for fruit. Tables of shoes and fabrics. Rows of clothing swayed in the breeze.

"This is a small local market," Tisha told her. "We come most every week, and you can get just about any staple foods you need. Down a bit farther they have the equivalent of a strip mall. That has a pretty nice little bookstore, a pharmacy, some upscale clothing stores. That sort of thing."

"Kochi has a huge spice market," Delilah told her. "It's famous. We could take you to see it sometime if you'd like. But this little town probably has anything you truly need."

"Especially since Ms. Vanya cooks for us twice a day," Melanie reminded her. "You just need snacks and whatever you might specifically want for yourself."

Tisha patted her stomach. "Yeah, no one goes hungry on Ms. Vanya's watch."

Overwhelmed, Olivia watched the steady flow of foot traffic wandering up and down the market. No clue where to start, she felt the urge to climb back in their borrowed car and return to her little room. So many people. And so many of them eyeing her.

"What would you like?" Chris prompted her.

She turned the question over in her mind. Had anyone ever asked her that? Growing up, she and Mom made do with whatever they could afford, what Mom had coupons for or found on clearance. She and Scott hadn't needed to be that thrifty. And yet he'd pinched pennies even worse than her frugal mother. Anytime she'd asked about finances, he'd claimed they were broke and frowned on buying anything frivolous. *Do we really need that?*

"I . . . don't know. What do you guys think I should get?"

Chris laughed, but she noticed the way Tisha's eyes cut to her, narrowing shrewdly.

"What do *you* like, girl?"

What did she like? What *did* she like? Scott had long ago decided she had terrible taste and made all the big decisions to "save her from herself." She remembered him chuckling on occasions when he hosted receptions for invited speakers at the university. "I chose the furniture. God knows what we'd have if I left Olivia to her own devices. Poor thing." She had squirmed internally, feeling small enough to crawl into a cupboard to hide and wishing she could—anything to escape the uncomfortable glances the other professors sent her way. They probably all wondered how someone like her wound up with a department chair to begin with. Someone who couldn't even furnish a house like a normal adult.

Now she squirmed as the other teachers all waited for her to answer what ought to be a simple question. *Come on, say something.* She thought back to breakfast—dry corn flakes and toast, with black tea to drink. "I kind of like to have fruit with my breakfast."

She waited for one of them to tell her smart people started their day with protein and carbs, not sugar. But no one did.

"To the fruit stand!" Chris declared, pointing forward and striking a pose.

"Our very own Marco Polo," Aubra said, clutching his bent arm. "Lead on, intrepid explorer!"

Tisha stayed beside her. "You feeling okay today?"

She blinked eyes as dry as sandpaper. "Yeah. Didn't sleep well. But yeah."

Everyone they passed stared, curious eyes wide with apparent fascination as necks craned for a better look. Could they all see her for the fraud she knew herself to be?

At the fruit stand, the vendor leapt from his low stool at the sight of them. "Yes! Hello!"

The variety and unfamiliarity of the tropical fruits startled her. Mom had done her best to keep the house stocked with healthy foods. But healthy meant expensive. Yes, she had some money on her for this sort of thing, and even some tucked away back home. But she wasn't being paid while she was here and had no sure employment when she went home. *Do you really need that?* Frugality seemed prudent. She could surely manage a bunch of bananas.

"Okay, rookie," Melanie said, "the rule is, if you can peel it, you can eat it."

"Got it. Some bananas then, I guess."

"Lady want banana?" the vendor asked.

"You can pick the bunch you want," Delilah told her, then helped when she hesitated. "That one!"

The vendor placed the bundle on the table.

"What else?" Chris asked.

Too many decisions. What if she picked the wrong thing and they all shook their heads, mortified by her inability to handle the simplest task? She shrugged. "I guess that's enough."

"Come on! You're new. Try everything! Give her some of your best pomelos, a couple of guavas, a mango, a custard apple . . ."

Her head bounced back and forth watching the vendor scurry about collecting the selections Chris pointed at and assemble them into a growing pile. Guava? Custard fruit? Those sounded exotic—and expensive.

"That should do for today," Chris finally declared. "How much?"

The vendor squinted, contorting his face. "One hundred eighty rupee."

Reaching into her purse, Olivia did a double take. One hundred eighty rupees? That was only around . . . three dollars. For that stack of fruit? That couldn't be right. She glanced at the others, startled to see all four of them giving the vendor a disgusted look.

"One eighty?" Chris asked. "No way!"

The vendor shrugged, gesticulating as he launched into a language she couldn't understand.

Chris held out a couple of paper notes. "One hundred fifty."

Olivia scrabbled in her purse, checking for the proper bills to pay with. "I'll pay—"

The vendor wobbled his head in a tiny figure eight and accepted payment from Chris. "Lady come back?"

"She'll come back. We all will," Chris said.

"Best fruit," the man told her, handing over her fruit in a plastic bag.

"Where to next?" Chris asked.

She scurried after him, cheeks flushed. Did something about her scream poor? Why did he think she couldn't afford her own food? Because she didn't give that taxi driver money for nothing? She could take care of herself. She'd worked hard to lift herself up. Sure, she wasn't wealthy, but she didn't need charity. Or did he think she couldn't do the math? Scott had always jumped in too, sighing heavily, shaking his head at her hesitance. But she wasn't totally helpless. "You didn't need to do that."

His brow furrowed. "Do what?"

"Pay for my fruit. I have money. I could've paid."

He waved a hand. "Don't sweat it."

"Really, I—"

"Besides, I want some too. I'll share. You get it next time. Yeah?"

He didn't shake his head or roll his eyes or call her "poor thing." She saw nothing malicious in his eyes but still felt uncomfortable. Why had he paid? What did he want from her?

Tisha looped an arm through hers and whispered, "It's no big deal. We do this all the time. Don't read anything into it." She turned to the other girls. "Who's ready to decorate a room?"

They all hopped and whooped in excitement, then led her to a stall with fabrics and handicrafts. Immediately, a piece decorated with a peacock jumped out at her. "Oh, wow. I love this." She pinched the fabric between thumb and forefinger and admired the work. Gold thread embroidery and sequins accented the peacock print. *Olivia, do we really need that?* She let go and tucked her hands behind her back, embarrassed. "But I don't need it."

"This type of dye work originated here in India," Delilah told her. "This is stamped on and then embellished with the hand stitching."

A homemade piece of unique artwork like this? She'd never be able to afford it. She cast one last glance over her shoulder before moving on to find some simple bedding in her price range. Something less frivolous.

"Hold up," Melanie said. "I thought you liked this one?"

"I love it but—"

"How much?" Melanie asked the vendor.

"It's okay," Olivia protested again. "Really. It's much too nice. I don't need it."

The vendor sized them up, eyes gleaming. "Two hundred forty rupee."

Olivia stared at him, incredulous, quickly working the math from rupees to dollars. That couldn't be right. She worked it again. And again. Roughly four dollars. Four dollars?

She reached for her money, feeling like a thief, but unable to resist. Better to pay and walk away before he realized his egregious error.

The others moved to intercede as she extracted two hundred-rupee notes and two twenty-rupee notes and held them out, waiting for the vendor to come to his senses but hoping he didn't. The vendor frowned and seemed startled. He eyed her warily, mirroring the look on her own face, she suspected. He took the money and handed her a folded bedcover.

Beaming, she started to walk away with her treasure, but the vendor called after her, "Lady!"

She cringed. He'd realized his mistake. And now she would be stuck paying the true cost, whatever that turned out to be. Scott's disapproval welled up inside her, pointing out a smart person would have given this more thought and not bought on impulse. She shook her head, annoyed that Scott still managed to insert himself into her life after walking out of it. *Oh, well. It's beautiful, and I want it.* For once in her life, she would splurge on something for herself and to hell with it.

She turned back. He gestured to the stall.

She shook her head. "I don't . . ."

He tipped his head and gestured again.

She looked to her own group, desperate for some guidance and hoping they could offer it.

Chris's smile, which she was starting to suspect was a permanent fixture on his face, combined with the look in his eyes, told her she'd messed up, though she didn't know how. Tisha's face conveyed sympathy while the other girls either giggled or covered their mouths to hide their reactions. Why did she always screw up the simplest things? Scott must have been right. It was better for him to make decisions.

"Let me guess," Melanie finally said. "You didn't read about haggling either."

"What?"

"You overpaid, girl," Tisha told her. "By a lot."

"He's telling you to come pick out something else," Chris said. "Something more to make up the difference."

"That's highly unusual," Aubra said, "so don't expect it to happen again."

"We're foreigners, and very obviously so," Delilah said, her Southern twang heavy. "Nothing has a price tag. Brace yourself to haggle. Opening price for a foreigner is at least twice what they really want. At least."

"And the price they want from us is still inflated," Chris said. "Like back at the fruit stand. He probably would have settled for one hundred twenty, without hesitating. But a local would pay more like ninety rupees. You can always send Ms. Vanya to shop for you once you've gotten the hang of it and know what you want. She tells the vendors what the price is going to be, not the other way around."

All five of them broke into hearty laughter. She felt like an utter fool. Her heart sank. "I'm sorry you overpaid at the fruit stand. I'll pay you back."

He held up a hand. "I wouldn't think of it. Besides, the fruit looked extra fresh. Worth it."

"You surprised him when you handed over his first asking price," Melanie said. "He didn't know how to react."

Tisha threw an arm around her shoulder. "It's an acquired skill. We all overpaid the first few times we shopped. It's a rite of passage."

"And honestly," Delilah added, "if you're happy with the price and feel like you're getting a good deal, who cares? Like you said, it's cheap compared to back home no matter what."

"You just don't want to set yourself up as a clueless rube," Melanie said. "That's all. Haggle a little bit at least so you don't look like an easy mark."

"Be glad you got an honest vendor your first time who doesn't want to take advantage of you," Aubra said.

She considered this new information, processing as best she could. "But . . . it only cost four dollars. This is worth so much more than that. I thought he was calling me back to charge more."

"In the States it's worth more than that," Chris said. "But here in India, entire families live on a few dollars a week. The truly impoverished scrape by on a dollar a month."

"A dollar a—" She stared at the vendor. "How? How can they possibly?"

"We can discuss economics at dinner tonight," Tisha suggested, taking her by the shoulder and steering her forward. "For now, choose some more bedding. You're scaring this poor man."

Chapter Five

That night, exhausted yet somehow also rejuvenated, Olivia stood in the middle of her transformed bedroom. No longer bare and dismal, it now burst with color and character, all of which she'd chosen. Scott's disapproving frown and patronizing head shake continued to rear up, attempting to shame her for this nonsense. But she pushed him aside, enjoying the happy little warm glow in her chest. Her space reflected her personality, even aspects she'd forgotten all about until today, along with newly discovered likes.

Peacocks for instance. She'd been drawn to anything with peacocks. In addition to the bedspread now draped over and hiding the plain metal bedframe, she'd discovered matching sheets. The vendor had happily handed over a set to her when she pointed at it—two flat sheets with the same beautiful vibrant green and blue peacocks stamped over them, plus a matching pillowcase. Remembering what they'd told her about prices and cost of living, and still feeling like she was swindling this man, she palmed him a few extra rupees when no one else was looking. As Chris had said, it was her dollar, and she could do as she pleased. The man had pressed his palms together around her hand, bowing low in thanks. It felt good to do as she pleased.

When she'd spotted an incredible piece of artwork with a classic Indian woman surrounded by peacocks, she had to have it. The vendor told her it was painted on marble. She couldn't resist the framed work, picturing it hanging in her new room and later taking it back home. Then she'd seen a similar one with a highly decorated elephant painted on the light gray marble, and similarly framed in gold-painted wood. A perfect set. Once she discovered the prevalence of elephant motifs, those called to her as well. Decorative elephant pillows sat at the head of her bed, complementing the peacock bedcover.

Chris surprised her with a set of two stone-inlaid, green marble elephants—a mother and a baby. Certain they were outrageously expensive, carved from marble and inlaid with colorful, intricate stonework, she attempted to refuse. He assured her they were prolific and cheap, souvenirs intended to entice tourists as a reminder of the Taj Mahal. "But the Taj Mahal is white marble, which is what most tourists want. The green is cheap. But still beautiful. And they had your name all over them." She held them in her hand. He had no idea how the sight of the mother and baby caused her heart to ache with sorrow. "They are beautiful," she'd agreed. "Thank you so much." She'd also noticed how Aubra's jaw tightened while the other girls admired the gift.

Guilt stabbed at her, accepting gifts from a man. How would Scott feel if he knew? How was the department chair faring as a divorced man? He probably moped around, presenting a stoic front, humbly accepting quiet words of sympathy as the long-suffering martyr. He would do that. She wondered what story he'd concocted to explain the divorce. What did he tell people about her? Thoughts of Scott brought back thoughts of reality, a reminder of the events of the past year, and quelled her good mood. Nothing good could come from dwelling on her ex. She went back to admiring her finds, hoping to recapture the fleeting happiness.

She'd found a peacock purse, embroidered tapestries Chris had helped her hang on the walls, and a wooden elephant incense burner plus stacks of spicy incense to scent her room. A square wooden lamp was another must-have purchase, particularly since it matched her marble artwork so well. The panes in the four sides of the lamp, where she would have expected glass, were instead translucent panels, painted with women surrounded by peacocks. The lightbulb inside shown through the images, illuminating them from behind.

She'd gushed over delightful tablecloths and matching cloth napkins, selecting a set with parrots, elephants, and camels all over it for her mom, imagining it draped on her mom's table as well as the look on her mom's face when she told her the price. Olivia shook her head in disbelief each time a seller quoted a price to her, still unable to adjust to the low cost of everything. The vendors took her shocked reaction as part of the bargaining process, which worked in her favor as she learned to haggle under her new friends' guidance. *Mom would love this.* And, she realized, she loved it. The low cost, the bargaining, walking away feeling like she got an amazing deal. She could picture her mom's face with each incredible steal. How amazing it would be for her to be able to afford things without always scraping and pinching and counting every dollar every month. And the shared delight of her fellow teachers, nodding their support at favorite items, agreeing she should get it, admiring her choices, all helped drown out Scott's continued disapproval.

Which made her wonder why he had always displayed annoyance when something made her happy.

At a stall selling shoes, she stopped to look at the leather sandals on display. Every woman they'd passed seemed to wear sandals with a loop over the big toe. The design appealed to her. Unable to resist, she tried on a few until she chose a favorite style in her size. She wore them rather than have the vendor wrap them up for her. Walking away, she told Scott's frowning countenance in her mind that she didn't want to hear his opinion. She liked these sandals, darn it, and so did the other teachers, and she was weary of questioning her every thought.

The others insisted she buy a supply of mosquito coils and the little clay dish to burn them in at night. "That way you won't need netting over the bed but can still sleep in peace," Melanie instructed. Skeptical of burning a chemical poison every night, she'd questioned this idea. But they'd reassured her it was simply a desiccant that would dry out mosquitos but not harm her in any way. They also assured her the risk of malaria in this part of the country was low—low enough not to take the prophylactic pills that carried a slew of potential side effects—but they all still needed to exercise reasonable precautions.

Aubra had spoken up then. "I keep suggesting we all take up the old British remedy of gin and tonic. The quinine in the tonic water is an anti-malarial. It's medicinal."

Everyone else in the group gagged and retched. "Ew! No gin!" By then Olivia's defenses had begun melting, and she'd ew-ed and laughed along, marveling she remembered how to laugh and delighting in the wonderful lightness a little laughter left in its cleansing wake.

They'd crammed back into the car after loading her treasures into the trunk and headed off to the strip mall farther up the street. The concrete buildings were a step above the street stalls, though nothing at all like a store back home.

They showed her the pharmacy, where medications that required a prescription back home were available for purchase. "As long as you know which medication you need," Tisha told her, "you can just come buy it. And for pennies on the dollar compared to what we pay in the States." You simply walked up to a counter and asked for what you needed.

They wandered through a book and stationery store. And though expensive by comparison to the open-air market, the quality struck her as better and the low costs continued to surprise her.

Their last stop for the day was a clothing store. All four girls urged her into it. "You must be burning up in those jeans," Delilah commented. "I remember when I first arrived and wanted to keep wearing my Western-style clothes too. But you'll be glad you switched. The temperatures here won't get much cooler, and this is so comfortable."

Delilah wore a sari, her lithe, willowy frame allowing such a thing. Olivia refused to even try one on. Her OB-GYN had dubbed her the "queen of stretchmarks" and under no circumstances would she expose her belly. Delilah assumed she had body image issues and pressed her to feel comfortable in her own skin. Easy for her to say.

Delilah held up a red and gold version. "You might wind up loving it!"

Olivia continued to shake her head, embarrassed but stubborn. A young saleswoman came to her rescue, attributing her refusal to modesty, of which she apparently approved.

The woman gestured to her own outfit, the same style Tisha, Aubra, and Melanie wore. "*Shalwar kameez?*" she asked, leading her away from the saris.

"We were getting there," Tisha said. "We wanted you to enjoy the full experience. We all at least tried on a sari."

Sure, and you're all younger than I am and don't have scars to worry about.

"I wouldn't come out of the changing stall, though," Tisha said. "I get it. But, girl, these outfits are so comfortable, I may never go back."

The soft drawstring britches and accompanying matching tunics came in every color imaginable, more fabrics than she knew existed, and all embroidered, embellished, dyed—the sheer magnitude of options made her head spin. She couldn't decide, each one more sumptuous than the last. Surely this would be when prices reflected the stunning craftsmanship, time, and effort that went into the handcrafted item.

The saleswoman sized her and then showed her to a fitting room, where she tried on a slew of options, and also taught her how to wear the matching *dupatta* that accompanied each outfit. The long scarf-like rectangle of fabric draped across the chest and over the shoulders, the ends dangling down the back. It could also be used to cover the head or shield your face. The saleswoman adjusted it until Olivia got the hang of it herself.

Tisha, Aubra, Melanie, and Delilah all had strong opinions about what she should wear and brought outfit after outfit. The saleswoman consistently brought heavily sequined and beaded pieces to her. Chris was no help in choosing from among the mind-boggling options. He told her she looked stunning in every one she tried on and suggested she choose whatever she liked best. She'd blinked at him, silently digesting this and trying to wrap her brain around a man who suggested she decide. What if she wound up disliking what she chose? What if they looked bad on her but no one would tell her the painful truth? Scott had kept her from these difficult situations, stepping in with a sigh and choosing for her. But Scott left her, and now she had to fend for herself. Ultimately, she settled on four outfits, none too flashy or fancy since she would be teaching impoverished children and didn't want to appear to be flaunting wealth she didn't have.

And yet, the total cost for all four outfits shocked her. She turned, wondering if she ought to pick up a couple more while they were here.

"We'll go shopping again," Tisha told her, laughing. "I remember though. It's exciting the first time."

"And there are other stores," Delilah said.

"Cheaper, even," Melanie said.

"Cheaper than this? How can that be possible?"

"These ought to get you through the first week," Chris said. "And yeah, we can try some other stores later."

She so loved the soft emerald-green outfit with beading along the neckline that she wore it out the door. Not only was the outfit far more comfortable, but also she liked blending in a smidge more—as much as she could with her skin tone that didn't match.

She hung the other three sets of *shalwar kameez* in the open not-quite-closet space and stood back to admire the room, now fully adorned with peacocks, elephants, and camels. The previously bare walls held embroidered tapestries and painted marble artwork. The lamp on her nightstand cast a soft glow over the room. She breathed in the soothing fragrance of cedarwood incense. The girls had even offered guidance to improve the bathroom space with fancy botanical soaps and shampoo, a small table for storage, and a hanger over the showerhead to hold all her toiletry items. They'd also reminded her to grab a trashcan for "that time of the month" when things would get a little messy without one.

Her growling stomach along with footsteps elsewhere in the building sent her to check a clock. Dinnertime. Her room transformation project had taken all day, which she'd spent happily preoccupied with new people and decorating.

This would do. She liked her new space, uniquely designed by her and for her, to reflect her likes and no one else's. Simple, but cute and fun. Scott's annoying disapproval attempted to rear up again, but she squashed it. She liked enjoying the moment, liked feeling okay about herself while it lasted.

She also liked her co-teachers/housemates. She'd never been a social butterfly and the realization she had melded into a group of friends surprised but delighted her. Scott had convinced her over the years that church was for chumps and had alienated her from friends one by one until her suggestions for lunch or coffee went unanswered. She'd listened to him when he listed off her friends' poor influences on her. And listened when he hinted that Olivia couldn't keep friends due to her own insufficiencies. "It's not my fault your friends don't want to spend time with you anymore," he'd said, more than once, when one of her friends claimed it could be challenging to keep friendships going after marriage. But she also remembered one friend asking if she could come without Scott, then losing interest when she could not. Scott preferred to accompany her.

But this little group of people seemed to enjoy her company today. Scott's voice in her mind attempted to tell her to give them time and once they knew her better, they'd drift away too. She hoped not. She looked forward to dinner not simply for the food to slake her hunger, but also eager for company, even after spending much of the day with her new friends.

She could manage the limited diet as well. She'd flirted with the idea of trying out a meat-free diet in the past, but Scott had always adamantly insisted he wanted meat included in their meals. In fact, he expected his meals to revolve around the meat, with additional items as sides, not the star of the show. And no matter how many times she showed him articles extolling the health benefits of vegetables and fruits in the diet, Scott had insisted she was wrong. India's cuisine offered her the perfect opportunity to branch out, try new things, see what she'd been missing. She'd be forced to go all in and see what happened, but the idea excited her. What did a person eat if a piece of meat wasn't the primary focus of the meal? She was about to find out.

She could do this. Only one question remained: Could she cut it as a teacher—not a professor, a teacher—and offer a small group of children the chance at a better life? She was about to find that out, too.

Chapter Six

The children sat silently, staring up at Olivia with wide eyes. They appeared terrified of her. One little girl cried. They were young. God, so young. And potentially mute judging from the absolute silence in the room. Not so much as a cough disrupted the perfect quiet. They all watched her, waiting.

She'd expected to be paired with a co-teacher, at least for the first week. The ad she'd responded to had stated specifically "training supplied, no experience necessary." What training? She didn't get any training. The school headmistress had led her to the classroom, wished her well, and left. She had nothing prepared. Even Chris and Tisha, who'd promised to be on hand for support, had scurried off to their own classrooms. Her hopes that maybe at least the oldest class of pupils, fourteen to sixteen, would file in first had also been dashed. A class of six- to nine-year-olds peered up at her, clearly waiting for her to do something. The mental residue left behind after living with Scott for six years laughed at her.

Come on, get your crap together. These kids needed to trust and respect her. Standing here gulping like a fish out of water would not instill confidence. She breathed deeply. What would she do in a college course?

She hiked a smile into place. "Good morning."

The children shuffled on their hard wooden benches, sat up straight, and appeared intrigued. "Good morning," a few shy responses echoed back to her.

She let out a sigh. She'd engaged them. That was something. Okay, now what? Turning to the chalkboard, she wrote *Good morning.* She turned back but no one studiously scribbled the words into notebooks. Come to think of it, none of them had notebooks. Damn it. Okay, back up a step.

She pointed to herself. "Mrs. Day—" She nearly choked, halting mid-introduction. She still, somehow, had not fully adjusted back to her maiden name. "Ms. Montag."

Twenty pairs of eyes blinked at her.

Forcing a bright smile and chipper tone of voice, she tried again, this time resting a palm on her chest. "Ms. Montag."

No one repeated her name, but one little girl ducked her head and grinned sheepishly—and possibly muttered something. She pointed to the smiling girl, nodding furiously. "And you?"

The girl sat up straight again, still smiling but also still silent.

Deciding to give it one more go before giving up, she pointed to herself again. "Ms. Mon-tag." She drew the word out slowly, over enunciating to the point she felt as though she insulted them. But she reminded herself they were learning, and it was a process. She pointed to the little girl again. "You?"

She saw the girl's mouth move and faintly heard sound. She cupped her hand to her ear and leaned cartoonishly forward. "What?"

Giggles burst across the room. Giggles! Even the crying girl's mouth curled slightly as she hiccuped a breath.

The girl repeated herself, this time speaking up. But Olivia didn't understand what she said. She heard the girl, heard the name, but she couldn't catch the word and make sense of it. The sound was too unfamiliar. Too . . . foreign.

Scott laughed at her in the back of her psyche. He'd been the youngest department chair appointed in the college's history. And yet she'd never managed to secure a full-time job as a professor. Adjunct, sure. But never the coveted tenure-track, full-time positions. Intelligent and hardworking, Scott landed a job straight out of college, probably helped by the article he'd submitted and published in *Nature* with his doctorate professor. It wasn't even his research. He'd worked in the lab and his professor allowed him second author on the paper. But things always seemed to work out for Scott. Olivia worked as hard, and yet never made it farther than adjunct professor. Scott of course implied regularly that she wasn't as smart as the other applicants and that was why she was relegated to adjunct positions. Never mind those other applicants who landed the jobs she applied for were all men. Never mind that the department gave lip service to equality, diversity, and inclusion but virtually every department chair and the majority of the full-time faculty were men.

If Scott could see her now, all these children staring up at her expectantly. Poor things stuck with her. Why had she thought for one moment she could do this? If she couldn't even pronounce their names, how could she possibly hope to connect with them and teach them? How foolhardy and arrogant of her to race across the world, trek to their tiny little piece of it, and believe she could make any difference whatsoever. Smart people didn't do things like this. Mortified, she opened her mouth to attempt pronunciation, knowing she would butcher it, making a fool out of herself and embarrassing the child.

The girl, possibly correctly interpreting Olivia's hesitation, jumped from her seat, slowly pronouncing, syllable by syllable, over enunciating as Olivia had done. "Esh. War. Ee. Uh. Aishwarya."

Olivia tried it. "Aishwarya?"

The girl clapped and nodded.

"Aishwarya!" She did it. She could do this. She pointed to herself. "Ms. Montag." She pointed to the beaming little girl. "Aishwarya. Who else?"

Fortunately, most of the names were easier to pronounce. Or

perhaps her confidence had returned, and she didn't feel as scared of trying them. She had no trouble getting each child to give their name after Aishwarya got the ball rolling. Only the little girl who had been crying remained quiet while her classmates waved hands in the air and volunteered names.

Olivia squatted in front of the little girl's place at the long desk when everyone else had given their name. "And you?"

The poor thing looked terrified, but quietly said, "Lakshmi."

"Lakshmi. Beautiful!"

She'd broken the ice. Now what? She looked around the room. No books. No cubbies with supplies. She didn't have crafts or worksheets. How could she impart the ability to speak English fluently on these children?

She turned to the chalkboard and drew a simple flower—simple because her artistic skills were dreadfully rudimentary. Under the picture she wrote FLOWER. "I like flowers," she said. The children repeated, or at least attempted to repeat, her words. She held the chalk out. "Aishwarya? What do you like?"

The girl sprang from her seat, took the chalk, and proceeded to draw a picture of a dog. Very clearly a dog. "Good job!" Under the drawing she wrote DOG. "D-O-G. Dog. Aishwarya likes dogs. I like dogs."

The children repeated her words back to her.

A little boy ran to the front. "Me! Me!"

Ah-hah! So they did know some English already. Good to know. What was his name? "Aru, do you want to draw? What do you like?"

The boy drew a ball, which she labeled BALL. The class understood the game and seemed to enjoy it. The children ran forward, eagerly contributing to the collection of favorite things on the chalkboard. Each picture she labeled, pronounced clearly, and had them repeat back. She also continued to repeat, "I like—" and whatever the children drew. Soon they repeated the entire phrase. She was getting somewhere. Did they comprehend? She had no idea, but comprehension could come later. For now, they were saying the words, getting the feel of English in their mouths. If nothing else, it was a start, and she could end the class feeling like she'd accomplished something.

She checked her watch. She'd managed to fill nearly the entire class time and breathed a sigh of relief. Looking around the room, she realized shy little Lakshmi had not drawn anything—the only student who had not. She held out the chalk. "Lakshmi? Can you draw something? What do you like?"

Lakshmi, eyes still red and bleary from crying at the beginning of class, rose from her seat and plodded forward. The girl took the chalk and drew a stick figure of a woman, complete with long triangle dress to indicate female.

Olivia stared at it. She liked women? She liked her friends? She wanted her mom? This one wasn't as simple and obvious as the other children's drawings had been. "You like . . ." She struggled to fill in the blank.

Lakshmi completed the sentence for her. "I like Auntie!" she cried out, throwing her arms around Olivia's legs.

Auntie? What? She stared down at the girl who smiled up at her. Stunned, Olivia patted the girl's back. Whatever was happening, she'd take it. This was a huge improvement over tears.

The other children jumped from their seats and ran to the front, all echoing, "I like Auntie!" and rushing to hug her.

The headmistress appeared in the doorway to tell her class was over, time to shift. Seeing Olivia standing in the center of a giant group hug, the woman smiled and nodded. "A good first day, I see."

Good? It was wonderful, she thought, tears pricking her eyes. She patted the children's backs and never wanted the hug to end.

The students waved and called, "Goodbye, Auntie!" as they scurried out the door. Sorry to see them go, she now felt eager to see them again tomorrow.

The headmistress, Mrs. Gupta, approached and tipped her head. "Already calling you Auntie? Well done."

The lilting, musical quality to Mrs. Gupta's words lifted her spirits even more. "I don't feel like I did anything too great. But I enjoyed it. Auntie is a good thing? I mean they all hugged me, so I assumed."

"It means they accepted you and are showing you respect. You have been welcomed as they would welcome their own family. Yes, a good thing."

The headmistress adjusted her *dupatta* and left as the next class filed in. This class consisted of middle-grade, ten-to-fourteen-year-olds. Drawing pictures on the chalkboard and repeating the same sentences over and over likely wouldn't cut it with this class. As if to prove they were more advanced, the children took their seats, and one little girl in the front read her name on the board and said, "Good morning, Ms. Montag." The rest of the children repeated the phrase.

No teary faces in this older group. Each of them sat stock-straight, waiting for her to impart knowledge. Unsure where the class would go, names seemed like the best starting place. And they couldn't move forward until they started. She took a deep breath.

"Good morning! You know I am Ms. Montag. I'd like to know your names." She pointed to the girl in the front row who had read her name from the board. "What is your name?"

"My name is Aditi." The girl's head bobbed with each syllable. But she got it.

Olivia repeated a few times with minor corrections until she said it correctly. "Aditi."

She should have realized it was too easy. The other children didn't seem as quick to grasp what was being said to them. Some said their names after glancing at Aditi, some said nothing and looked to Aditi for help. The girl then rattled off words in another language, which resulted in all the students sharing their names. Instead of the euphoric success she'd felt with the younger class, Olivia felt out of the loop and a bit frustrated when the students gave their names. This wasn't a result of her teaching or instruction but Aditi coming in with an assist. Ideally, she could switch back and forth between languages as the little girl could, but she couldn't, leaving her distant and removed. This was a disadvantage. If the children had a crutch, they would fall back on that rather than learning English.

The repetition of the phrases "What is your name?" and the corresponding responses "My name is . . ." reminded her of college Spanish. In those classes, she'd been the student, lost, listening to sounds that meant nothing—until the day things clicked and her brain could connect the words and phrases with something that made sense. She remembered the Spanish professor, how she'd always smiled and laughed and kept the atmosphere light, even when some students grumbled and didn't want to participate and clearly resented the language requirement necessary to earn a degree. The professor repeated and repeated and repeated until they got it. That would be her role model. She would do the same. Resenting Aditi, who clearly only wished to help, would get her nowhere. Starting tomorrow, she would ask the little girl not to intercede, but not today. Today they all just needed to muddle through.

In order to truly communicate in English, the children would need to be able to not only speak it, but also to read and write it. Her Spanish professor had always written on the board. Olivia picked up the chalk and wrote "What is your name?" Then below that she added "My name is _____"

She tapped the chalk under each word as she recited the sentences. She wanted the children to write the phrases as well, but the empty classroom offered nothing but chalk and board. So today they would speak. And she would evaluate how much hesitation was shyness and fear of a brand-new teacher, and how much was true confusion.

What could she talk about with them? She needed something simple and easily understood. She glanced outside, noting the temperature of the room crept steadily up as the sun progressed in the sky. This afternoon would likely be sweltering and unbearable. Already, perspiration developed under her arms and soaked the underside of her bra.

The sun! She could draw the sun. And she could ask silly questions and maybe get the students playing and laughing. She remembered her Spanish professor doing that as well—asking preposterous questions until they all realized she was being ridiculous and farcical and then laughing as they shouted, "No!"

On the board she drew clouds—a big blanket of storm clouds across the top, which she shaded with slash marks to turn them into dark storm clouds. Then she slashed angry raindrops falling from the clouds. She turned back to find the children leaning forward, watching intently, brows furrowed. Yep, she was doing this. They were going to discuss the weather.

"Is it raining today?" she asked, contorting her features into cartoonish confusion.

Heads cocked, furrowed brows furrowed even more, faces scrunched in thought as they attempted to work out what she said to them. Aditi turned to stare out the window, then looked at Olivia as if she might be crazy.

Olivia nodded her head. "It's raining. Yes?"

Aditi's eyes narrowed suspiciously. "No. No raining."

Olivia made a huge show of appearing surprised. "No?" She walked to the window and stared out, then slapped her hand to her forehead. "No! It's not raining! The sun is out!"

The children exploded into great big belly laughs at her exaggerated antics exactly as she had hoped. "No!" some of them yelled. "No raining!"

She returned to the board and drew a huge X over her clouds and drops. "No rain!" She drew a sun and wrote SUN. She heard the children repeating, "No rain!" and "Sun" while she worked.

"It is sunny today," she said as she wrote the words. And everyone repeated it back to her. "Aditi, do you like sun? Or do you like rain?"

"I like sun!" the girl answered.

Olivia would need to offer something more to the girl, who was clearly more advanced than most of the others.

Without prompting, the other children offered their opinions. She continued through the class time, drawing and pantomiming various weather conditions—wind, clouds, snow. Snow confounded the children as most of them had lived in this tropical region all their lives and truly had no concept of frozen water falling from the sky. They laughed and shouted "No!" at her, sure they'd caught her being preposterous again.

When the headmistress appeared to announce it was time to move on, Olivia did not stand in the middle of a group hug. The children told her goodbye and that was all. But somehow, she found the class period just as satisfying, even without the hugs.

Chapter Seven

At dinner that evening, Olivia told the others all about her first day, pleased to be able to share what she considered an overall success. She dove into her potatoes and cauliflower, famished after a long day, realizing she hadn't taken time for lunch. "I was kind of worried at first, especially when one little girl cried in the youngest class."

Tisha tore a piece of *chapati* and scooped rice with it. "Lakshmi? Yes, she cried at me too. I think new faces scare her."

"Yes, that sounds about right. I remember her being upset when I took over too," Melanie said.

"You know the teacher you replaced left quite suddenly," Delilah told Olivia, "so it may have been especially disruptive for Lakshmi."

"What happened?" Olivia asked. "Is the woman okay?"

The girls exchanged glances. "She was local, not a Westerner like us," Tisha said. "Before she disappeared, she confided that she was pregnant."

"And she didn't want to teach anymore?"

"She isn't married," Delilah said.

"Oh. She needs a paying job instead of a volunteer position?"

"No. You're thinking like an American. Present day American. A pregnant, unmarried woman in India is in serious trouble. We . . . we're not sure what's happened to her, but we're sure it isn't good."

Olivia put down her fork. "What do you mean?"

"Well, women are expected to marry as virgins here. A pregnancy proves she isn't one. On top of that, her parents were actively arranging her marriage. She's educated and smart, and they'd found a good match for her. The pregnancy ruined that."

"She didn't want to marry that man," Aubra said. "Like Melanie said, she's educated and smart. She knows Western countries don't arrange marriages. She agreed to bow to tradition and allow her parents to arrange her marriage but then she didn't like the man. She loved someone else."

"That's so sad," Olivia said. "What do you think happened to her?"

"Honestly?" Tisha said. "She's probably been forced to abort the pregnancy and is being hidden from the boy she loves."

She nearly choked. "A forced abortion? That's . . ." She didn't have words. She couldn't comprehend. Simply could not wrap her brain around the idea of anyone being forced to terminate a pregnancy. Of course, she knew she was biased. Her experience with pregnancy had left her reeling and with a firm grasp of just how tenuous and precious life is.

"Yes, I know. But it happens here. Gender bias results in forced abortion too."

"Her parents forced her to end the pregnancy? Rather than let her marry the baby's father?"

"We don't know that for sure. We're guessing," Delilah said.

"But . . . why?" That's what bothered Olivia so much. The why, the how. How could anyone do such a thing?

"Most women don't have many options besides getting married, having children, and operating the house. Particularly in more rural areas like this one. Things are changing here, but not quickly. India is an old, old country, with thousands of years of history. You don't change thousands of years of gender bias in a day."

"What do you mean by 'gender bias'?"

"Baby girls are considered a drain on impoverished families," Tisha said. "Girls take resources away from the family and yet don't offer any return on the investment. Once a marriage is arranged, the daughter leaves and becomes part of her husband's family."

Scott would love that, she couldn't help but think. He hadn't liked the close relationship she and her mother shared. He'd frowned at suggestions of spending holidays with Mom, preferring to spend them alone. She'd never understand his sour attitude after they married or his insistence she needed to grow up and stop leaning on her mother.

"Plus, the marriage itself is expensive. The woman's family pays a dowry to the man's family and pays the cost of the wedding," Aubra said.

"Whereas sons will provide for the parents in their old age," Delilah said. "My women's studies paying off. We discussed this cultural difference. The man's family receives the dowry, gains the woman who provides free labor around the house plus grandchildren. And the man's parents will live with them once they're unable to care for themselves. It's their retirement plan."

"Parents pay men to marry their daughters?" Olivia asked, not sure she understood correctly. Surely she misunderstood.

"More or less, yes," Delilah said. "Cash doesn't necessarily constitute the dowry, though some amount is typical. The dowry could also include appliances, furniture, or a house. And if a family wants to arrange a good marriage, they will pay a higher dowry. Men with university degrees and status and steady incomes command higher dowries. The practice is officially outlawed, but in general, the laws have been ineffective at stopping the practice. Women have historically been completely socially and financially dependent on male relatives and then their husbands after marriage. And unfortunately dowry abuse is real.

With any luck, her parents will salvage the marriage arrangement. Or at least find her someone."

"But she loves another man. Why won't they let her marry him?"

Aubra looked around the table. "Did anyone ever hear exactly why her parents disproved of him? I know she hinted at them not liking him, but now I can't remember why. If she ever told us."

"I never heard," Melanie said.

"She really didn't discuss it much," Delilah said. "I didn't pry but I was curious and tried to get her to talk about him a couple times."

"Okay so why don't they simply elope?"

"Oh, girl, you're still thinking like a Westerner," Tisha said.

"Remember," Delilah said, "she can't marry if her parents don't pay her dowry. Unless the groom and groom's parents agree to forego it. Which apparently her beau's parents weren't willing to do. In their minds, they invested heavily in him and his schooling, preparing him for the best match they could hope for, and now they expect to collect. If his parents demand a dowry and her parents don't approve of the match, then the marriage will never happen."

"She should forget all that, take her baby, and run away then," Olivia suggested. "Why does she need a guy anyway? You said she's educated and smart. She can get a job and take care of herself instead of being forced to have an abortion and marry a man she doesn't like."

"It's just not that simple," Tisha said. "You're still thinking like we've been raised to think. Women here don't have much recourse. Society generally frowns on single mothers or women in the workplace. Who would hire her? She'd be an outcast with no family and no support. Where would she live? How would she live? You heard us talking about why we ask Chris to drive us around and take us shopping. We've encountered some problems. Aubra tried to drive us once and men yelled at us and told us to get off the roads, that we made them unsafe. The stereotypical 'woman driver' caricature is taken as fact. Combine that with the belief that women shouldn't be outside the home unchaperoned plus the common belief that all Western women are tramps and ready to hop in bed with any men they meet, and it didn't go well."

"It's a different country and a different culture. So many things play into this—tradition, economics, religion." Melanie shrugged.

Everything they said made sense and nothing they said made sense. She couldn't believe Melanie shrugged off the situation as if it were nothing. Except what could any of them do? A couple of Western women up against the entire continent's deeply entrenched belief system, many thousands of years old? Might as well spit into a hurricane and hope to knock it off course. They wouldn't change a thing.

The scenario they described left her nauseated and unable to finish her dinner. But they were right—this wasn't her country or her fight, and she was getting worked up over a young woman she'd never even met. The situation tormented her though. She looked around the table and watched the rest of her co-volunteers return to their food. They'd moved on. Why couldn't she?

In her mind, she pictured the woman literally dragged to a clinic, struggling and protesting then held down while her pregnancy was terminated. She imagined the young woman weeping for the lost baby, something she was entirely too familiar with herself. She wanted to find the woman, wanted to offer her comfort, hold her and rock her and tell her it would be okay, all the while knowing it wouldn't be.

She knew it wouldn't be because she still wasn't okay, nearly . . . oh God, it was nearly a year later. She quickly tallied up the months and confirmed that. Nine months, somehow an eternity and no amount of time at all. The exact amount of time the pregnancy had spanned, a huge life-altering shift in itself. How could so much have changed when so little had happened? A year—less than a year even—since her life turned upside-down completely.

No, that wasn't right. Shattered. Her life had shattered completely. And now here she was in India, trying desperately to form the broken bits back into something she could recognize as her life. Or *a* life. Any life, really, at this point. She'd been unable to function for some time, heart lacerated by the jagged shards. She'd finally forced herself to move, attempting to gather the pieces.

But even though she was here, moving through life, and she was showing everyone a good, solid front as if she had all her crap together, she was not okay. What if she never felt okay again? What if the huge canyon of grief rent by one horrible day, one horrible event, one atomic bomb of grief and devastation could never be traversed? Would her life be forever divided in two by one calamitous event, the years before spent as her original self, the person she remembered and longed to be again, and the years after this new, hollowed-out, aching version of herself?

She knew the teacher she'd replaced would never be the same either. Strange how one shift in life could cause a domino effect, leading from one life change to another to another, collapsing in a pile of debris kicked off by what at the time seemed like a tiny tremor, a slight quiver, a challenge to overcome, sure, but manageable. Then it turned out to be enough to cascade into an earthquake that resulted in an avalanche that left you buried and lost forever.

"You okay?" Tisha pulled her from her thoughts.

She nodded. "Yeah, just . . ."

Chris, sitting next to her like always, had tensed up and gone silent. "I'm with Olivia. Let's talk about something else. As the sole male of the group, I feel like I'm about to be ripped apart as retribution for thousands of years of female subjugation. And I personally have never so much as insulted a woman, so I feel like that would be grossly unfair."

"No one is going to rip you apart!" Aubra laughed.

"Yeah, who would drive us around then?" Melanie asked.

"Chris is right," Aubra went on. "He's the last person to atone for sins of the past. He's a perfect gentleman."

Olivia had the feeling Aubra wished Chris wasn't such a perfect gentleman and would attempt to try a few ungentlemanly things with her. The girl was so obvious. Surely Chris had caught her vibe by now. Was he simply not interested? And why was she wasting any thought on the dynamic anyway? Who cared?

Tisha caught her eye. "It's a lot to adapt to, I know. We can't change anything, though. We're here to teach and that's all. Remember how happy you were a moment ago, telling us about your day. What else went well? Sounds like you really did great straight out of the gate."

She picked up her fork again and cast a grateful glance at Tisha for bringing her back. *Focus on the positive.* "I mean, I don't really know for sure, but I felt good about it. Not at first, especially not with Lakshmi crying, but by the end they hugged me and called me Auntie."

"Auntie on the very first day?" Chris said. "That's awesome!"

She blushed a bit at his praise, feeling heat creep across her cheeks.

"They call all the teachers Auntie," Aubra said.

"Of course," she said, quickly dismissing Chris's compliment. Tension emanated from Aubra, and Olivia couldn't cope with tension. Especially petty jealousy over what the kids called the teachers and how soon, fueled by Aubra's obvious crush on Chris that apparently went unrequited. Olivia wanted no part of that drama. Period. "I assumed it was something standard. I didn't even know why they were calling me that at first. Mrs. Gupta had to tell me." She giggled a bit to show Aubra how silly she found the entire situation.

"Still, that's great," Chris insisted, though she wished he had picked up on the social cues and let it go. His emotional intelligence didn't seem terribly high.

She changed the subject. "One little girl is remarkably bright. Aditi. She blew me away."

The other teachers all spoke at once, agreeing and nodding.

"She's brilliant," Aubra said. "Bloody hell, she stuns me how smart she is."

"Excellent at math too," Chris said.

"And she's exceptionally kind," Tisha added. "Not that any of the kids are mean. She just always seems to notice when one of the other kids is down and goes out of her way to cheer them up."

"She isn't a snot either," Delilah said. "Not an arrogant bone in her body. She will help explain to the other kids whenever they're not quite grasping a concept."

"She's amazing," Melanie agreed.

This was why she was here. To stop feeling horrible and help the kids in this little school in a little town in rural India have a chance at a better future. They weren't her children, and she wouldn't be here long enough to see the outcome or follow up on what became of them. Maybe her six months here would amount to a great big nothing. But she had to try. She knew, somehow, deep down, that the trying would mean something, and perhaps even benefit her in ways that attempting to forget and move on had failed.

Would she change these kids' lives? Probably not. But she would damn sure give them her best effort. And right now, she knew she was no more prepared for her second class than she'd been for the first. Okay, maybe a little bit more prepared since the first-day nerves and anxiety were behind her. But as far as presenting a lecture—no, lessons!—she had nothing. This was something she could focus on. She would shove everything else into a closet in her mind—all the worry and fear and the horrible events that brought her here and the poor teacher she'd replaced who could have been beaten or worse for all she knew but she really couldn't think about that right now because even starting to think about it was bringing tears to her eyes and derailing the awesome plan she'd thought of.

Nope. Stop that.

She pushed all the depressing thoughts into the closet in her mind and mentally leaned hard to close the hiding place, now crammed and over-stuffed with all the things she simply couldn't deal with right now. Right now, she needed to focus on the kids she had agreed to teach. And she knew how she was going to do it.

As the others cleared the dishes and left for their rooms, she turned to Chris and asked, "Do you think I could catch a rick-shaw to that nicer market we went to?"

Chris frowned. "Why do that? I'll drive you."

"I hate to keep imposing on you."

"It's not an imposition! Seriously. Please let me. You've been in the country less than a week. If you got lost or, heaven forbid, something happened, I'd feel personally responsible."

"You know, everyone keeps saying it's totally safe here," she said, one eyebrow up. "And yet I'm supposed to be chaperoned and can't go out alone."

"It is! It is safe. But no sense inviting trouble, right? Come on! Where are we going?"

"To that bookstore we saw when we went shopping. I need some supplies."

Chapter Eight

"Hey, sleepy. We're here."

Olivia jolted awake to discover Chris nudging her and coaxing her awake. "Oh, my God! I fell asleep on the way to the market?"

"It's the jet lag. You're worn out. Aren't you glad I brought you instead of a stranger in a rickshaw?"

Was she glad? Her mind reeled at the thought of how horribly she could have been taken advantage of by someone. She'd been unconscious. Totally out. And completely vulnerable. Wouldn't Scott relish this turn of events if he knew? *Wow. Smart.* She shuddered at the thought and placed a hand on Chris's arm. "Absolutely. Thank you so much."

He glanced at her hand resting on him and beamed. "Anytime! I mean it."

She blinked and shook her head, a bit disoriented from dozing off, then climbed out of the car. She admired her new sandals as they slapped along the concrete parking lot, trying not to think about the little shiver contact with Chris had prompted.

"What brought you to India?" Chris asked.

The question caught her off-guard. Chris had kept things light, and she preferred it that way. She didn't want to share. She didn't even want to think about it. The question cracked open the mental closet she'd stuffed all the awful memories into. Opening it and examining them, reliving them, sharing them with anyone—but most especially this guy she barely knew—would only make her miserable. Just considering his question opened the door enough that all the painful memories and past issues she didn't want to think about oozed out, beckoning her to remember. Her dad's drunken rages, her mother's teary face, the struggle to escape it all. The hours of labor, a swaddled baby, a distant husband. She shook her head and frowned, slamming the door firmly closed again.

"Oh, you know." She left it at that, realizing her vague response didn't answer his question but hoping he'd let it go.

He didn't. "I *don't* know. That's why I asked. You teach college classes, not young kids. I'm just curious what prompted the decision."

The closet creaked open again, all the mess she'd crammed into it threatening to spill out. Why was he so nosy? Her heart hammered a bit. "Why did *you* come?"

He walked quietly for a moment before answering. "Some things happened. I wanted to get away and put some distance between me and some people. But I've also always wanted to travel and do something good in the world and this offered a way to do both."

That wasn't what she expected to hear. "That's pretty similar to what brought me here. The distance part, anyway."

"Have any siblings?" He seemed to understand that was as much as she wished to share. Maybe his emotional intelligence was higher than she'd first thought.

"No siblings." *Thank goodness.* Her mom had struggled plenty trying to raise one child on her own. She couldn't imagine the stress more children would have added. Besides, that would have been someone else her dad would have hurt. She shuddered at the thought and wondered how she would have reacted, watching him treat a younger sibling as he'd abused her. She liked to think she would have intervened, or at least tried to, as Mom had tried to protect her. When he really got going, though, sometimes nothing could calm him down or deflect his rage. She remembered lying in her bed one night, woken yet again by his screaming fury, accusing her mom of cheating on him. She'd curled on her side, stomach churning, terrified for her mother, listening for the smacking sounds that indicated he'd moved on from yelling to hitting—and hoping he wouldn't come after her when he tired of beating Mom. That night, though, after a vicious verbal beatdown, after screaming at Mom what a terrible wife and mother she was, Mom cried and sobbed and pleaded, begging him to be quiet "before you wake Livvy." Then she gave up and simply started agreeing with him. "Yes, you're right. You deserve so much better than me," Mom had said. And it must have worked. She never heard smacking or any thudding sounds to indicate he had grabbed her by the arms and was shaking her as he dug his nails into her arms and bashed her against walls and counters. Olivia knew the feel of those angry fingers digging into skin.

She'd relaxed when the screaming stopped and no hitting began. But then she replayed over and over her mother agreeing with him, lying and telling him he was right, that she was terrible and he deserved better. And that made Olivia's blood boil. She knew her mom was a good person and a good mom. At the time she hadn't even been old enough to understand the allegation of cheating but knew for a fact now how outlandish that claim was —he'd left them both at home with no car, wouldn't give her access to the checking account, and Mom always took care of her. She'd never once seen her mom anywhere near another man. When and how she could possibly have cheated on him only a drunken mind could have imagined. None of it was ever true. Olivia had no idea what demons her father wrestled with that resulted in such misery and fury. But she knew neither her mother nor she had ever done anything to add fuel to the fire. They simply suffered the burning rage. Thinking back, she realized she wouldn't have blamed her mom for seeking love and kindness from another man. Mom deserved better. She deserved love. But Olivia also knew Mom had never received the love she deserved—or ever sought it. After leaving her father, Mom devoted her life to raising Olivia in a safe, male-free environment.

Walking along beside her, Chris shared a bit more. "I don't have any siblings either. Anyway, I finished my degree, and some things happened that I kind of wanted to get away from. I figured before I started working on a career, I'd take a hiatus and go see the world. But once I got here, I stopped. The kids are just . . . wow. They blow me away. Have you traveled at all before?"

She glanced sideways at him. That was the second mention of "things happened" and she wondered if he wanted her to ask for details. She didn't want to share her own, but he seemed to be opening the door. As for where had she traveled? Almost nowhere. She'd never been on a vacation at all until her honeymoon. Mom hadn't been able to afford such a luxury. She and Scott had taken a few vacations, but never anything big. Work didn't allow for lengthy time off and synching their leave never quite worked out. Even when they did manage it, it wasn't far or for long. They'd always been saving for something or dealing with an unexpected expense and would decide they couldn't spare the funds. Funny, she had more money after their divorce than she'd had while married. Not that it would last forever. Eventually she would want her own place again. She would have to get a full-time job. These were the things she didn't want to worry about right now. Couldn't Chris see that? Why was he relentlessly badgering her with personal questions?

Thankfully, the bookstore offered an out. "Here we are," she said.

"Sure enough." He opened the door for her. "I know you can open doors yourself. Not implying you're weak. I open doors for all friends, male or female. I am a gender-neutral door opener."

In spite of herself, she laughed. "Thank you. I appreciate it."

What had someone said to him that left him feeling defensive about being polite? It hadn't even occurred to her to be offended. But someone in his past must have been. She opened her mouth to ask, considered how she'd just shut him out, and closed it again. Not fair to pry when she refused to share.

She stepped inside the bookstore and inhaled deeply, the scent of shelf after shelf of books relaxing her like nothing else in the world.

The shopkeeper called out to them and tapped his watch. Chris held up a hand and nodded.

"What's wrong?" she asked.

"He wants to close soon. They don't stay open as late as we're used to back home."

"Oh. I wanted supplies for tomorrow, though."

"That's fine. He's not throwing us out. He just wants us to move along."

"Fair enough." She hadn't made a list, but she'd thought back to what she could remember of kindergarten and first grade and knew what they needed.

She descended on the art supplies, scooping up scissors and packages of construction paper and glue. She grabbed pencils and erasers, crayons, colored pencils, markers. Something called pastels caught her eye and she decided her kids needed those too. When her arms were so full she couldn't hold anything more, she dumped the armload on the counter near the register, then went back for more. Each trip, the shopkeeper's eyes grew wider and wider.

Chris laughed and held out his arms. "How can I help?"

"Let's go look at books." The book selection did not disappoint. She found coloring and activity books. Penmanship books. Simple readers. Flipping through, she noticed British spellings and phrases. *How cute.* With each selection she counted out enough that each student could have their own, even if they wouldn't have exactly the same books. The store wasn't large enough to carry that many copies. Maybe the shopkeeper could order for her.

As she rested another stack of books in Chris's arms, she discovered him watching her, eyes soft, almost quizzical, a gentle smile curling his lips. "What?"

He looked away, shaking his head. "For someone who worries about money as much as you do, you're kind of going overboard in here, aren't you?"

She lifted a box of pastels from a nearby shelf. "This costs a quarter. A quarter. For ten dollars, every student in my youngest classes can have their own. He doesn't have that many on the shelf, but they can share. I'll get more if they run out. I came to teach, and I intend to do a good job. If I spend a hundred dollars in here, which I doubt considering how cheap everything is, I will consider it an excellent investment. The kids deserve it."

He raised an eyebrow. "Okay. Now I know why you came to India. And I'm impressed."

She went back to the shelves. Impressing him wasn't her goal. "You haven't bought anything for your classes?"

"I teach math, mostly to the older high-school-aged kids. Remember? We don't color much. Besides they're all boys. No interest in crafts. I think the other teachers may have bought some things. Not this much though. You know the school has a supply closet, right?"

"Mrs. Gupta showed me. They have a nice supply of plain white paper and white chalk. Which reminds me . . ." She added colored chalk to her growing pile. Glancing at her watch, she indicated to the shopkeeper she was nearly done.

He bobbled his head in a figure eight. "No, lady, no. Okay. Okay."

Chris grinned. "That means take all the time you need. For you, he'll stay open as long as you'd like."

"I really am nearly finished. I think."

"You've bought nearly everything in stock," Chris joked.

Why were his classes all boys? That seemed weird. Maybe the

school segregated the genders at a certain age. That would make sense. She'd ask who taught math to the high school girls and offer to buy anything they might need.

But for now, she needed to finish what she was doing. Her middle-grade classes posed more of a challenge. The ten-to-fourteen-year-olds were much too advanced for crafts. Especially Aditi. She needed something to challenge them. Without a defined plan and with no personal teaching experience to draw from, once again she thought back to her college Spanish courses. Those had been presented in units, which they'd spent a week or two covering and learning. She made a mental list of the units she could remember off the top of her head—foods, travel, health and illnesses—then brainstormed for more. Anything that might help with that she and Chris picked up—magazines and newspapers, stickers. When she spotted a set of food stickers, she decided to start with that. What could be more fun than talking about foods and comparing their cuisine to what she ate back home? She grabbed as many lined notebooks and composition books as the store had on the shelves, plus activity books that seemed age appropriate. Once she ran out of ideas for units, she could shift over to reading YA books.

She picked up a copy of the first Harry Potter book. "Do you think they'd enjoy reading this? I wonder if he can order twenty copies for me."

"I think he will gladly order anything you ask for," Chris said. "But we can also drive into Kochi if you need to. It's a big city and will have everything. It's a drive but I can take you."

She looked through the shelves but kept coming back to the Harry Potter. She'd heard good things about it and kind of wanted to read it herself. Maybe the kids would enjoy it too.

Okay. She surveyed her spoils, and nodded with satisfaction, feeling quite accomplished. She asked the shopkeeper to order twenty copies of *Harry Potter and the Philosopher's Stone*—the British title, she realized, which made sense since everything imported came from England—and added one copy to her stack. After all, she needed to read it herself to prepare.

The total cost of her supplies left her feeling like a thief and the shopkeeper looking like he'd just won the lottery. She even paid in advance for the twenty books he agreed to order.

Chris helped her tote the bags to the car and load them into the trunk.

She climbed in and breathed a sigh of relief. "Now I'm ready for tomorrow. Thank you so much for bringing me."

"Anytime. I can't wait to see Mrs. Gupta's reaction."

"She'll be happy, right?"

"I think so. Although now your classes will have a huge advantage over others."

That thought had never crossed her mind. How would the other children feel? She didn't know exactly how many children attended the school, but she knew she didn't see all of them. "If this causes a problem, I guess she can dock my pay."

"Ha! Good one."

"Actually, if it causes a problem, I'll come back here and buy supplies for all the other classes too."

She meant it. She'd never been one to donate to charity. She'd been the recipient of charity. She knew most of her Christmas gifts growing up had come from donations to angel trees and that her mom had depended on food pantries and free lunches from the schools. Why hadn't she and Scott ever adopted a child from an angel tree? Just been too tied up with their own lives and plans? They weren't rolling in cash, but they could have helped a child with less. Maybe it had simply never occurred to her that she could turn her life around and be the one giving instead of receiving. Now that it had occurred to her, she would make up for it. These supplies would make a major impact on her students' lives.

Charity is for chumps. You're going to need that money. Smart people don't—

Shut up, Scott!

The sum of money in her bank account back home combined with the incredibly cheap prices here left her feeling wealthy for the first time in her life—and it felt good. She could buy without stress, without guilt, without wondering if this purchase would impact a greater need later in the month. Without Scott asking her if she really needed it. Yes, she wanted to scream at him. Yes, she really needed this.

Chapter Nine

Olivia wove through the classroom, winding between the desks and benches, peering over her students' shoulders as they hunched over their work.

She could not believe how far she'd come in a matter of a few weeks, how comfortable she'd grown with the routine here at the school. Remembering that first day, how she'd been stricken with anxiety and self-doubt, fully believing herself unable to offer these children a thing, she smiled at the little surge of pride that swelled in her chest. She'd done it. She'd quelled that doubt and figured it out. And now she had memories of faces brightening with understanding, children learning words and phrases, hugs and smiles.

A hand shot in the air. "Ms. Montag! Teacher! See me!"

Lakshmi. No longer teary and terrified, the girl proved to be nearly as sharp and advanced as Aishwarya in this class and Aditi in the older group.

See me. Olivia couldn't stop a smile from curling her lips. The girl meant, "Look at my work," but considering they all bent over construction paper renditions of themselves, the phrase actually applied nicely.

She squatted beside the girl's seat. "Let me see."

She'd been up quite late last night, cutting out forty paper dolls she'd sketched and traced onto brown paper. She gave the children construction paper so they could cut out and label clothing for their paper people. She drew examples on the board along with the word for each—shirt, pants, skirt, socks, shoes— and instructed them, "You can design your own, but cut out one of each and write the name of the piece of clothing on each one."

Every student had immediately started working, not a confused face in the group.

"Lakshmi, this is beautiful. Good work!"

The girl to Lakshmi's left crinkled her nose. "She made boy pants."

Olivia frowned. "I wear pants." She stood and held out the sides of her loose britches. "See?"

"That is *kameez*. She made boy pants. You can see her legs."

Brow furrowed, she looked again at what might offend the girl about Lakshmi's paper person. The bottoms of the pants reached the knees, leaving the paper doll's shins exposed. Boy pants. The girl meant shorts. Olivia sighed. She knew the importance of ensuring clothing covered her limbs. Short sleeves were acceptable on women, though she'd noticed long sleeves in the market, even though this was the hottest part of the year. Exposing a leg was completely taboo.

"Well, we are only pretending today. Lakshmi won't wear boy pants, will you?"

Lakshmi hunkered down, shoulders scrunched to her ears, and giggled. "No!"

Olivia shook her head and continued around the room, reviewing their work. *Boy pants*. She may have adapted and settled in, but she knew her time here was finite. She loved wearing *shalwar kameez*, fancy and formal without wearing a dress. But she also felt as if she wore a costume and missed the comfort of a pair of jeans. Though women might wear the Western option in big cities, rural India did not accept them. Olivia wanted to be accepted and not seen as offensive. After all, she was a guest in the country, here to quietly help, not stomp around offending people with her Western ways, attempting to change beliefs.

She paused by a little boy named Dev, his paper person catching her attention. He had dressed himself in blue pants and blue shirt on which he'd colored a red S inside a red shield. A red cape hung behind the doll.

"I think I know who Dev is dressed as," she announced. She reached for his paper person. "May I share?"

Dev's face split into a grin and he thrust his work at her with a nod.

"Who is this?" she asked, holding it up for the class to see.

"Superman!" one of the boys answered.

"Yes! Do you like Superman?" Heads nodded. Last week they'd studied colors, and this presented an excellent opportunity to revisit and reinforce.

"Superman wears what color pants?" she asked.

"Blue!" the class yelled.

She walked to the board and wrote the word as a reminder. "That's right. Blue. And what color shirt?"

"Blue!"

"Yes. Very good. Superman wears something we didn't talk about. He has a cape. C-A-P-E. Cape. What color is his cape?"

One little girl spoke before the others. "Rose!"

"Well, a rose can be this color. But the color is called . . ."

"Red!"

"Very good! Good work today, boys and girls."

"Auntie!" One of the girls waved her hand frantically.

"Yes?"

The girl held up her own paper doll, dressed as Superman too.

She smiled. The girl must have hoped for some extra attention like Dev and quickly modified her doll's clothing. "Priyanka is Superman too."

"No!" the class responded forcefully. "She is a girl. A girl cannot be Superman."

Gender separation again. "Well, okay. Priyanka is Supergirl."

"No!" The children laughed, sure they'd caught her being silly. "Girls are not super!"

The quick and certain responses sobered her. The kids weren't playing. This no longer had anything to do with using the correct gender. These kids were telling her what they wholeheartedly believed—that women weren't anything special. No woman could be a hero.

Mrs. Gupta appeared in the doorway and though she crossed her arms, she beamed at the children.

Thank goodness class was over. Olivia wasn't sure what to do with this latest turn. "Okay, class, you can keep your paper people. We will talk about clothes again tomorrow."

The children scrambled out the door, some calling, "Goodbye, Auntie!" over their shoulders.

Mrs. Gupta, rather than turning to leave as she normally did, approached her. "Your application said no experience, but you are doing quite well with the children."

"Thank you." Her cheeks warmed at the praise. Mrs. Gupta worked with all the volunteers who came and went and had no reason to compliment her if it wasn't true.

"Thank you for flying here so quickly. We cannot remain open without volunteers."

The short notice likely had something to do with how amenable they'd been to her, with no experience. They'd been desperate, so desperate that any warm body would do, anyone willing to upend their life and step in on short notice. Perhaps that was the qualification that landed the job for her. She was okay with that. "I understand the previous teacher left very abruptly."

Mrs. Gupta's eyes narrowed. "Yes, she . . . became very sick."

Olivia nodded slowly, silently communicating she understood. Apparently, this wasn't discussed openly. "I hope she will be okay."

Mrs. Gupta nodded gravely and turned to leave, but not before Olivia noted the brief sadness that filled her eyes.

The mid-grade students were filing in and taking her seats. Olivia shook off the melancholy the exchange left behind and focused on the children.

As Aditi passed by, the girl held out the copy of Harry Potter she'd lent to her, allowing the girl to take it home. Olivia had already finished reading it, but the class copies on order hadn't come in yet.

"I finished," Aditi said.

"Already?" She'd sent the book with the girl only a few days ago.

Aditi ducked her head and nodded.

"So fast!" The girl truly astounded her. "I could not put it down. Did you like it?"

Aditi nodded again. "It is good. I want to read more."

Olivia made a mental note to return to the bookstore and order the next book. If she remembered correctly, the fourth book had recently released. She remembered seeing signs for a midnight costume party book release event at the bookstore she frequented back home. Perhaps she could get the next three and keep her reading. She could ask Mrs. Gupta if an accelerated school existed for advanced children like Aditi. But even if it did, that type of school likely wouldn't be free, like this one.

This school had intentionally been located in a rural area, built entirely with donated funds and staffed by volunteer teachers, allowing children from impoverished families the opportunity to learn English for free to prepare them for better opportunities —and perhaps the chance to break out of poverty.

Though Olivia read articles complaining about the homogenization of the world and losing cultural identity, the best jobs required fluency in English. If these kids wanted a shot at them, this was their best start. Their parents knew that and sent the children, hoping for better futures for them. In the few weeks she'd been working with them, Olivia had grown fond of and attached to these kids and wanted the best for all of them too.

The children took their seats while she erased the board from the younger group and wrote JOBS at the top.

"Did everyone think about what they want to be when they grow up?" she asked.

Heads wobbled in tiny figure eights.

"Did everyone write about their job?"

More wobbling.

"Good! I'll go first. I am a teacher. I help boys and girls learn to read and write English. Who wants to go next?"

One of the boys raised his hand.

"Go ahead, Kunal."

He stood and read slowly from his paper. "When I grow up, I want to work at a hotel. I want to help people when they come to India. I know English and can talk to the tourists in English."

When he sat back down, she clapped. "Very good. Kunal wants to manage a hotel. Wonderful!"

She called on one after another, listening to their dreams of being teachers, taxi drivers, shop owners. One little girl said she wanted to be a nurse and help sick people in hospital. "Aditi, what about you?"

The chair scraped the floor as the girl stood. "When I grow up, I want to be a doctor. I want to go to university in England and then go to the United States. I want to help people when they are sick. I want to give them medicine and make them feel better again."

That was an excellent goal for this brilliant girl. She knew Aditi would have to work hard and even then, so many things would have to go right for her. But she wanted a bright future for Aditi, and all the others. She beamed. "Aditi will be a doctor and Surithra will be a nurse. Maybe you can work together."

The class giggled.

"All wonderful jobs. I'm so happy you are thinking about your futures and that you are here at school learning, working hard toward your goals. Let's talk about some other jobs people might have."

She turned to the board and began writing various professions she thought would be fun to talk about and prompt discussions with the children.

A loud booming noise startled her so badly she jumped and dropped her chalk, which broke to pieces on the floor. She spun around to find twenty pairs of frightened eyes looking to her for reassurance and guidance. She stared back, no idea what they'd just heard.

"What was that, Auntie?" The fear on Aditi's face rallied her, forcing her to maintain a calm demeanor.

Some of the boys stood, but no one knew what to do.

She took a deep breath and went to the window, trying to keep her voice steady. "Goodness. What was that? I think I felt the building shake." Could it have been an earthquake? The ground wasn't shaking. Other voices in the building indicated she wasn't the only one confused and alarmed.

Heads swiveled to stare outside with her. No additional noise assaulted her straining ears.

Darkness rolled over the school, thick clouds blotting out the sun's bright scorching rays. The sky opened up and torrential rainfall pounded against the buildings and parched dirt courtyard. Rain was good, surely, but this had blown in so suddenly. And the noise she'd heard had sounded like an explosion, not thunder.

Something seemed off about this storm, about the rain itself. She couldn't pinpoint what it was but felt certain something strange was happening. She walked along the entire length of the wall, staring out the windows, transfixed by the storm. The outside world appeared discolored by a filter, strange hues twisting into shadows while the rain tapped on the roof and windows. When she got to the door, she saw other teachers amassing in the hallway.

"What's happening?" she asked.

Tisha shook her head. "That's what we're wondering."

"Did you hear that noise?"

Melanie nodded emphatically. "Crazy, right?"

Mrs. Gupta appeared. "Is everyone okay?"

"Yes. Just shaken," Delilah said.

Chris joined them, forehead creased in confusion. Aubra hurried to his side. "What's happening?"

"Come on, guys." Chris gestured outside. "We've all seen storms before. It's not monsoon season, but a tropical storm can happen out of season."

"But that noise," Aubra said. "That sounded like an explosion."

"And maybe it was. A transformer blew once, and I remember it made a loud noise." Chris spoke with such authority. Olivia wondered how long he'd been here. She would have to remember to ask him.

"Not like this," Mrs. Gupta said. "Not like this."

"'And in that moment, like a swift intake of breath, the rain came,'" Delilah said.

"What's that one from?" Chris asked.

"*Other Voices, Other Rooms*. Truman Capote."

"Strangely applicable," Melanie muttered.

The children, apparently unable to control their curiosity and excitement, streamed from the classrooms in wiggling, giggling torrents, bobbing and jockeying for position to peer out the doors. Eventually one of them burst through the door and stood in the rain, holding his hands out. The others followed.

Olivia stared hard at the water. Something was off, something . . .

A tub sat outside the buildings, intended to collect rainwater. Though she and the other teachers didn't drink anything but purified bottled water, she knew the staff used rainwater for cleaning and for laundry. The water collecting in it wasn't right. She bent low, trying to determine what she was seeing. She glanced up at the children playing chase in the courtyard as the rain continued to pelt down. The children's uniforms included white shirts—white shirts currently turning red.

"What in the world?" She ran out into the tumult, droplets

pelting her skin while wind whipped her hair violently. She grabbed the first boy she encountered, Dev, by the shoulders. No question. The rain was staining his shirt red.

Dev held out his hands and grinned at her. "Teacher! It is raining. It is raining red!"

The children laughed and joined him. "The rain is red!"

That's what was off, what was wrong with this storm. The rain fell blood red. She turned to the other teachers. "It's red! The rain is red! What is this?"

Chris ran to her side, clutching at her *shalwar*, streaked with crimson rivulets. "It is! It's red. What would cause this?" he asked, as if she had any insight into this bizarre storm.

She shook her head. The tubs and jugs in the courtyard filled with the red-hued rainwater, shimmering like containers of blood collecting from a bleeding sky.

She had no idea what was happening, what could cause this, but an eerie shiver started at the base of her spine and traveled all the way up, filling her stomach with dread. What were these children being exposed to? What was drenching them as they dashed about playing? Chemicals? "Children! Get back inside! Now! You cannot play in this. Go! Inside!"

The other teachers joined her, scrambling around the mud, corralling the grinning children.

Utter fear clutched Olivia once they'd successfully ushered them all back inside and stood staring at the red rain pummeling the earth.

"I think Cormac McCarthy described this best," Delilah said. "'Shrouded in the black thunderheads the distant lightning glowed mutely like welding seen through foundry smoke, as if repairs were under way at some flawed place in the iron dark of the world.'"

Chapter Ten

The rain stopped. The storm passed. But Olivia couldn't stop thinking about it. She and the other teachers had finished out the day's classes as best they could after such an all-consuming disruption to the day derailed their lessons, then piled into the car and drove aimlessly around the town, searching for evidence and answers. Everywhere they went, red-tinged puddles shimmered in the late-afternoon sun drying up almost as quickly as they'd accumulated. Women pulled splattered and streaked laundry from clotheslines. And everywhere people marveled at the sudden storm burst that gave every appearance of drenching them all in blood.

How far did it reach? Did their little town alone experience this bizarre event? With no radio or television available to them, and dial-up internet slow and spotty at best, they had no option but to wait for the morning papers and glean what they could from the articles in those. Presuming the event had been large enough to attract the attention of the media.

While they were out and in town, Chris let her run into the bookstore to check on her order. To her delight, not only had her requested books arrived, but also the shopkeeper pointed out the next three books in the series on the shelves. He smiled so proudly, she was sure he'd ordered them with her in mind. She took a copy of each, not only because she enjoyed the first and wanted to see what happened next, but because if Aditi had already finished the first, she needed something more to keep her challenged. But Olivia would read the second book prior to passing it along. Best to preview it before handing over to a student.

She climbed back into the front seat of the car. Chris turned into traffic.

Aubra pressed her face against the window. "That's her! Look! She doesn't look pregnant. But she's still here."

The others twisted in their seats and craned necks.

"Who is it?" Olivia asked.

"The teacher you replaced," Melanie said.

Olivia spun in her seat but caught only a glimpse of the young woman as she walked down the street, eyes down, no apparent interest in anything. Olivia recognized that look.

As Chris parked the car and they all headed inside for dinner, she gave thanks for so many witnesses to the bizarre storm. Otherwise she might start doubting her sanity, questioning what she'd really seen. Then again, one glance at the stains on her top, darkening deep crimson as they dried, offered all the proof she needed. Would they wash out?

The deep crimson breathed new life into moments she'd tried to bury, memories she'd held down, strangled the life out of, knowing they would suffocate her if she didn't smother them first. Her brain closet creaked open, puking out blurred and hazy recollections to torment her with—a lifeless body, gray-blue skin, no blood circulating to pink the tiny cheeks, followed by six weeks of postpartum bleeding she'd agonized through, wondering if it would never end.

That teacher's face, the mourning and misery she wore like a shroud as she walked down the street. Olivia knew it well—the look of someone crushed under the weight of enormous loss, no direction, no knowledge how to even begin to recover. One foot in front of the other would keep you plodding forward, but it didn't help you move on.

Chris nudged her, offering her a platter of biriyani. Lost in thought, she didn't remember walking from the car to the dining table.

One foot in front of the other.

She scooped food onto her plate and passed it on.

Tisha accepted the platter, asking, "What's up? You okay?"

She tried to shake off the stupor. "Yeah. Today was weird."

The other women chimed in agreement.

"The rain looked like blood. It was—"

"I know!"

"The real red tide, right?"

They all laughed. So she wasn't the only one thinking that.

She glanced at Chris. "Not going to suggest we change the subject?"

"Chris is totally metro," Tisha said. "He is not the least bit perturbed by periods or discussions revolving around them."

She nearly dropped her spoon in her *dal*. "Seriously?" Scott couldn't tolerate the "p" word or the sight of feminine hygiene products. She'd half expected him to pass out in the delivery room. As it was, he stayed by her head the entire time, refused to look below her chin, and looked peaked the entire time.

"He's so enlightened," Aubra said, and though she tried to sound nonchalant, Olivia saw the longing in her eyes. "A true renaissance man."

Chris shrugged. "It's natural. Biology. What's to be bothered by?"

She met his eyes. "My turn to be impressed."

"Part of life. Like sweating and farting."

"And there it is!" Delilah said. "Table manners, please!"

A lull fell over the table, all of them eating quietly. Olivia could not stop thinking about the young former teacher, and how she had looked so morose, and wondered if anyone offered her understanding and support. She remembered how listless she'd been for months, inconsolable, despite her mother's attempts to rouse her from the intense depression she fell into. Scott made it worse. He wandered around the house like a specter, sleeping with his back to her, scrunched as close to the edge of the bed as possible without tumbling over the side. When he looked at her, she saw crests of accusation buoyed atop waves of hostility and frustration. Her mother kept insisting they needed to lean on each other, hold each other up, be each other's strength. But when she reached for him, he pulled away, no strength to offer her, leaving her to wither in her grief, while he drowned himself in a bottle.

"What's her name?" Her voice startled her.

"Who?" Melanie asked.

"The teacher. The one who got pregnant and left."

"Oh, Meena."

"Do you know where she lives?"

They all shook their heads. "No. Frankly I was shocked to see her today."

She nodded and dropped the subject, focusing on finishing her food.

The lights went out, plunging them in complete darkness, pitch black. Groans filled the dining room.

Tisha sighed beside her. "Honestly, meals are the worst for power outages."

"Nah. Sitting on the toilet at night is the worst."

"Chris!"

"Hey, if we can discuss periods over dinner, I think bowel movements are also on the table. Pun intended."

The ridiculousness of the situation, Meena's haunting face, and the ease of delightful company after a strange day all combined to trigger a laugh—a deep, uncontrollable laugh that percolated from a place within her that had been abandoned and gone fallow. Once she started, she couldn't stop. The others joined her, setting off another round of unfettered hilarity until tears leaked from her eyes.

Olivia took deep breaths and composed herself. "Goodness, I

haven't laughed that hard since—" She stopped short of completing the thought and ruining their evening. The moment got away from her.

"Since?" Tisha asked.

"Nothing. But seriously, now what? It's gotten dark outside. What do we do?"

The kitchen door swung open, and Ms. Vanya shuffled into the dining room, carrying a candle in one hand, shielding the flame with the other.

"When we lose electricity," Tisha said, "we switch to candles. Ms. Vanya keeps them on hand and lights the candles in our rooms."

"I don't have any candles," Olivia said.

"We forgot to tell you to get candles!" Tisha said. "How could we forget that?"

"Oh, no! We did forget. I'll grab an extra from my room," Chris said.

"Meanwhile," Aubra said, "the night is young, and I have a new shipment of chocolates from my parents that just arrived yesterday."

They clustered around the candle, moving slowly, taking cautious steps. The darkness outside was unlike anything she'd ever experienced—no streetlights, no soft glow from windows, no ambient city lights. She held her hand directly in front of her face and saw absolutely nothing. Complete, utter pitch blackness.

Chris's voice in the darkness said, "Here you go!"

She couldn't see his face, had no idea who he spoke to or what he meant.

He moved into the anemic glow of the single candle and checked each face until his gaze landed on hers. Before she knew what was happening, he'd grabbed her hand.

She jerked away from him. "Hey!"

His features morphed from delight to horror. "I'm so sorry! I didn't mean to startle you. I should've thought. Here, this is for you." He lifted a candle in front of Ms. Vanya, into the feeble light. "For your room. You can borrow the holder too, until we get one for you."

Of course. He was being thoughtful and generous. He'd never been anything but, and yet she continued to make assumptions and hold tight to suspicions. She'd learned the hard way to suspect ulterior motives from men. But not from him, and he didn't deserve it. "Thank you, Chris. I—"

He didn't let her apologize. "I'll take you to the market after classes tomorrow, okay?"

She nodded and he disappeared from sight, swallowed up in the darkness, back into the desolate building before she realized he couldn't see her reaction.

Ms. Vanya lit candles in each girls' bedroom before bidding them all goodnight.

Olivia watched for Chris to reappear, to join them for chocolates, before remembering boys weren't allowed in their building. She thought about him alone in the dark in the other building, no other guys to interact and chat with, for the first time considering how isolated he must feel. No wonder he always eagerly jumped at the opportunity to accompany them out into town.

Aubra welcomed them all into her room, where they sat in the floor, clustered near her nightstand with the candle casting a warm glow over them.

"I always love an impromptu girls' night," Melanie said.

Aubra passed around boxes of assorted Cadbury's chocolates. The other Americans insisted she notice the royal seal: By appointment to her majesty the queen . . .

"That makes it sound so serious and official," she said. "Cadbury makes me think of Easter commercials and nose-twitching rabbits laying eggs."

"Yes!" Melanie laughed.

"Good lord. What?" Aubra asked, and Olivia wasn't sure which she enjoyed more, Aubra's horrified face, all traces of British decorum gone, or falling onto Tisha's shoulder again in another fit of helpless, teary laughter.

She wiped her eyes. "I can't remember the last time I laughed so hard. I feel like a kid again." Except she couldn't remember ever laughing so hard as a child, and she'd definitely never had a group of friends or a sleepover. So really it was all new.

Tisha's fingers dug into an open box of chocolates, the packaging crinkling at the intrusion. "Why so serious normally?"

Olivia glanced over, lured in by a sense of false security the soothing darkness blanketed them with, and met Tisha's probing gaze. She glanced away quickly, shoulders rising and falling in a helpless shrug.

"Don't psychoanalyze her, Tisha," Delilah teased.

"I'm a counselor, not a psychiatrist," Tisha said.

She'd never asked the others about their lives before teaching in India. She didn't want to think about hers. Didn't want to open herself to return questioning.

She shook her head. "Several reasons, I suppose."

"Do you have a guy back home?"

She squirmed and shook her head again.

"What do you think of Chris?" Melanie asked.

She swore she felt Aubra's gaze bore into her. She shrugged. "He's young. Like all of you."

Tisha cackled. "Girl, I bet I'm older than you."

"No way. Nope."

"Thirty-two."

"Get out. You do not look thirty-two. I thought all of you were just out of college."

"No," Delilah said. "Not any of us. Tisha is hiding." Her southern drawl rolled over the words, as if relishing a decadent dessert instead of airing someone's dirty laundry.

"I . . ." She truly didn't know what to say.

Tisha shook her head. "It's okay. We've all confided in each other. I'm here to get away from an abusive boyfriend. Ex-boyfriend. How's that for irony? I work for DHS as a counselor, specializing in domestic abuse cases, and hid what was happening in my own home. Or didn't want to see it. Anyway, I'm trained to recognize the signs of battered women. We're here for you. That's all. And we all have demons we're wrestling."

Battered. The word sent a sharp jab into her sternum as though she'd been poked. Her father used to do that—poke a finger into her breastbone until she cried, then grab her arm and shake her, admonishing her to stop fussing, his voice growing louder and louder. She remembered her head lolling, teeth rattling, as he shook her, yelling, "Shut up!" When Mom appeared and yelled at him to stop, he turned on her. Always. She'd been the bait to lure her mother into a fight, a screaming match that escalated to justify his angry slaps, punctuated by his insistence that she deserved it, that she'd made him angry. Olivia had always stood there watching, frozen, tears streaming down her face.

She dropped her head, hid her face in her hands, tried to deny the tears leaking from her eyes.

Tisha pulled her into a hug, holding her fiercely, rocking her gently. Delilah, Melanie, and Aubra scooted close and draped themselves around her.

"It's okay," Tisha crooned. "It's okay to hurt. We're here. We know."

Chapter Eleven

As Olivia's young class filed out the door, she erased the board and placed workbooks for the next class at each seat. She glanced repeatedly at the door as the next class trickled in, watching eagerly for Aditi to appear and take her seat, feeling like she might burst with excitement. She'd stayed up late the night before, reading the second Harry Potter book by candlelight. She imagined the girl's face when she saw the book, knowing how it would light up with delight.

Her middle-grade students entered and took their seats, greeting her with shy smiles. She instructed them to continue their lessons and watched more intently for Aditi. No one had far to travel from one class to another in the tiny school, and the girl typically arrived right away.

Eventually she had to start class. Her eyes kept flicking to the door as she discussed the four seasons and weather in America. But Aditi never appeared.

When Mrs. Gupta signaled the end of class, Olivia met her in the hallway. "Aditi was absent today. I hope she's not sick. Do you know?"

"She is not sick," Mrs. Gupta said. "She will not be back."

Olivia opened her mouth to ask for additional information, but Mrs. Gupta turned on her heel and spun away.

She continued through her classes, concern for Aditi gnawing at the back of her mind, fueled by Mrs. Gupta's terse response about the girl's wellbeing.

Chris showed up at her door when the last class of the day ended. He helped her erase the chalkboard, gather up supplies, and straighten the room. "I thought maybe we could run to the market before dinner? Go get a stockpile of candles for your room?"

"Oh, yes! I'd forgotten. Thanks for the reminder."

He seemed atypically quiet on the drive. Normally she longed for silence, longed for the safety of keeping to herself. But today she found it unbearable.

"So, you're a math major." She already knew this bit of information. It was a statement, not a question. Something to break the stillness and hopefully lead to light conversation.

"Yes. Master's degree. No PhD. Eventually I expect to teach. I had planned on community college, like you. But maybe I'll check into high school math. The upper-level courses like Calculus. These kids are getting under my skin, you know?"

"I do know." Warmth flooded through her at the discovery of more they had in common. "How long will you stay here?"

"I only planned to stay two months initially."

Disappointment turned her stomach inside out, envisioning life here without him. How strange to think she'd disliked him such a short time ago when he picked her up at the bus station. She hadn't considered how painful leaving behind friends would be. But then she hadn't expected to form friendships. "Are you thinking of leaving earlier now?"

He laughed softly. "I've been here a year already, so no."

"Oh. Oh!" She let that sink in. "Not to be rude—and please tell me if it's not my business—but how?"

They'd arrived at the market. He parked and turned to her,

stretching an arm along the back of the seat. "What do you mean?"

He'd drawn up one leg, his posture and gentle demeanor so relaxed it would put even the most hardened attitude at ease. She tried to ignore how adorable he was in the male version of *shalwar kameez*. Averting her eyes, she debated how to discreetly ask her question. She couldn't, so she just went for it. "Are you independently wealthy? I mean—"

His laughter filled the car. "Oh, boy. I wish." His face fell, and he looked away.

She recognized that turning inward, going somewhere else mentally, somewhere unpleasant and painful. She should have left him alone. Prying into other people only dislodged their pain. Chris normally maintained such a bright, positive outlook, she'd assumed he hadn't been through anything horrible. His smile and eagerness to help labeled him a fortunate soul in her mind, someone unmarred by tragedy and abuse. But the look on his face she'd just witnessed made clear she'd been wrong. She opened her door and started to get out. "I'm so sorry. I didn't mean—"

He rested a hand on her arm. "No, no. It's okay. You're a fellow volunteer. You know our housing and basic meals are free. Our living expenses are extremely low once we get set up."

"Sure. I get it. I paid for my travel over here out of some . . . money I'd saved up."

"Me too. And I lived frugally during graduate school, kept loans to an absolute minimum, worked part time as a teaching assistant, got financial aid and grants, so I didn't have a lot of debt weighing me down. It doesn't take much to keep going."

"Well, sure. But we need a little money, right? I mean, I'm using up savings to be here, but that's finite. Eventually I'll need to go back and work. Did you just have a lot saved up?"

He laughed again. "No. In fact I'm using this hiatus to work on paying off my loans, while our financial responsibilities are so negligible."

"But—"

"I tutor students," he explained. "It pays reasonably well. The income is enough to live on here and still make student loan payments."

"By tutoring? I didn't think anyone around here could afford something like that."

"Oh, no! I tutor online. Students back in America. At night here, after dinner but before bed, it's morning there and I can answer last-minute questions and offer tips before they head to school. Then I get up early in the morning and catch them after school. I make myself available to anyone who needs homework help for a few hours."

She never would have guessed. His work ethic was incredible. "Wow. You work a lot. Really."

"It's worth it. Doesn't pay a fortune, but it pays. And I've always had to make money stretch, so it's no big deal." He glanced away again.

"Me too," she confided. "Things are so cheap here. It feels strange being able to afford things. My mom would—" She stopped herself, not ready to share too much personal information yet.

"Yeah. Mine would too. Except she's distracted with other things now." He clenched a fist, squeezing his eyes tight. When he opened them again, he smiled. "Sorry. Shall we?"

They meandered through the market, stopping at stalls and perusing the proffered wares of the vendors, even those who didn't offer candles. She got the feeling Chris needed to decompress, that he perhaps needed a break. But the silence weighed on her.

"Do you think the tutoring service needs English tutors, too?" Hoping to lure him back into conversation, she dangled the most recent topic in front of him.

"Oh, yeah! Definitely. You want to try it?"

"A source of income is extremely tempting."

"I'll email you the info. The only frustrating thing is when we lose power. The dial-up internet is always a little slow, and you'll pay per minute. But it's a negligible expense. Losing power is the worst. I stay as caught up as possible, as a safeguard. But still, from time to time I miss an assignment or question when I can't get online. I hate that. Hate leaving my kids hanging. You know?"

She did. And she saw him in an entirely new light. Flustered with the increased heartrate he seemed to be prompting, she nodded and looked away. She simply was not ready to deal with that.

"Here we go. Candles!" he said.

She picked up several boxes along with some candlesticks and insisted on paying, even though he offered. "I already owe you," she reminded him. "And now that I know you're on a fixed income—"

"Hey, now! Them's fightin' words. Disparaging a man's net worth is nearly as bad as calling him short. Or husky. Or weak."

She twisted her face into a frown and looked up at him. "You're not any of those things so why would I?"

He curled an arm. "I used to go to the gym regularly. None around here. I've definitely lost some muscle mass this past year."

He'd *lost* muscle mass? He looked pretty darned good. "A buff mathematician? You're supposed to wear glasses and a pocket protector and be a skinny little nerd." She laughed and elbowed him, then looked away. What was she doing? Was she *flirting*? Was he? Why else would he flex for her and apologize for his physique—which did not require any apology.

They arrived back at the car. He opened the door for her before getting into the driver's seat. She still hadn't adjusted to sitting on the opposite side of the car.

"It was just my mom and me growing up," he said as he pulled into traffic.

"Me too," she admitted. "In fact, I moved back in with her about a year ago, after—"

Silence hung between them for several minutes.

"I can tell you don't want to share," he said. "I get the feeling something bad happened and you needed to get far away too."

Too?

"I really, really hope no one put their hands on you." He squeezed the steering wheel, and she saw his jaw tighten.

"It's not that. I promise. At least not recently."

He relaxed a little. "Not recently?"

"My dad . . ." She shrugged and stared out the window. "My mom was his primary target, not me. I don't really like to talk about it. Sorry."

"I tried to keep it secret, too, when I was little. The whole reason I started going to the gym was to be strong for her. He's not my bio dad. Never knew him. But after a string of shitty boyfriends, she let the shittiest of all move in. He won't marry her, but she won't throw him out. No matter what he does. This has gone on for years. Last year, he put her in the hospital."

"Oh, my God! Is she okay?" Though her father had terrorized her mother, he had never hurt her so badly it put her in the hospital. She supposed she should be grateful for that. But it wasn't any underlying compassion that stayed his hand. He didn't want hard proof of his abuse.

"She was, once they stitched her up. I called the cops to have his ass thrown in jail. But she wouldn't press charges. They released him, he went right back, and she let him in. She called me for help. She always called me for help. Locked herself in the bathroom and called me, crying, pleading for me to come handle it. Same thing we'd been doing for years. And I went. I always went. I told her to stay in the bathroom and wait for me to get there. But she didn't listen. When I got there, he was smacking her around. She was still black and blue from the last beating and there he was smacking her around again. I hit him. Knocked him on his ass."

"Good," she said through gritted teeth. His story had propelled her back in time and pulled up old recordings of Dad throwing Mom around. Her fists clenched, nails digging into her palms, itching to pummel her father for what he'd done to them both. But she remembered her inability to change anything, too. She wished someone had been there to knock her dad on his ass back then and put a stop to it.

Chris glanced at her. "You've been there. I can tell. Here's the thing though. After I pulled him off and punched him, she threw herself over him and yelled at me to get out before she called the police on me."

"What? How could she do that? It doesn't make any sense. She called you!"

He nodded, a grim half-smile on his face. "I'd been seeing a counselor and finally accepted what she'd been telling me. I can't save my mom. My mom has to decide she wants better for herself and until she does, we will keep going through the same cycle over and over. Because I can't tell her no when she calls me crying."

"Who could? You'd be a pretty callous jerk."

"But I can't fix her problem. *She* has to throw that man out. And I had to stop running to her rescue."

She saw where the story was leading. "That's why you're here, isn't it?"

"Hardest decision I ever had to make. Mom wouldn't break the cycle, so I had to. I can't run across town at her beck and call anymore. It was killing me slowly, seeing her like that. My counselor said it's the same with family members of addicts. We want to help, but ultimately we can't stop them from making bad decisions."

He'd run away too. And if she was honest with herself, from a far worse situation. She'd misjudged him. "Is she . . . okay?"

They'd arrived back at the school complex. He parked the car and turned to face her. "I don't know. I severed all contact with her when I came. And maybe that's part of the reason I stay. Maybe I'm scared to go back, afraid of what I'll find."

"I'm so sorry." She didn't know what else to say.

"Tisha is a good listener. I talk to her some. She's a counselor, you know."

"Yes. She told me. I think she was trying to get me to open up to her."

"Well, whatever you've been through, she can help. At least a little. I mean, I still struggle with guilt. But . . ." He shrugged. "Shall we go inside?"

He was finished talking, she could tell when he opened the door and got out. The little car had functioned as confessional, and now they were moving on. But she could not absolve Chris of the heavy burden he carried.

Guilt. She knew how grappling with that day in and day out wore you down, exhausted you in a wrestling match of sorts. Her own guilt always pinned her. She'd never yet bested it.

She got out of the car too, and grabbed his arm as he passed her by, staring at the ground. His brow furrowed. Without a word, she opened her arms wide and threw them around him, pulling him into a fierce hug. He didn't deserve to suffer from his mother's behavior.

He rested his head on her shoulder, relaxing into the embrace, and curled his arms around her in return. "Thanks."

She didn't want him to get the wrong idea. Or maybe she did. Her jumbled thoughts yelled at the emotions churning in her guts to get their act together and knock it off. She didn't know what she wanted. For that matter she didn't know what *he* wanted. But he needed to know the truth. "I . . . uh—I'm divorced," she confided, waiting for him to stiffen in response.

Instead, he shrugged. "We're all adults with lives. People our age generally have been married. Or come close at least. I never got that serious with anyone because my mom got jealous anytime I dated someone."

"Jealous?" She tried to imagine her mom jealous of Scott instead of supporting them and encouraging them to seek help, to lean on each other during troubled times. On the contrary, Scott had been jealous of Mom.

"Yep. Another woman took my attention away from her."

Sounded like his mom had some pretty serious emotional

issues, in addition to the codependent relationship. But perhaps that wasn't surprising. What did it matter anyway? She wasn't here to get entangled with anyone. She came to escape emotional baggage, not to pile more onto the heap. Until she made peace with her own demons, the worst of which she had not shared with Chris, she would not become ensnared in someone else's.

Chapter Twelve

The latest Cadbury's care package from England resulted in another impromptu girls' night in Aubra's room, though this time with power. Olivia accepted the open box from Melanie and selected a piece from the assortment. She passed the box to Tisha and bit into her chosen confection—English toffee.

"Mmmm. The British know how to do chocolate," she declared, smooth cocoa on her tongue as her teeth crunched the rich, creamy toffee.

She wished Chris could join them. He seemed to drift into her thoughts quite a bit lately, and she found herself collecting things throughout the day to share with him during dinner. She liked telling him goodnight after dinner less and less. Particularly after what he'd shared with her this afternoon, she hated for him to be alone.

Aubra smiled at her, though it didn't reach her eyes, which remained cold and calculating. "Where did you and Chris go this afternoon?"

Oh, boy. How did she even know? "He drove me to the market for candles, that's all." She wondered if Aubra would be so fiercely jealous if she knew Chris's history with his mother. Well, she wouldn't be the one to fill Aubra in on the subject. That wasn't hers to share. Besides, Aubra had nothing to be jealous about.

But she did wonder if Chris was lonely, all by himself in the guys' building. It wasn't fair he couldn't even step foot in their women's housing, that he was stuck all by himself due to some archaic belief in the separation of genders. Unmarried men and women could fraternize without having sex. And honestly, where there's a will, there's a way. Meena's predicament illustrated that. She wondered if she could find out where the young woman lived and make an excuse to visit her.

At least they had power tonight. Chris probably busied himself with tutoring—

"Hello? Olivia?" Delilah snapped fingers in her face. "You're distracted tonight. What's up?"

She shook her head. "Zoned out. Sorry."

"We were talking about Diwali. It's still a couple months away, but we should celebrate the holiday with the kids. It's a big deal here."

"Oh! That's perfect. I plan to incorporate a holiday unit with my kids. American holidays will be easy, but I need to research Indian holidays. What did you call this one?"

"Diwali. Festival of the Lights," Aubra said. "It's one of their biggest holidays, although not as much in Kerala as the other states. My father used to travel to India on business quite a bit when I was growing up, so I'd heard about it already. I'm glad we're close enough to Kochi that this town celebrates it."

"Chris told us about it too. He said it was amazing," Tisha said.

"Oh, sure. Cuz he would have been here for it last year."

Aubra's eyes narrowed. "How did you know that?"

She waved a hand and shrugged, like *no big deal.* "He mentioned it at the market today."

"Anyway," Tisha continued, "Chris says it's a big deal that this town celebrates it. Fireworks, candles and lamps. Families gather to celebrate with food. Kids go door to door for candies and sweets. It falls at the end of October through the beginning of November this year."

The date jarred her, reminding her of an impending anniversary. She wasn't sure how she could possibly make it through the day. Maybe she should ask for it off, see if someone could substitute for her. She brought a hand to her forehead, noting anxiety building, a slow stirring she feared would build in intensity until she erupted like Vesuvius, belching destruction. She should definitely isolate herself that day.

"Okay, you," Tisha said. "Something is clearly up. What is it?"

She saw genuine concern and briefly considered spilling her painful secret. After all, Chris had assured her that Tisha would be wonderful help. But instead, she substituted another, albeit lesser, concern. "Aditi wasn't in class today. Did anyone else notice?"

The all glanced at each other, clearly aware of something she wasn't.

"Mrs. Gupta didn't tell you?"

Her heartrate kicked up a notch, fear and dread tangling in her stomach. "Tell me what? What happened to her? Was she in an accident or—"

"Nothing like that," Delilah said. "She won't be returning though."

"She won't be back . . . ever?"

Tisha shook her head. "She got her first period."

Olivia shook her head. She wasn't following or was missing something. "They don't let the girls come during their periods? She can come back next week, right?"

The other women shook their heads.

"No," Delilah said. "I know it's a shock. But once girls get their periods, at least in rural areas like this, their parents pull them out of school."

"Forever?" Olivia remained convinced this couldn't be true.

Tisha blew out a long breath. "It happens to all the girls eventually. Or at least the vast majority of them. Their education ends when they get their period. Surely you've noticed that the oldest students are almost entirely boys."

"It just didn't register, I guess. Why? Why do they do this to their girls?"

"Different cultural beliefs. Fear of menstruation. Lack of basic sanitation. No good feminine hygiene products. Or at least not affordable options."

"Speaking of sanitation, avoid going behind the building where they burn the trash," Delilah said. "Pads don't completely incinerate. I don't know about you, but I don't enjoy seeing my scorched, bloody remnants."

All the girls made faces and shuddered.

"Also, those sometimes attract wild animals, as close as we are to the jungle. Especially wild dogs. So, yeah, try to steer clear of the burn piles."

Wild animals. *Tigers.* She remembered reading something about tigers. "Do we need to watch for tigers here? Or wear masks on the backs of our heads?"

The others laughed.

"Don't wear a mask," Aubra said. "Just be aware and don't go out alone at dusk or dawn."

"I've never seen a tiger around here, if that helps you feel better," Tisha said. "So don't worry about that too much."

"Snakes, though," Melanie told her, "are everywhere. And they can get into the pipes. Always approach a toilet with caution and look inside before you sit on it."

Olivia waited for more laughter, but none came. They were serious. Great. Now every time she sat on a toilet, she'd be worried about a snake slithering up through the pipes and biting her butt.

Snake slithering through pipes. *Harry Potter and the Chamber of Secrets.* She'd never get to put that book into Aditi's hands.

She thought back over the past month, how a student had declared girls can't be superheroes, how extraordinarily bright

Aditi was, Aditi's dream of one day being a doctor. All of that now ground to a halt because she got her period? "This can't be right. I have a book for Aditi. How can she be completely finished with school? She's never coming back?"

"We've seen it happen over and over," Melanie said. "Don't get too close to any of your students, but especially the girls. You'll just be inviting more heartache."

Now they told her. Now when it was too late. She couldn't allow this to happen. "What happens now? Can she go to an all-girls school? Surely it's not really the end of her education. She wants to be a doctor. She's so smart. She could be one."

Four pairs of eyes watched her with empathy. They understood. They'd been through it. And they had no happy endings to share.

"Look, some parts of the world are worse. Some places ban menstruating girls and women to isolation tents. At least here they stay home."

"But it seems like such an extreme measure. We don't drop out of school back home."

"Not now we don't. In the past some girls did. Now we have clean, running water. Pads and tampons—thin and discreet. Washing machines for our clothes. We can clean up if anything leaks. Here they use rags and strips of old torn up cloth like women used on farms back home, like my grandma tells me she had to use growing up. Sometimes they resort to leaves. Eventually they'll probably catch up, but for now, this is how they handle things."

Olivia shook her head. She simply could not wrap her brain around this. "That just can't be right. I mean, come on. I've seen female Indian doctors in America. They must have gone to school here."

"In one of the bigger cities with a more progressive family, sure. But here? No. In rural parts of the country, the girls are expected to marry, have babies, and take care of their husband's house and children. Education is considered frivolous for them, since they won't get jobs anyway. Once they start menstruation, they stay home with their mothers and start helping run the house. On-the-job training basically, to teach them the skills they'll be expected to know in a few years. It wasn't much different in the States not that long ago."

Tisha rested a hand on her arm, sympathy in her eyes. "I know, but imagine how mortified Aditi, or any of the girls, would be to come to school with nothing but rags, leak all over their britches, and have no way to clean up. And what would they do with the bloodied rags in the middle of the day?"

Memories of heavy bleeding, so much blood, soaking her overnight pads, seeping through her pajamas, their sheets, billowing Rorschach blots spreading into meaningless but indelible stains, rushed back to her. She remembered Scott pinching his face in revulsion, as if she somehow had any control and could have stopped this from happening. Guilt and shame burned her neck and cheeks as she remembered ripping the sheets from the bed and scrubbing the bloody mess in the sink until her fingers glowed red and raw, sobbing at the injustice of it all.

The others nodded. "This is how they handle things. This is their way."

Olivia didn't accept that. She couldn't.

Indignation filled her at the thought of the little girls in her class chided and ostracized. Because their bodies bled, according to nature's design. She clenched her fists. "I'll give Aditi all the pads I have—everything I brought with me. I can buy more at the market." She gestured to the other young women. "What about you? We can distribute ours to all the girls as the need arises."

Aubra cringed. Melanie and Delilah wrinkled their noses.

Tisha grimaced. "You haven't seen the pads in the markets around here, girl."

"And you don't want to," Aubra said.

"They're expensive, thick, and won't absorb a thing," Delilah said.

Aubra made a face as if she smelled something horrible. "So

you walk around waddling with this horrible nappy between your legs all day—"

"—and blood runs off the surface and down your leg. I understand why the women use rags instead. I swear the pads are coated in water repellent."

"We had the misfortune of trying them," Tisha said. "I brought some from home but not a year's worth. When I ran out, I tried the local product and was shocked. Now we drive to Kochi and buy imported product—and pay many times what we'd pay at home."

"Well," Aubra said, "chocolates aren't my only care packages from home. Mum sends me some."

Olivia pressed on, sure the solution was somewhere in front of them. "Okay, so we get people to ship to us. Or . . . or overpay here. I just took on some tutoring. I'll have a little income."

Those forlorn eyes all stared back at her again. Delilah clucked her tongue, a silent *Bless your heart* evident in the sound.

"And what happens when we all leave and go home?" Tisha asked. "They'll be right back in the same situation."

Jarred, she slumped, caving in on herself. Like her marriage, like her own devastating loss, nothing could be done.

"I'm sorry. We did everything we could. It wasn't enough."

No happy endings waited for Aditi—or Olivia either, she realized. Why in the world had she entertained the notion they existed at all?

Chapter Thirteen

The next morning when Olivia woke up early, she checked online and discovered she had several new students who had reached out to her for tutoring. She responded to email, answered questions, assured those who needed papers proofed quickly that she could get to them in the next twenty-four hours. If she continued to add students at this rate, she might need to stop taking new students. She hadn't expected them to find her this quickly. Though delighted as well as surprised, she couldn't allow the side work to interfere with her main teaching.

She glanced at the clock and discovered she'd nearly missed breakfast. She signed off her account and disconnected the internet (the meter would continue to count the minutes if she forgot, and though it wasn't exorbitantly expensive, she didn't want to pay for more than she used). Making a mental note of which of the tutoring students needed responses first, she scurried about the room, gathering up what she needed for her classes today.

Shoot. She'd meant to email her mom. She really needed to check in with her, let her know she was adjusted and doing well. Even enjoying the teaching. Later. After class.

Switching gears, she looked over her lesson plan as she dashed across the courtyard and into the dining room.

"There you are!" Tisha said. "We were worried. Wondered if you were sick or something."

"No, I'm okay." She lifted the cup of lukewarm tea resting at her place and gulped it, not bothering to sit. "I lost track of time."

No time for cereal, she decided, so she took a remaining piece of dry toast to crunch on the way to her classroom.

Quick footsteps preceded Chris catching up to her halfway to the school building. "You really okay?" he asked, nudging her arm with his elbow.

"I am. Really. Got busy with tutoring and lost track of time." She sunk her teeth into the toast, biting off a third of the slice and immediately regretting her over-estimation of how much she could manage at once.

"I worried that . . . maybe after what I told you yesterday . . ." His brow furrowed above downcast eyes, his mouth twisted in remorse.

Realizing the completely wrong conclusion he'd jumped to, she chewed faster, trying to empty her mouth. The dry toast formed a wad and seemed only to swell and threaten to choke her. She couldn't speak, so she widened her eyes and shook her head.

When he wouldn't look up, she poked him and forced the dry toast down. "Seriously, I haven't given it another thought."

"I thought maybe it was too much."

"Not at all. We all have our issues and baggage, right?"

He lifted his gaze from the ground. "Yeah?"

She envisioned him alone in the men's housing again, replaying their conversation all night, worried he'd said too much, gone too far—while she ate chocolates and worried about Aditi with the other women. With no one to talk to, he must have really worked himself up, poor guy. She rested a hand on his upper arm and squeezed, hoping he could sense she meant every word. "Absolutely."

He seemed to melt with relief. And finally smiled. "Okay. Good."

She noticed him start to reach out—to hold her hand? *Oof.* That wasn't her intention. Encouraging friendship was one thing but veering into anything remotely romantic was a whole different thing. She turned and headed toward the school building again. He walked her the rest of the way to her classroom.

"I'll see you at dinner," she assured him.

His eyes searched hers. She knew what he was looking for and knew he wouldn't see it there. She liked him. She did. She wanted to maintain their budding relationship but wasn't ready to cross the line into anything serious. Not now. She appreciated how easily he'd accepted her divorce, accepted her baggage. He didn't judge her or show any sign of shock. Maybe she worried about it too much. Still, how would he feel if he knew—

"Let me know if you need anything," he said.

She could tell he meant it and appreciated his support. "I will."

He gave her one last smile before leaving for his own class.

Aditi's empty seat haunted her, distracted her throughout class. She went through the motions of teaching, but each girl's smile and bright eyes, eager to soak up everything she presented to them, left her distracted and fighting tears. They would all disappear, one by one, all suffer the same fate of growing up and being hidden away at home until their fathers married them off, relegated to wives, mothers, homemakers. They all had dreams. How could she in good faith encourage those dreams, knowing what she knew? If these girls wanted to stay home and do nothing else, fine. So be it. But not one girl had said she wanted to stay home and care for her husband and children. How unfair to dangle prospects and possibilities in front of them, knowing they could never have that.

By lunchtime, she'd realized she could not allow herself to grow attached to these kids, could not take any more emotional fallout from losing them one by one. Much like she held Chris at arm's length and would not, *could* not, let him close enough to hurt her, she would not let the children past her barriers either. It was the only way. Otherwise, each lost child, each potential future snuffed out, would erode her heart, chipping away little pieces until nothing remained to beat in her chest. What would she be without a heart? A bitter, desiccated husk, unable to feel, to connect, to love.

No, she'd been there once before. Never again. Better to put her heart into hibernation until she got back home and could safely wake it slowly as she unpacked and examined her time in India and where she wanted to go next. For now, she would shut down.

She lined up her class and escorted them down the hall to the little room that functioned as a cafeteria. Chris passed her, leading his older charges back to class, their lunchtime over. His face lit up and he waved when he saw her. She offered a smile in return. And then spotted Aubra glaring at them both, as if any of this reflected back on her. She hadn't encouraged his attention. For crying out loud, she hadn't dated in . . . how many years? At least a decade. More years than that by now. She had no tolerance for middle-school drama when she was in college. She darned sure wouldn't get swept up in any now. Chris needed to grow a backbone and tell Aubra to take a hike. And Aubra needed to accept that Chris harbored no feelings for her, suck it up, and move on.

But she wouldn't get drawn into it. She held her head high and stared straight ahead as she passed Aubra, pretending not to notice the younger woman's gaze. She refused to be stuck in the middle, used as a scapegoat by both parties.

Outside, the sun beat down, baking the earth in the court-yard. She took the *dupatta* from her shoulders and draped it over her head to shield herself from the intense heat of the midday rays. Her sensitive skin normally burned easily. But thanks to the *shalwar kameez* that covered her arms and legs plus the thick haze of smog that nestled over them, filtering the sun's light and UV waves, her exposed skin had browned, but not burned. Thanks to the pollution, she blew black mucous out of her nose every night. But she hadn't burned.

She didn't run and play with the children—her children, as she'd grown to think of them—as she had before. She stood to the side of the courtyard, alone, determined to remain aloof—from the children, the other teachers, and Chris.

The boys tore around the yard, playing tag, kicking a ball, using a stick to play an approximation of what she'd learned was cricket. The girls skipped rope or watched longingly as the boys ran about, yelling, laughing, playing. One little girl, Prisha, even struck a batter's pose and swung each time a boy stepped up to bat in the impromptu game. She looked like she could hit a wicked googly. Or whatever the phrase was.

Prisha discovered Olivia watching her and immediately clutched her hands behind her back, as if caught doing something she shouldn't. Olivia smiled at her and nodded in the direction of the game, hinting the girl should join in. Prisha looked stricken, shook her head, and stared at the ground.

Of course. The girls didn't mix with the boys. She looked closer at the girls, their frayed jump ropes, quiet demeanors, and downcast eyes. For that matter, the boys played with sticks and rocks and a ball so scuffed and deflated it thumped and careened sadly with each kick. Why didn't they even have decent playground equipment? Surely none of this would be very expensive—

One of the little boys in her class took a tumble and landed hard on his palms and knees, inertia sending him skidding a few feet across the ground. He got up and brushed himself off, but the sight of blood must have been too much for him. Instead of returning to the game, he stood still and began to cry.

She rushed to his side and knelt to inspect his wounds. His hands and knees had been skinned, dirt lodged in the abrasions. She rested a hand on his back and led him to the building, wondering what sort of first aid might be available. She hadn't thought about that before, but it seemed like something critical at a school. She hadn't been introduced to a school nurse, so she tried Mrs. Gupta's office. Finding no one, she took Dev back to her classroom and cleaned up his scrapes.

The boy kept crying, which seemed out of order for the level of his injuries. Sure, skinned palms and knees hurt. She knew that. She remembered from when she was little. She soothed and reassured him, but no matter how many times she uttered, "There we go, it's not that bad," he was absolutely inconsolable. Her options were limited, with no Bactine or Neosporin, nothing to deaden the pain of open wounds. But she wiped him off with a damp tissue, gently dislodging the dirt and debris stubbornly packed into the raw, red lines. With no bandages to cover the exposed pink skin, she applied pressure until the scrapes stopped bleeding. She didn't understand most of what he said but thought maybe she caught "torn pants" between rattling breaths. Seemed like rather an overreaction. If the knee torn out of his pantleg upset him this much, she should get a sewing kit. She was no seamstress, but she could use needle and thread well enough to close the rip.

She got another tissue, blotted his face, and instructed him to blow his nose. By the time she got him cleaned up and somewhat calmed down, recess was over, so she left him in his seat, still sniffling and upset but no longer wailing. She went to retrieve the rest of her class. As she knew they would, the kids had continued to behave themselves and follow the rules even in her absence. They were such good kids. She watched them put away their frayed jump ropes and deflated ball, and leave their sticks and rocks in little, organized groups. She wanted better for them. Every one of them.

Prisha threw her arms around Olivia's waist and squeezed tightly. "I love Auntie."

She placed a hand on the girl's back and squeezed back in a gentle hug. "I love Prisha."

Her plan wouldn't work. How could she stop herself from

caring about these kids? It was a good idea but completely unfeasible.

The children lined themselves up, and she led them back inside, fighting tears and wishing she could do more.

Chapter Fourteen

At dinner that night, Olivia mentioned Dev and told the others how hard he had cried over skinned knees and palms and a torn pants leg.

"He ripped his pants?" Tisha asked. "Well, that's why he was so upset."

"The school requires the children to wear uniforms," Delilah said.

Melanie nodded. "It's a huge expense on poor families. Huge. Dev probably has one shirt and one pair of pants."

"Buying another pair," Tisha said, "would be like a whole 'nuther back-to-school shopping trip for us back at home when we were little. It's just too big an expense. And unexpected. He might very well have gotten in trouble when he got home. Some of his tears may have been due to anticipating his parents' reactions."

"This is awful," Olivia said. How many shocks could she take? "Why does the school even require it? I thought we're here to help these kids get ahead. Not cause additional burden on the families."

"Hey," Tisha said, "it's free otherwise. A school that teaches their kids and makes them fluent in English, all at no cost? The uniform is each family's investment. Something so that they have some sort of stake in the kids' educations."

"And they do have their pride," Aubra weighed in. "If they can't buy new, embarrassment alone might cause them to pull the boy out of school."

"Pull him out? That's such an overreaction!" Olivia said. "Can't his mother sew the rip? Surely the moms here can sew."

"Of course. And then every day he will arrive in the same pair of torn and repaired pants. And everyone will know his family can't afford a second pair."

"But if all the children are in the same boat, who cares?"

"It's an accepted illusion. They can all pretend to have five sets of clothes, until something shatters the fiction."

"The red rain stained all their shirts. They didn't all freak about that."

"Bleach," Melanie said. "A white shirt can soak in bleach."

"So if the parents are too embarrassed about not being able to buy another pair, they'll just keep him at home? No more school for him?"

"Well, not here anyway," Aubra said.

The tears she'd interpreted as an extreme overreaction to a skinned knee actually reflected his fear of getting in trouble combined with the knowledge the torn pants might result in no more school for him. These kids deserved a break. She lost her internal struggle not to get involved and turned to Chris.

"Would you please drive me to the market again?"

She expected him to be mildly annoyed, but Chris looked downright delighted to be recruited as chauffeur again. Trips to the market was turning into their thing, which of course Aubra noted.

"You two sure do find a lot of reasons to go to the market together."

Whatever. Let her be irritated. What difference did it really make? She needed to go to the market, and everyone had been abundantly clear that Chris needed to accompany them when they went. The other girls could come if they wanted to. Nobody was stopping them. But no one spoke up, aside from Aubra's snide comment.

At the market, she bought a couple of new soccer balls, some jump ropes, and an actual cricket set for the boys. After a moment's hesitation, she asked for a second set for the girls. She would learn the basic gist and rules of the game and then teach the girls so they could play too. She would make mistakes and get things wrong, but after all they were only playing during recess. No one was trying to qualify for any world championships here.

At the tiny pharmacy, she requested a huge box of bandages, resulting in some confusion over what exactly she was asking for. Chris interceded and told the man behind the counter she wanted plasters.

"They use the British term here," he told her. "Aubra filled me in. Now you'll know for next time."

While the man went to retrieve the plasters and other assorted first-aid items she'd asked for, she debated whether or not to open a discussion about Chris and his admirer. Her questions might be interpreted as a way to gauge his interest and availability for herself. Which wasn't the case at all. But there was a chance he was utterly oblivious to Aubra's obvious-to-anyone-else affections. Maybe she'd be doing Aubra a favor by letting him know and giving him a nudge. Although honestly, she couldn't believe anyone could be that clueless. Finally, she decided to simply plow ahead.

"So. Aubra is nice."

One side of his nose wrinkled, and his brow furrowed. "You really think so? She's a little bit of a diva truth be told. Too high maintenance for me."

Oh. That shed some light on things. He was aware of her interest. "Well, I don't know her that well. She's been nice enough to me though. Gives me chocolates on girls' nights." She left out the bit about the passive-aggressive comments and behavior. "I guess you already know she has a crush on you."

It wasn't a question. She looked down at the counter and then examined all the medications on the shelves behind it very closely, uneasy about making eye contact.

"I know. I feel bad about it, but it just didn't work out. Like I said, she was just too high maintenance for me. And wanted to move way too fast. When she started insisting I go to England to meet her parents, I had to break it off. I just wasn't ready for that, you know? And I don't know how I would have handled an international relationship like that after teaching here ends. I mean, I told her I wanted to keep things light."

Well. This shed a whole new and much brighter light on the situation.

"You guys dated?"

He tipped his head, confusion in his eyes. "I assumed you knew. Figured the other teachers would've filled you in on the gossip."

No. Not a word. She didn't know what to say. Hearing him say Aubra wanted to move too fast and that he wasn't ready for a serious relationship made her think maybe she'd been misreading cues. Maybe he was simply a really nice guy who liked helping people.

The man behind the counter returned with her antibiotic ointment, pain relieving cleansing spray, bandages, thermometer, and other assorted items. She picked up a pouch to store everything in and added that to her pile of purchases. She would keep them all in her classroom and function as school nurse as long as she was here. And then leave it with her replacement when she left.

A pastel package caught her eye. "And I'd like some pads, please," she told the vendor. She wanted to see these things herself. She glanced sideways at Chris, but he didn't cringe. If he was at all bothered by her request, he hid it well.

However, as nonchalant as Chris appeared to be about the subject matter, the man behind the counter tensed. His lips flattened into a line. Without a word and without looking directly at her, he went to the shelves and pointed. She asked for one of each, curious if every option was truly as bad as the other teachers had led her to believe. The vendor's attitude confused her. Why should this be any different than her request for a box of bandages? Or the packages of tissues he'd retrieved for her? No one was ostracized and given the cold shoulder for buying toilet paper. Why did female hygiene products carry such a stigma?

She had been taught as a young girl to "be discreet" with her pads and tampons and to keep them out of sight. It wasn't something discussed ever. She could even remember her mom burying packages in the shopping cart underneath other items in the basket. Why were girls and women made to feel embarrassed about their bodies? This seemed akin to the unspoken agreement that everyone pretended the children all had entire wardrobes of clothes at home, even though everyone knew better. Girls and women should pretend not to have periods and refrain from discussing anything about them or brandishing product in plain sight that would then dispel the fantasy? She never felt the urge to trumpet her time of the month or discuss details about it. But no woman or girl should feel shamed or ostracized for it.

The man returned to the counter with one of every type of pad sold at this rural little market and dumped them beside her other purchases as if he expected them to contaminate him. He took out old newspaper and quickly wrapped each package, hiding the product from view, then tallied her total and accepted payment, though not with a smile.

"Wow," she said as they walked away. "He turned downright chilly, didn't he?"

"That was a lot of pads." Chris laughed. "Maybe he was afraid you were about to bleed all over the sidewalk in front of his shop."

She couldn't help but laugh too. "Where can I buy school uniforms?"

Her question appeared to give him whiplash. "We'd need to go back to the more upscale market where we got your clothes when you first got here. There's a bigger and slightly nicer pharmacy over there too. I don't know if you need more pads, but you'd be able to get nicer ones. Maybe some overnight options if things are that dire."

She caught the gleam in his eye and burst out laughing. Okay, there was a difference between being comfortable with pads and making suggestions and knowing where to buy the better options. And joking about periods like they're no big deal. "I'm not . . . these aren't all for me. I'm trying to figure out how to help Aditi. And eventually the other girls."

"I figured. I'm only teasing you."

"Still, how do you know where the best pads are? That doesn't seem normal."

"The other teachers talk. Remember, I drive them around. We've even driven all the way to Kochi to stock up on crates of them. I felt like a smuggler." He laughed again. "Sorry. This just doesn't bother me."

"No, please don't apologize. It's refreshing." Scott hadn't been nearly so easy-going. She'd never thought much about it, but the squeamish attitude was downright silly in retrospect. Were smart people disturbed by periods? She almost laughed out loud at the thought of asking him that. And the look on his face if she'd turned his own weapon on him.

As they turned to leave, she spotted a young girl walking with a man and woman and did a double take. "Aditi!"

The girl turned at her name.

Olivia hurried to her. "I'm so happy to see you! I have another book for you."

"Hello, Ms. Montag," Aditi said. The girl's demeanor seemed far more subdued than it had been in class.

She held out a hand to the woman she presumed to be Aditi's mother, who balanced a baby on one hip and clutched a toddler by the hand. "Hello. I'm Aditi's teacher at the school. I'm so happy to meet you. She's a wonderful student."

The woman stared at the ground.

"No, Auntie. No English," Aditi said.

The man interceded. "Aditi does not go to school now."

The scowl on his face unnerved her. "I understand that, but maybe you could reconsider. She's very smart and has so much potential. And I have another book for her—"

"No!" the man insisted. He grabbed Aditi and pulled her away. "No more school. And no more books with girls learning magic and tricking people. She stays home now."

Learning magic and tricking people? Oops. He didn't approve of the book. Still, Aditi deserved to return. "If you give her the chance, she can be so much more than a wife and mother. Please think about it. Wouldn't you like to see your daughter be a doctor or—"

"No more!"

The man's tone startled her into silence. Her heart thumped against her ribs, the scared-rabbit thumping she remembered from her childhood when her father screamed at her mother and threw her around the house.

She watched in silence as the man led his wife and children to a pale blue scooter. They all piled on it and rode away.

Dumbfounded, she stared at Chris.

"Sheesh. He reminds me of some of my mom's boyfriends," he said, patting her on the back in a gesture clearly meant to comfort her.

"Yeah. Reminded me of my dad too. I'm so glad my mom got away from him." They walked in silence. Her thoughts dove back into her childhood memories, landing on the time her father scooped her up off the floor where she played with toys and shoved her on a shelf in a closet. He'd closed the door, telling her she could stay there until she learned a lesson. She'd been about three years old at the time and had no idea what would happen to her as she cowered on a high shelf in the dark. She'd cried and cried. Her mother eventually found her, pulling her off the shelf and into a crushing hug, crying until tears soaked her hair. And then of course came the screaming match with her father and the subsequent lashing out. Thinking back on it, she knew her father had been drunk and spoiling for a fight. Locking a toddler on a shelf in a closet, terrorizing and scarring her for life, had been a means to getting what he wanted—an excuse to fight with Mom, which then gave him an excuse to smack her around. But why? Why did he drink? Why did he abuse them instead of cherishing and loving them? Why couldn't he face down his demons and be a man instead of making himself feel stronger by picking on the weak? Only, as it turned out, her mom wasn't weak after all. She was the one who found strength to stand up and make life better.

Chris nudged her with an elbow. "You okay?"

She shrugged. "Yeah. Just remembering things I wish I could forget."

"I understand that. Try not to let that guy get to you."

They passed a newsstand. One of the newspaper headlines grabbed her attention.

SCIENTISTS BAFFLED BY RED RAIN—CAUSE UNKNOWN

Cause unknown? How could that be? She stopped and picked up a copy and scanned the article. The inexplicable downfall had been on her mind since the day the sky opened up and drenched them all with crimson droplets, staining their clothes rust red. And no one could explain why?

SKY RAINS BLOOD

Another headline in a different paper. She picked up a copy of every English-language paper available at the newsstand, determined to learn everything she could about the bizarre phenomenon. She should look it up online as well, in case she could find more up-to-date information than what trickled down to this little community.

"Have you heard anything more about this?" she asked Chris. "It would be nice to know what we were drenched with."

He shook his head. "From what I've heard, no one seems to know anything."

"How can that be?"

"I guess some things just defy explanation."

That wasn't good enough for her. She needed to know what it was, what caused it, what happened. Was it toxic? Harmless? How would it affect her later? She'd had her fill of hearing that sometimes things just happen, and we don't know why. She needed a why. "Just because" wouldn't cut it.

She paid the man for the papers and clutched them to her chest until they were back in the car. While Chris drove to the more upscale market, she devoured the front-page story, but was disappointed. The article revealed that scientists at Kerala University had been unable to definitively determine what stained the rain red. It detailed some tests they'd run, but that was all. An article in another paper hypothesized that the red rain was the result of dust storms in Saudi Arabia. And a third paper postulated that the unidentifiable material found in the rain must be extraterrestrial in nature, perhaps introduced into the atmosphere by a meteorite.

Extraterrestrial living cells from a meteorite? The article went on to claim that scientists had not been able to match the material extracted from samples of the red rain to anything on the planet. Could that be true? She read and re-read the articles, hoping for something to offer a glimmer of explanation.

Nothing. No one understood the bizarre phenomenon. She refolded the paper and leaned back, closing her eyes. Weary of nothing making sense in her life, she needed someone to figure out what had happened. She needed answers and resolution.

Chapter Fifteen

Olivia stood quietly, lips pressed together, as Mrs. Gupta spoke with her. Apparently, some of the parents of the children she was trying to help had called the school with complaints. They didn't like their daughters coming home excited about having been taught to play cricket or with books where girls went to school and learned to do magic and broke the rules. And even Dev's parents were inexplicably up in arms over the new pair of pants she'd gifted him with.

"This is India," Mrs. Gupta told her, "not America. We know in America people have many things. But not here. Please adhere to our ways. Do not try to make the children into little Americans. When you leave, they must be content to continue in our ways. I know you mean no harm, but I must ask you not to give the children so many things."

Little Americans? Was she trying to Americanize the children? That wasn't her intent. They were here to help the children, to give them a chance to break the cycle of poverty. Teaching them English and giving them an edge in the job market was her job, not her idea. She frowned slightly.

"I'm sorry, Mrs. Gupta. I know I've only been here a little while, but I love these children. It tears me up when they stop coming to class. The money for Dev's new pants wasn't a huge expense for me, and I wanted him to be able to come to school. No one knows I did that. His parents can pretend they bought them. And yes, I bought the kids in my classes some supplies and some playground equipment. Can you consider that my donation to the school?"

"I must ask that you make no more large purchases."

How could she explain it wasn't large to her? That she was happy to do it. Could she stop? "I'm sorry, Mrs. Gupta. I'll try to do better, but I can't promise that. I want to help them."

Mrs. Gupta took a deep breath and seemed unsure how to proceed with this response. Olivia still couldn't believe anyone would chastise her for better equipping the children. She thought she'd been doing a good thing. She'd felt happier than she had in a long time, and now to be criticized for her behavior left her feeling foolish.

"If this is a problem," she said, "if you need me to leave . . ."

Mrs. Gupta's hard expression softened. "No, of course not. Nothing so radical. We are grateful you came to teach on such short notice. But perhaps you did not have enough time to prepare and understand how we do things here. India likes to take care of India."

Ah. They didn't want her charity. She didn't see it that way, but she supposed she could understand. No, actually, she couldn't. She couldn't believe she was being reprimanded for trying to help children stay in school. As always, no good deed went unpunished. She'd told herself to stay out of it, to keep her distance. This is what she got for not listening to herself.

"I will try to do better," she said. The words scratched the inside of her mouth like sawdust, dry and rough.

"I will tell the parents I spoke with you." Mrs. Gupta smiled reassuringly.

Olivia felt anything but reassured. Dismissed, she trudged across the courtyard and to her room. She clicked the door closed, lit a stick of incense, and sat at the tiny desk. She needed to check in with her tutoring students. She had a couple of papers to proof that she knew of, plus whatever had hit her inbox during the day while she taught. Her fingers clicked across the keys as she entered her information into the dial-up modem.

While she waited for the connection to establish, she breathed deeply and looked around the room. This was how she wanted her room when she went back home. In fact, she would pack everything up and take it with her. She could ship it or get another suitcase and check it when she flew home. But she wanted these things surrounding her back home too—the tapestries, the bed cover, the sweet little lamp with the peacocks on it, the elephants that Chris had given her. These wouldn't simply be souvenirs to keep the memories alive—these had become part of her.

She'd known already that she loved animals, but Scott had always disparaged her for it, telling her zoos were for kids and implying she was childish and immature for enjoying them so much. But the elephants and camels and peacocks surrounding her soothed her soul and delighted her, helping her to relax after a long day. The soft glow cast by the wooden lamp enveloped the room in a warm ambience, easing her mind and encouraging calm. The tension in her muscles eased.

The wisp of smoke from the stick of incense curled upward and suffused the room with the grounding scent of patchouli. She breathed deeply, luxuriating in the heady fragrance. She'd never used scents in the house she'd shared with Scott. He didn't like fragrance of any sort. He used unscented soap, insisted on unscented laundry detergent and dryer sheets, unscented deodorant. He hadn't liked her to wear perfume, so she didn't. But now she could do as she pleased, and she realized she loved incense. Patchouli, cedarwood, sandalwood—she loved the earthiness of them. They stirred her soul.

Staring around the room, she realized the house she'd shared with Scott never felt like home, never felt like hers. She'd lived in the place for ten years and not once did she feel as at home and surrounded by things that delighted her as she did in this tiny, simple room in rural India. Scott always wanted final say on anything they bought together. Furniture, decorations, wall art— he would ask her what she liked but never act on her response, pretending to mull it over before picking his favorite anyway. Always. Come to think of it, the same applied to deciding what they would watch on television. Eventually she'd given up even offering an opinion when he bothered to ask. Knowing her input would be dismissed, she eventually told him to make decisions. He would anyway. Consequently, nothing ever reflected her, her style, her personality, her likes. No wonder she hadn't cried when they sold the house—it never felt like hers anyway.

She never could have brought any of this into the house she'd shared with him—his house. He wouldn't have approved. Would she have picked any of this while married to him? What would she have picked? She realized she didn't know who she was anymore. All those years of marriage, of giving in to someone else's wants, of not making any decisions of her own, had left her unsure of who she was and what she liked. She'd lost sight of herself, given up, forgotten who she'd been before. But now she wasn't sure if she was remembering or something else.

Like Chris, she'd needed distance and a clean break from everything that held her back. Had she on some unconscious level known she needed to get away and find herself? Was she finding herself? Or was she moving on, transforming into a new person?

When she went home, she would get her own place, something her very own, and she would decorate it however she pleased. She'd fill it with eucalyptus and burn incense if she wanted to, when she wanted to. Never again would someone ask her if she really needed something or wrinkle his nose at her choices or tell her smart people didn't do the things she did.

Constantly implying she was dumb, making decisions for her and insisting it was for her own good, rolling his eyes and apologizing for her in front of others, Scott had rendered her a self-doubting, indecisive mess. How could he have thought so little of her? Why did he look annoyed when something delighted her? Why did he even want to marry her in the first place?

Internet connection established, she navigated to her email and discovered a reply from her mom. Though still not pleased with her decision to race off to India, Mom was glad to hear she was enjoying her time. She hit reply and shared a few recent developments, how the children's English was improving and how she taught the girls to play a simplified version of cricket. That brought back unsettling thoughts of being rebuked. She debated for a moment before typing a brief version of Aditi leaving school and why. And she mentioned Chris, but only briefly and didn't even stipulate he was a guy for fear Mom would get the wrong idea. Then again, maybe she should let her think that. Some day she might want to pursue a relationship again—this time with someone who liked her the way she was, who didn't always demand his own way, perhaps someone who actually enjoyed seeing her happy.

How would Mom handle that? For that matter how would Mom handle her moving back out? She recognized how easily they'd fallen into an easy rapport living together as they had when she was growing up. But she needed her own place again eventually. She couldn't live with Mom forever.

She moved on to tutoring, but her mind drifted again to Aditi. The pads she'd bought at the market were every bit as terrible as the other teachers had warned her. They hadn't exaggerated one bit. Plus, considering she'd paid roughly the same amount for a small package of ten pads as she'd paid for Dev's uniform pants, the cost would inhibit local families from purchasing them, even if the quality was better. If they couldn't afford clothes, no one would shell out that kind of money for feminine hygiene products. What did women do around here? Were ripped rags the only option? Surely there had to be an effective but affordable alternative to allow the girls to stay in school.

Knowing she ought to focus on proofing papers for her tutoring students, and still stinging from Mrs. Gupta's rebuke to stay out of India's business, she opened a new tab and typed in a search. The few results the search returned shocked her. Ripped up old clothing and rags were a luxury option compared to animal dung and dirt, which apparently some of the poorest women in the world resorted to using. She discovered that only around twenty percent of women in India had access to and could afford to purchase pads. Horrific statistics of women contracting infections as a result of non-hygienic materials shocked her. Many of the women who contracted infections suffered permanent damage to their reproductive systems.

She shuddered, thinking of Aditi and the other girls in her classes facing this sobering future. Handing out pads wouldn't work. If giving a male student a pair of pants got her in trouble, how would parents respond to her distributing pads to their daughters? Nothing good would come of that. The other teachers didn't seem to have a problem with the way things happened here. And she'd just been told, basically, to butt out and leave it alone.

So why couldn't she stop looking for options? Everyone was right—when she went home, India would continue on as it had done for thousands of years. Who was she to think she could change things? And why did she even think she should? If everyone else was happy, why was she fixating on this?

Smart people know when to quit. Funny how Scott's encouragement to quit and to give up only ever applied to her. Time after time when she'd been turned down for a full-time position at his university or any community college in their town, he'd shaken his head. *Why don't you stop applying? It's just too upsetting to you when you don't get the job. Maybe it's time to look for a different job.* It was like he didn't want her to succeed.

The last thing she needed to do was take up another hopeless cause. Anytime she tried to do anything, she failed. Scott made sure she understood her limits and kept her from getting hurt.

She shook her head and closed the tab. She needed to send back papers to her tutoring students before dinner time. It wasn't her business. She needed to stay out of it.

Chapter Sixteen

In addition to the usual bowls of *dal*, cauliflower with potatoes and peas, rice, and plate of *chapatis*, the teachers passed a platter of chicken, murmuring comments of delighted surprise.

"Wonder what the special occasion is," Melanie said.

Chris shared a look with Tisha, who nodded. "Ms. Vanya sent us to the market to get a chicken, at Mrs. Gupta's insistence. She had to speak with a teacher today and doesn't want the teacher to feel unappreciated. She knows the teacher means no harm."

Olivia flushed and dropped her gaze to her empty plate, but not before noticing every eye in the room shift to her no doubt bright crimson face. Even with Chris and Tisha keeping the perpetrator anonymous, everyone in the room knew exactly who had rocked the boat and required a dressing down. Just like Scott used to tell her, *Smart people stay in their own lane.* Why did she keep causing trouble?

Tisha stabbed a leg from the platter. "I'm sure whoever it was acted out of kindness. And I for one am thrilled to see some chicken on the table."

"Me too," Delilah said, forking a breast. "It's not southern fried, but I'll take it."

The platter stalled at Olivia and Chris nudged her.

"Don't let that go 'round a second time," Melanie said. "I guarantee we won't leave leftovers. We're holding back to be polite and give everyone a chance for firsts."

Olivia took a piece and passed to Chris, who, she noted, had waited for all the women to take food before he put anything on his plate. Interesting. Scott used to insist on being served first. Apparently not every guy did that.

She rested her fork on the edge of her plate, still unwilling to make eye contact. Everyone else managed to navigate India fine. What was wrong with her? Why was she alone incapable of adjusting and following guidelines? Did she want to be sent home, exiled prior to the end of her agreed-upon term? Some of the other teachers had even extended their stays. Leave it to her to manage to get fired from a voluntary position.

For a moment, only forks and knives clattering against plates disrupted the silence. Did everyone always chew so loudly?

Chris cleared his throat. "I just hope whoever Mrs. Gupta spoke with understands they're not alone. We all got a talking-to at some point."

She glanced at him, afraid to hope that could be true, afraid he only said it to make her feel better.

"Yep," Tisha said. "This isn't the easiest place to adjust to. Some of us didn't adopt local dress as quickly as others did and our morality for baring our arms and wearing jeans like a man was called into question."

"Some of us tired of the men in the community talking down to us like we're morons," Delilah drawled in her deep South twang, "and overreacted when we reached the boiling point."

Aubra swallowed and seemed to struggle with herself. "Some of us loathed giving up our independence and being forced to let a man chaperone us everywhere and refused to comply until 'the talk.'"

Admitting as much must have been tough for her, especially now that she'd dated and been dumped by the man she was forced to depend on. Olivia's heart softened toward Aubra. That wasn't an easy situation.

"Especially since I'm the most qualified driver here, considering I'm the only person who learnt to drive on the right side of the road," Aubra said.

Everyone burst into laughter. Olivia couldn't help but join in.

"You mean the left side!" Chris teased back.

"You Americans always insist you're right." Aubra rolled her eyes.

"We did invent cars," Chris reminded her. "We get to make the rules for driving. You Brits insisted on changing them up."

Olivia could no longer tell if they were only playing or if perhaps the exes were now swiping at each other.

Melanie lifted her water glass. "What we're getting at is that we actually consider this meal a celebration of someone's huge and generous heart."

The others lifted glasses and clinked them together as Olivia blinked back tears pricking at her eyes.

"You guys," she said, swiping at a tear that escaped and ran down her cheek.

"We mean it," Tisha whispered. "So eat."

Her diet hadn't included meat since she'd left New Delhi, where she'd discovered tandoori chicken and loved it so much she'd eaten it repeatedly over several days. This dish was a curry of some sort, but equally delicious. She was surprised how quickly she'd adapted to a vegetarian diet here at the school. In fact, as she chewed the chicken, as delicious as it was, the texture felt foreign in her mouth, the meat greasy and heavy. How strange to change so quickly.

"We saw Meena at the market when we got the chicken," Tisha said, her voice serious. "I spoke to her a little, before her mother pulled her away from me. Her family definitely forced an abortion. She didn't get to have her baby."

Olivia nearly choked on her mouthful of food.

The lights went out. Everyone groaned.

"And the electricity is down again," Aubra said.

"Shoot. I have more tutoring to do tonight," Olivia said. "I wonder how long this will last."

Ms. Vanya scurried from the kitchen with matches and lit candles on the table. She picked up a candle and gestured for the girls to leave, clearly ready to accompany them to their building for the night.

"Looks like another girls' night," Melanie said, her bright tone indicating she was ready for it.

"We haven't even finished eating," Chris lamented.

Olivia saw the disappointment in his face, even by the soft candlelight. She imagined him once again relegated to his room, alone and lonely while they all chatted and spent the dark evening together. "Can't we stay here for now? It's so early. And then Chris would have some company this time."

Ms. Vanya looked confused.

"It's okay. You don't have to stay," Olivia reassured her. "We can walk ourselves back later."

The older woman turned a skeptical eye on Chris.

He held up his hands as if in surrender. "Hey. I won't break the rules. No boys in the girls' rooms."

Ms. Vanya nodded and returned to the kitchen, taking empty serving dishes with her.

The conversation returned to Meena. Olivia, still horrified, couldn't let it go. "How could her family do that to her?"

"She didn't marry the man her parents chose for her and they didn't approve of her choice. Without their approval, she had no dowry and no one to pay for her wedding." Aubra shook her head.

"Her parents hoped the man they arranged for her to marry would still accept her, but word got out about the pregnancy. It's impossible to keep things like that a secret in a small community like this," Tisha said. "Her reputation is ruined and now she has no future."

"Can't she and her boyfriend get married now?" Olivia asked. "What do you mean, no future?"

"She won't be allowed to teach with her shattered reputation," Delilah said. "She was pregnant out of wedlock, and no one will forget it."

"She also defied her parents," Melanie said. "They won't forget that either."

"Then she was forced to have an abortion for nothing?" Olivia asked. "I can't believe this."

"She couldn't have supported a child anyway," Tisha said. "How could she with no job? She managed to finish school but who will hire her? No one around here. And with no money and no husband and no support from her father, it's not like she can move somewhere else."

Olivia couldn't accept that. "But it should have been her decision. Not forced on her."

"Things aren't the same here," Melanie said. "You know that."

"Forced abortions are not unusual in India," Tisha said. "Haven't you read about it? Women carrying females are sometimes forced to abort pregnancies by in-laws eager for male grandchildren. Sex selection is very real here, even if outlawed."

She shook her head and pushed away her plate, appetite gone. "How could anyone do that?"

She withdrew into herself, thoughts of forced abortions and babies who didn't get a chance at life overwhelming her. She pushed away memories that struggled to surface, memories she didn't want to think about, didn't want to share, didn't want to remember. Closing her eyes, she gritted her teeth, pushing against the door in her mind where she locked away the painful memories and the emotional turmoil that accompanied them.

Tisha rested a hand on her arm. "You okay?"

Opening her eyes, she focused on the candle flame. The gentle and genuine concern in Tisha's voice weakened her defenses and the memories pushed back. Her resolve slipped. Somehow, she'd thought she could simply put it behind her and move on, start over, pretend it never happened. She'd even run all the way to India, trying to forget. But she couldn't escape. Nothing blotted the indelible pain from her heart. "I . . . I lost a baby."

Soft murmurs of sympathy rounded the table. She thought she sensed Chris tense beside her.

Tisha squeezed her arm. "I knew something was wrong. I thought maybe your ex-husband hurt you."

"Scott? No. He blustered and yelled and demanded his way, but he never hurt me. But then, I don't know, he just sort of crumpled after . . ."

"What happened? Would you like to tell us?"

A bead of melted wax dripped down the side of the candle, leaving a trail and hardening into a teardrop.

"She . . . had a birth defect. Something wrong with her heart. The doctors detected it when I had an ultrasound and warned me she might not survive. They . . . urged me to consider abortion, but I couldn't do it. I wanted to give her a chance." Her voice caught in her throat, guilt and grief choking her.

"I'm so sorry," Melanie whispered. "I can imagine what a difficult decision that was to make."

"Scott and I fought about it. He thought an abortion would be the merciful choice. He couldn't stand the idea of a newborn going through surgeries and coping with all the stress and pain, unable to understand what was happening and why." She drew a deep, shaky breath, trying to take control of the emotions threatening to take over her. If the dam broke, she feared she would break too, and never be the same again. "I was so sure she would make it. I turned our guest room into a nursery. I never once doubted I would bring my baby girl home."

She lost the fight and deteriorated into tears.

All the women rushed to her side, closing in on her in a massive group hug.

"It's okay," Tisha assured her. "Losing a child is a huge source of grief."

"I'm so sorry," she managed through gulps of air.

"Why are you apologizing?" Tisha asked.

"I didn't mean to share. I ruined dinner crying and blubbering."

"You have every right to cry about this."

"Don't apologize!" Delilah said.

Now that she had shared, the words tumbled out. She couldn't stop them. "I made the wrong decision. They rushed her off to surgery, but she didn't make it. Poor, poor little thing. I put her through that for nothing. They brought her to me after, so I could hold her and say goodbye."

Tisha stroked her hair. "Oh, sweetie, this was a decision with no right or wrong answer."

"Every outcome was shit," Delilah agreed.

"The doctors warned me," she sobbed. "I didn't listen. Scott kept saying he'd told me so. He wouldn't even hold her."

"What an asshole," Chris said.

She'd never heard such a harsh edge to his voice.

Chris remained in his seat, fists clenched, voice rough. "He should have held you, cried with you, mourned with you. Everything you went through, fighting to give your baby life, and he turned his back on you? Don't you spend another minute thinking you made the wrong choice."

His words shocked her. They were so contrary to the beliefs she'd clung to for nearly a year now, she couldn't accept them. Scott was . . . wrong? That thought didn't compute.

"You wouldn't have felt any better if you'd opted to have an abortion," Melanie told her. "You'd feel guilty that you didn't give your baby a chance at life."

How could she know? Olivia wanted to believe her, but Melanie probably just wanted to make her feel better. "That's nice of you, but—"

"No, I mean it. I know. I got pregnant a few years ago. While I was in college. Married professor asked me out to lunch, one thing led to another . . . yeah. I agonized over what to do. My parents were disgusted with me, told me they raised me better than that. Professor tried to deny it was his, threatened me if I told his wife or caused problems for him. If *I* caused problems for *him*! I decided I'd keep the baby. I didn't know how I was going to take care of it, but I was damned sure going to try. Next thing I knew, the baby was diagnosed with some condition, doctor told me he would be stillborn."

Seriously? She'd come all this way to India and managed to meet up with someone else who'd faced a similar predicament to her own? "Really? You too?"

"Except they told me the baby had no chance. None. Absolutely no chance of survival. I decided to take the abortion route rather than carry for nine months and struggle through labor for nothing. But abortions are illegal in my state, so I had to drive to another to find a clinic. Once I got there, I got yelled at by a crowd of protestors, all of them calling me a baby killer." Melanie's voice wavered. Olivia grabbed her hand, fresh tears stinging her eyes.

"Some guy on a ladder yelled through a bullhorn at me not to kill my baby, to trust God's plan and turn it over to God. I wanted to yell back at him that God killed my baby." Tears pooled in Melanie's eyes. "But now all I can think is that maybe, just maybe . . . what if some miracle could have saved him? Every year I wonder about that. I knew his due date. And every year I think about how old he'd be now, what he'd be like . . . I was so upset when I found out I was pregnant, but I didn't want my baby to die. If you'd had an abortion, I promise you'd feel guilty for not giving the baby a chance."

All the women cried with Melanie now. Olivia hadn't thought about it that way but could see Melanie's side. And it cracked open a glimmer of light. Maybe, just maybe, she hadn't made a terrible mistake?

"Both of you had to make terrible, painful choices, and you made the best choices you could," Tisha said. "Women always feel guilty. Stay home with kids, feel guilty for not having a job. Choose to work and take kids to daycare, feel guilty for not staying home. Whatever we do, the other option looks more appealing—because we can idealize it in our minds while we deal with the reality of the choice we made."

She'd never considered that perhaps she would have been equally unhappy had she sought an abortion instead of believing wholeheartedly that her baby would survive the heart defect. She'd painted the guestroom in vivid primary colors, selected a crib, decorated with a jungle motif, complete with giraffes, zebras, elephants, and lions, all smiling and eager to welcome her baby girl into the world. Holding the poor helpless thing, the tiny lifeless body, a piece of her had died too. Returning home to the nursery she'd lovingly prepared, staring into the empty crib that would never hold her sleeping child, all the animals smiling up at her, she'd felt like such a fool.

She'd turned to Scott, desperate for comfort, for forgiveness, but he'd turned away. He blamed her, convinced she deserved the pain she'd wrought on them. If only she'd listened to him. Maybe her marriage wouldn't have fallen apart.

But perhaps she would be equally tormented now, every day still wondering what if, if only. The storm of emotions she fought so hard to prevent broke over her. Her heart pounded in her chest. She couldn't catch her breath. Tears poured from her eyes. She couldn't live like this. This was exactly why she didn't discuss what had happened, why she never shared. Why she tried so hard not to even think about it.

"What did you name her?" Aubra asked, her voice barely a whisper.

Olivia blinked, fighting to shove the emotional mess back inside the closet and slam the door closed for good. She couldn't allow it to so much as crack open. Ever. She took a deep breath. "I didn't name her. Scott and I decided to wait, to see what she looked like."

"You must have had a favorite. Something you were considering."

She did have a name quietly picked out that she never shared with anyone—not her mother and not Scott. She'd been waiting to tell them once the baby was out of surgery and recovering. Once the doctors had assured her the little one had defied all odds, that she'd been correct to hope and believe and fight for her baby. She'd imagined it over and over, triumphantly telling them she'd known all along and had a name ready—imagined snuggling the baby and whispering her name to her.

She shook her head emphatically. "No. Everything happened so fast. She was simply called 'baby girl'."

"Oh, girl, you have to name her."

"What's her birthday?" Melanie asked.

Fighting the impending panic attack, she managed to answer. "October twenty-eighth."

"That's during Diwali this year," Chris said.

"I know." Should she tell them how worthless she'd be that day? How could she even face it?

"We have to celebrate her birthday," Tisha said. "We can get some pink balloons and—"

"No, I appreciate the thought, but no. Thank you."

"But it's her birthday."

"It's also the day she died." Her voice cracked. She couldn't talk about this. Couldn't think about it. Wished she could erase it from her memory. She jumped to her feet. "I'm tired. I'm going to my room."

Chapter Seventeen

O nce she'd stumbled across the pitch-black courtyard and fumbled her way into her room by the flame of a lighter, she banged her shin against the dresser and then her desk. Her hands shook as she lit candles. So much for girls' night. She needed to be alone.

She slumped onto her bed and breathed deeply in the pale, flickering light, drawing her arms about her. Discussing the loss of her baby had opened the wound, fresh and raw, painful once again. Why couldn't it scab over, heal, and go away for good? Weary of hurting, exhausted from the constant ache it left on her soul, she longed for relief. Another wave of tears trickled down her cheeks.

She knew the teachers meant well by suggesting she celebrate the little one's birthday. That was the problem—everyone always meant well. How could she be angry at people who reached out to her in compassion and sympathy? She couldn't. But the teachers simply couldn't understand. How could she ever, ever think back on that terrible day, remember her lifeless, gray baby swaddled in a receiving blanket, and feel anything but devastation?

And now she couldn't stop thinking about Chris's reaction to her description of Scott's behavior. All this time, withdrawn and closed in on herself, unwilling to discuss what had happened, replaying the days following the delivery and death over and over. She had wept as the nurse wheeled her to the waiting car idling in front of the hospital, Scott stone-faced behind the wheel. He hadn't even gotten out of the car, just sat there as the nurse hovered, watching her climb in on her own then handing her the overnight bag she had so carefully packed several weeks before. The unused "coming home" dress remained untouched inside. The car seat she had so painstakingly researched and selected for its highest safety rating remained buckled in the backseat, the beige fabric and cheerful animal print waiting to nestle a baby who would never come.

The dynamic between her and Scott had shifted, and in the days, then weeks, then months that followed, she came to realize it would never shift back. Nothing would ever go back to the way it was. When he packed up and moved out, he had said little, and she'd merely nodded. Why would he stay? She didn't want to stay. Her life had become a blur and she a sleepwalker in a nightmarish world she didn't recognize, a reality that couldn't possibly be her own. She couldn't even say she'd been spinning her wheels because that implied an intent to gain some traction, a desire to move forward. She felt neither in the aftermath. She had simply stopped, incredulous that the world kept turning after her baby died. How could the sun continue to rise and set as if nothing had happened? Returning to their house with empty arms, standing in the doorway of the nursery she'd carefully prepared, racked with guilt, she'd struggled to remain standing long enough to collapse into bed. And all this time she'd believed Scott's attitude and behavior justified.

What an asshole.

Was Chris right? Had Scott been out of line? Not one of the other teachers looked horrified with what she'd shared. Not one had suggested she'd made the wrong decision. They all expressed sympathy and praised her for trying. Melanie went so far as to say she'd feel at least as bad if not worse if she'd gone the other way and opted to seek an abortion.

She shuddered as she thought of Meena forced to abort her baby. Meena had not faced a choice at all. The unfairness of it crushed against her chest, squeezing until she could scarcely breathe. Women forced to get abortions. Girls forced to stay home when they started their period. Babies born with heart defects for no reason whatsoever, who didn't get a chance at life.

She longed to call her mom. Mom had always been supportive and strong, even when Olivia's life fell apart. Mom tried to help her work through the ordeal, urging counseling. *"Get help from a professional, sweetie,"* Mom had said. First marriage counseling to try to preserve that relationship, then grief counseling when she couldn't move past the loss of both baby and husband. She didn't see the point. What could anyone say that could make her feel better? In a span of six months her life had completely upended, washed away like a sandcastle in a wave. Her future disintegrated, leaving her to navigate a world she no longer recognized without a map or a compass—or even a ship. She'd fallen overboard into an ocean while a storm raged about her. Though her mom believed a counselor capable of throwing a lifeline, she didn't believe it. She already knew these were horrible experiences for anyone. She didn't need someone else to tell her that. But knowing something to be true in your mind did nothing to resuscitate a drowned heart.

She didn't need to talk about her grief. She didn't want to think about it. She'd come to India to put distance between her and the broken shards of her shattered life. That was the best way for her to "get over it" and move on. Whether anyone else understood that or not, that was what she needed.

Olivia listened as her students read stories they'd written. The power had not returned until early this morning. She'd slept so fitfully that when her little lamp flickered on in the early morning hours, she'd roused herself and worked frantically to catch up on the tutoring she'd been unable to do the night before.

Exhausted, out of sorts, and underprepared for class, she opted to let the children spend their class times today writing their own stories about anything they wanted to write about. Her youngest classes she'd given construction paper as well, folding the paper into rudimentary covers and stapling it all together. She congratulated each smiling pupil for writing their very first book. A glimmer of the happiness she'd felt in her first weeks—getting to know the children, watching them light up as they learned—shimmered in her dark mood.

For the older classes she put less emphasis on illustrations and simply let them write. The absence of Surithra from the same class as Aditi stole away the brief spark that lit her day earlier. Distracted and shaken, she only half listened as her students read their creations, concerned the girl was the latest victim of menstruation.

Surithra's empty desk reminded her entirely too much of an empty crib.

A boom resounding so heavily through the building that the windows rattled, shaking her out of her thoughts and back into the classroom.

Shadow blotted out the sun, covering the schoolhouse in an eerie pall, a reddish hue that cast a surreal atmosphere, as though she'd dozed off and now sleepwalked through a nightmarish landscape.

Giggling, the children wiggled from their seats and scurried to the windows, clinging to the sills as they peeked through the glass panes into the looming red glow.

Slow, intermittent drops thudded the parched, packed earth outside before the onslaught opened full force, driving wind swirling from nowhere pummeling the building while angry droplets sluiced against the windows.

Red splotches threw themselves against the glass in a kamikaze effort to gain entry before sliding downward, crimson trails forming in the wake.

Splattered by backsplash from the sills, the children squealed in delight.

"Auntie, it is raining red!"

No. Not again.

Before she knew what was happening, her class morphed into a pack of squirming, leaderless puppies and oozed amoeba-like out the door.

"No!" she called. "Come back!"

Damn! Why hadn't she bought an umbrella? Probably because without referring back to the newspapers for confirmation of her sanity, she could easily convince herself she'd imagined the previous occurrence. The sky rained down blood on them, for Pete's sake. This could not be real. And yet, another glance out the windows assured her it was.

She took a deep breath and launched herself into the hallway, only to negotiate a churning sea of bodies undulating toward the door that led into the courtyard. Unable to stop the flow, the current carried her along until she found herself thrust into the torrential downpour.

The children raced about, darting like minnows, suddenly shifting direction with no clear stimulus interrupting the trajectory, turning to charge pell-mell in another direction.

What in the world—or perhaps out of this world—fell on them? What toxic chemicals seeped through their pores?

Priyanka, Aishwarya, Tala, and other girls not in her classes, stood in place, mouths open, tongues lapping at the red droplets while crimson rivulets soaked their white tops, forming two-dimensional stalactites which cut triangles down their torsos.

Blood. All she saw was blood. Blood-soaked earth. Blood forming in pools. Bloody children.

Blood staining her hands.

She brushed strands of drenched, stringy hair off her forehead and willed her feet to move from where she stood planted, rooted to the spot.

Racing around the courtyard, she shooed the smiling, delighted children, attempting to drive them toward the door and inside to safety. God knew what the open-mouthed children were swallowing, but it couldn't be good.

"Inside!" she called to one after another. "Get inside."

The other teachers joined in the ludicrous chase, a cross between herding cats and a game of keep away. But it was too much to overcome.

This had to be an omen. The sky had inexplicably opened up twice now and stained this town and their children, marking them for life, indelibly branding them as lower, less than, fated for a life of servitude and poverty.

She had thought—no, wholeheartedly believed—that her presence could influence this culture, older than she could fathom and set in its ways, immovable as granite, and give these children a fighting chance.

Mud sucked at her sandals, red droplets slapped her face, and she realized what a fool's errand she'd set herself upon. Who was she to help anyone? She couldn't save her baby. She couldn't save her marriage. She couldn't save herself.

She'd run halfway around the globe seeking to leave her problems—herself—behind. But here she stood, exactly the same, a childless, divorced failure.

Accepting defeat, she stopped running. Mud oozed into her sandals, the squishy muck working its way between her toes as she sunk, stuck. The almost brown color the bizarre rain rendered her previously beautiful emerald *shalwar kameez* reminded her of bloody childbirth. Drenched and miserable, she gave up.

The other teachers managed to wrangle the children inside, but still she stood, glad the red rain hid her tears.

With the last child successfully steered back inside the building, the other teachers noticed her and called out for her to come inside out of the rain. What was the point? What was the point of anything? She could buy a whole new outfit, but the children couldn't buy new uniforms. And the stain would never wash out.

Chapter Eighteen

At the market on Saturday, Olivia walked with the other teachers as they perused the stalls and debated purchases. She didn't need anything, and only accompanied them because they'd refused to take no for an answer. She knew they were worried about her and had been since the second instance of red rain. On one level, she greatly appreciated their concern, though it rather baffled her. Why did they care? Still, she hadn't been able to shake off the funk that overwhelmed her since.

Tisha in particular maneuvered to meet up with her when no one else was around, and her gentle attempts to encourage conversation were perhaps more transparent than she realized. Olivia knew what Tisha was trying to do and recognized the kindness behind it, but she didn't want to talk. As a counselor, Tisha probably couldn't stop herself from attempting to intervene, but she didn't want to talk about her past problems. They could stay firmly in the past. No more meltdowns.

However, she soon regretted her reluctant decision to join them as the shopping did not, as they'd predicted, snap her out of it. If anything, it only made things worse. The open-air market teemed with families. Saturday was a big shopping day. When she spotted Aditi with her family, her heart lurched. The girl's father glared at her, as if daring her to approach. She didn't. A caustic exchange was the very last thing she needed.

Then the other teachers spotted Meena with her mother, a pinched and sour-looking older woman, nothing like Ms. Vanya with her warm smile and welcoming demeanor. When they pointed her out, Olivia couldn't stop herself from staring. Like herself, the young woman ought to be toting an infant in her arms. Her breath caught in her throat, and she fought an urge to run. What was wrong with her?

Meena caught her staring. Olivia quickly managed a smile and lifted her hand in greeting. The young woman took in the others in the group, then understanding seemed to dawn on her. She nodded at Olivia, but grief clouded her face. She'd made the connection and identified Olivia as her replacement. Guilt tugged at her. But she'd had nothing to do with that situation, and nothing she could do would fix the enormous injustice that befell Meena.

For days, she'd reverted back to simply going through the motions, sliding back to that place she'd hoped to leave behind and never revisit, where she simply existed, barely. The other teachers insisted she join in the planning meetings, excitedly preparing for Diwali, the Festival of Lights. In addition to the plans they had for their classrooms, the teachers took great delight in sharing ideas for decorating their rooms. Even Chris got in on it, which especially surprised her. Scott had certainly never shown an iota of interest in planning or decorating for holidays. Mostly he'd harrumphed at her attempts at festivities, rolling his eyes anytime she got excited. And apparently the town would do something together as well, though she wasn't clear what exactly it would be. That was on her though, since she'd only half listened. What did she have to celebrate?

At least no one had attempted to get her to open up and share since the night she'd had the meltdown. They seemed to understand the need to leave the subject alone.

At the news stand, headlines jumped out at her about the second occurrence of red rain. She peeled away from the group and paused to skim an article before paying the vendor for a copy of every English-language paper he had. She intended to scour every one for useful information. Maybe one of them could finally shed some light on what the heck they were all being exposed to. Not knowing left a simmering anxiety stewing in the back of her mind. How could the other teachers maintain such a cavalier attitude about it? She heard more giggling as they happily discussed plans for the holiday.

"Olivia!" Tisha called. "Diwali is like Christmas here. You have to participate."

"It's beautiful," Chris said. "Lasts for five days. I'm so glad I'm still here and get to celebrate it again."

She didn't want to be a Grinch, or the Diwali version of one, but a festival of lights didn't strike her as anything she could enjoy at this point in her life. Where was the light in her darkness? The girls in her classes had no future. Her own future, so sure not even a full year ago, stretched before her, murky and unknown. One year ago, she'd been putting the finishing touches on a nursery, delighting in the kicks and jabs of the baby girl she carried. She'd been married, about to have a child, held a position as adjunct, and had fully expected to step into a full-time faculty position eventually. But now? Everything had changed, all for the worse.

Folding the newspapers and tucking them under an arm, she rejoined the group. She could accompany them while they shopped, regardless of her own opinion on the matter.

Soon, however, disappointment clouded all their faces. This was India, not America, where giant stores competed aggressively for disposable income, seeking to gain the upper hand for those dollars with earlier and earlier holiday displays. Though the teachers giddily made plans, no huge displays of Diwali decorations awaited their fists full of rupees. Finally, they happened onto a stand with strings of lights and bags of colored sand.

"Here we go!" Chris led the happy descent onto the stall.

"Everything needs to be brightly lit. We will all need lights for our rooms, our classrooms, the hallways—the courtyard! Last year we didn't do much with the courtyard but maybe we can manage more this year."

Olivia couldn't deny the allure of the light strings and envisioned them sparkling softly in her room—over the bed, around the door, adding to the glow of her peacock lamp.

Chris lifted bags of brightly colored sand. "I'm going to try my own *rangoli* this year. Ms. Vanya is incredible at making them. Maybe I can make a simple one."

"A what?" she asked, joining the other teachers in selecting several light strands, estimating how many she'd need. A tiny shiver of excitement pulsed through her. After all, who didn't get excited about setting up the Christmas tree, even if it was a bit early. She imagined the children's delight during the festivities. Time to put aside her own issues and focus on the children.

"They're called *rangoli*. Beautiful drawings on the floor made from colored pigment or sand. Everyone will have one in their home. Ms. Vanya made some for us around the school last year. So intricate. They're round with swirls of patterns in the circle. Incredible little works of art. You'll never believe they're drawn free-hand!"

She thought for a moment. "Can the kids make some?"

"Oof. Not with sand," Melanie said. "What a mess that would be."

"Yeah. I kind of tried that last year," Chris said. "Disaster."

"They can draw pictures," Tisha said. "Paper and crayons will do."

"What about chalk?" Olivia suggested. "Outside?"

"There's an idea! Anywhere on concrete would work great. Good thinking!" Chris beamed at her.

"And that would simply wash away next rainstorm," Delilah said. "No muss, no fuss. Especially once the monsoons hit."

"Let's just hope it isn't red again," Aubra said.

"Ever again," Melanie agreed. "It's so weird."

"My parents are convinced I'm having a laugh," Aubra said.

"I emailed my mom," Olivia said, "but she didn't say anything about it when she replied. Maybe she thinks I'm joking too."

She noticed Chris's face cloud over. He probably wished he could reach out to his mom to discuss the bizarre experiences they'd lived through. How would she feel if she couldn't talk to her mom? That would suck. She'd always been close to her mom and shared most everything with her. From what he shared with her, she suspected Chris's relationship with his mom had been similar before a man came between them and ruined it. Not for the first time, she was grateful to her mom for forcing her father out of their lives. And proud of her for the strength she found to do it.

"Who would joke about such a thing?" Delilah asked. "My boyfriend believes me, but he's convinced it's some sort of chemical warfare experiment gone wrong. And he's convinced there's a massive coverup since he can't find a single mention of it anywhere in any publications back home. Not a thing about it in the overseas news."

"I have every newspaper I could get my hands on," Olivia said. "But not one article offers anything definitive. Lots of wild conjecture."

"That's exactly why he's convinced of a coverup," Delilah said. "There's nothing anywhere."

"A friend of mine from back home has an internship in a lab at Kerala University," Aubra said. "They have samples of the rainwater they've been running tests on. He swore me to secrecy, but—"

"Get away from my wife!" A shouting man startled them all.

Chapter Nineteen

Olivia's head whipped in the direction of the altercation. She hadn't heard anyone shout since she'd arrived in India. Something serious must've sparked this exchange.

At the end of the market, just past the final stall, a man stood behind a simple card table. She couldn't tell what he had spread across the table, but she recognized the shouting man—Aditi's father.

She cringed as he shouted again, this time reverting back to a native tongue she couldn't understand, shaking a fist at the man behind the stall.

Her stomach tightened in on itself, as if she were shrinking back to her younger self, terrified of her screaming father. Even as she assured herself nothing threatened her, her body flipped into panic mode, heart pounding, pulse racing, fear infusing every cell in her body. Hormones cascaded, communicating loud and clear to her muscles that she needed to get out of there, as if a tiny megaphone in her brain screamed, "Run!" She grappled with the visceral response, attempting to regain control of her body. Her breathing increased to a race-running pace, though she stood absolutely still, terrified to move. Her body would not listen to reason.

Tisha seemed to notice her response. The woman placed a gentle hand on her arm and whispered, "Just breathe. Slow, easy breaths. Slowly in and slowly out."

Olivia tried to smile but feared it more resembled a grimace. She didn't want attention. She shook her head as if to say she was fine.

Aditi held her younger sister by the hand and hid behind their mother, who jostled a wailing baby on her shoulder—and appeared to be pregnant again, judging by her swollen waistline. Aditi stared at the ground and stood still as a statue. Olivia suspected she was looking at a mirror into her past, that her younger self had resembled the young girl before her now, resolutely gazing anywhere but at the angry man, attempting to will invisibility as a protective shield, praying stillness would prevent becoming the next target of his rage. Her heart broke for her former student, knowing full well what life at home must be like and wishing she could do something to help. But like Aditi, like the remnant of her younger self cowering and quaking inside, she remained in the same place, helpless to intervene.

The vendor also watched the exchange and sucked in a breath through his teeth. "Not good."

Aditi's mother plucked at her husband's sleeve, clearly mortified. When he slapped her away and yelled at her, Olivia gasped. She noticed the others shuffled their feet, uncomfortable but unclear what to do.

"What's happening?" Chris asked.

"Strange man talk to wife," the vendor said. He tipped his head and clicked his tongue.

Olivia turned back and watched the scene unfold, unable to look away, despite the continuing emotional storm lighting up every nerve in her body. The continued shouting spurred her pulse, until blood galloped through her veins like a spooked horse.

More men joined Aditi's father, facing off against the stranger behind the table. The vendor said something she couldn't quite follow, but she thought she heard the words "beat him up." The stranger held up his hands, the universal signal for defeat and submission. Though she couldn't hear the entire exchange, and wouldn't be able to understand the words if she could, she understood the gist of it. Threatened with physical violence, the man gave up whatever he'd hoped to accomplish.

Aditi's father, indignation and fury still blazing in his eyes, grabbed his wife by the wrist and stalked away, dragging his family in tow behind him. The additional supporters he'd amassed drifted away in his wake.

Aditi glanced up at her as the angry ensemble paraded past and waved at Olivia, a sweet, secretive gesture that reminded her how much she missed having the bright girl in her class. She nodded in response, keeping the quiet exchange just between them.

"What was that all about?" she asked the vendor as she paid him for her light strings. A quick, sideways jerk of his head indicated he didn't wish to answer.

Her heartbeat slowed, now that the argument ended without further escalation. She could breathe normally again. She stared at the lone man behind his table. He lifted a hand in greeting. He seemed nice enough from a distance, and she had trouble imagining what he'd done to bring down such anger on his head.

Chris appeared at her elbow. "The vendor seems to think those guys were threatening to beat that man up. But he wouldn't say why, other than something about talking to his wife."

The other teachers joined them, all clutching their treasures.

She stared at the docile-looking man, curiosity piqued. "I mean, we have to go see what that was about, right? It'll drive me crazy not knowing."

"I thought I was the only nosy one," Delilah said. "I'll walk over if you will."

Tisha looked less enthusiastic about the idea. "Maybe we should stay out of it."

Melanie squinted at the man. "Maybe. But I'm with Olivia. This will really bother me. Besides, look at him. Chris can totally take him."

"Oh, thanks!" Chris said.

"For real, though," Delilah said. "Nothing ventured, nothing gained."

"That's not a literary quote," Chris chided her. "That's just a thing people say."

Olivia tried to maintain a neutral countenance and pretend they were simply continuing on their merry way, but couldn't stop glancing at the man, who watched them approach. He seemed awfully calm and laid back for someone who had just been threatened with a beating.

The man, probably in his forties she guessed, with dark black hair combed to the side and a clipped mustache, broke into a wide grin when they approached his table.

"Hello! My name is Mukesh. I am sure you ladies use napkins."

Napkins? How did he incite ire and fury by selling napkins? She edged closer to the table and blinked a few times, her mind struggling to make sense of the unexpected sight in front of her— pads prominently displayed on the table. Thinking back on her experience at the pharmacy, when that vendor behaved so strangely while selling packages of pads to her, things clicked into place. A little bit.

"You're selling pads?" she asked.

"And you're pretty ballsy about it, laying them out in the open like this," Tisha ventured.

The man, rather than looking abashed, smiled at Tisha. "You know the difficulties, what I am up against. No woman in India will discuss this subject with me. It is simply not done. But I am not selling pads, but rather the machine which makes them."

Exuberance infused every word he spoke. He handed a flyer to her. The flimsy paper left ink smudges on her fingers as she looked at it.

Olivia picked up one of the pads on display. A plain rectangle, nothing fancy, yet it seemed functional and perfectly fine. "And you have a machine that makes these?"

"Yes, madam. When I married, I knew nothing of a woman's menses. Have you tried to discuss this with Indian woman? They will look down at ground or up in sky. They will not look at you. When I married, I knew nothing. But I saw my wife try to hide the bloody cloths she used and asked her about it. That was when I learned that women bleed. It is normal. What woman can stop her body from bleeding? But a woman is made to hide and feel shame and men are not told about it."

"You were a married adult when you learned about menstruation?"

"In my thirties, madam, yes. I learned about sanitary napkin and went to my wife, so happy I have solved her problem, and told her about this and she said I am a fool. 'Yes, I know,' she told me. 'But if I buy these napkins at the market, it will take the money you give me for food. Then what will we eat?' Indian women are not as ignorant as I was. But they cannot afford the napkins. So I decide to make napkins for my wife, so she can be healthy and safe."

"And you've succeeded," she noted.

"Indian women deserve what women in other countries have." The man launched into his sales spiel. "Only ten percent of Indian women use sanitary napkins. Most women cannot afford even cheapest option from the market. Most women use cloth, but they do not have a way to sterilize them. They could lay them in the sun to dry, but that would advertise to the entire community that they are menstruating. The subject is simply too sensitive and taboo. But some women do not even have cloth. They use leaves or garbage or worse."

"Worse than garbage? What could be worse?" Melanie asked.

"Exactly, madam. Women with no sanitary napkins, who use cloths and worse, experience high rates of serious infection which sometimes results in sterility. And in India, a woman's worth is all contained in her pants—honor, discretion, virginity, and producing children."

"The girls in my classroom are disappearing," Olivia said. "They start their periods and they never come back."

"You are teacher?"

She nodded and gestured to the others. "We all are. At the English-language school."

Aubra felt the need to add, "She's new. The rest of us have been here for some time."

"Drop-out rate for girls is quite high. This is normal. Less in big cities, but higher for small communities. Girls are taught to stay home, forbidden to go out. That they are unclean. They cannot even hand something to their family."

"This is even worse than what I'd heard about," Tisha said, echoing the shock apparent on the others' faces.

"I knew we shouldn't discuss it with the children," Delilah said, taking a flyer, "but this is far worse than I realized."

"I mostly teach boys," Chris said. "I didn't know. I mean, I knew, but I didn't *know*."

Olivia glanced in the direction she'd watched Aditi's father drag her away. "How exactly does this work?"

"I install the machine and train women to operate it."

She cocked her head. "Women? Only women?"

He tipped his head, waving a hand for extra emphasis. "Only women, madam. Women operate the machine, make the napkins, and sell to other women. That is the only way."

She thought of Meena, helpless and dependent, no one in town willing to defy her father and employ her. Well, perhaps one person in town was. Her thoughts began to race as an idea clicked into place.

"You've installed these elsewhere?"

He tipped his head again. "Yes, madam. Most successfully. Not many people know yet, but someday I want to make India all napkin country. Yesterday a company offered me many U.S. dollars for the rights to my machine, to distribute the machine. I said no. I want to help women, not help Mukesh. If big company buys, they only want to make money. I only want to help women. You see? India needed high school dropout to solve this problem. An educated person would be smart enough to quit." His eyes lit up at his own joke, and he cracked a grin.

She laughed but then grew serious again. *Smart people know when to quit*, Scott's voice echoed in her mind. What would Scott think of Mukesh? Because he seemed pretty damned smart to her.

"And the women where you've installed machines, they use the pads?"

"Madam, yes. It is most successful. The women have income source, have napkins they can afford to buy. Everything is better. They go to other villages now and talk to women and show them napkins are much better. Someday, my dream is India will be all napkin country."

"You did this for your wife?" Tisha asked. Olivia heard wistfulness in her tone and thought she understood. Her heart melted to hear a man demonstrate such concern and devotion.

Olivia mentally compared this man to Scott. Mukesh had learned about periods and set out to make life better for his wife. Scott wrinkled his nose in disgust at any mention of "that time of the month" or "girl things." The man couldn't even bring himself to say the words pads or tampons. Mukesh may joke lightly about being uneducated, but she found him far more enlightened than the highly educated department chair she'd been married to.

"For my wife, yes." Mukesh looked down, a shadow crossing over his face. "My mother too. I quit school in ninth grade after my father died. My mother could not get a good job, cleaner only, and could not support us, so I quit and took factory job. I wish job like this had been available for my mother."

Chris nodded. "I was raised by a single mother, too. It's tough." Doubt tugged at the corners of his eyes and furrowed his brow. Was he questioning his decision to let her handle her issues alone, in the face of Mukesh's determination to make life better for his wife and mother?

Olivia tucked a loose strand of hair behind her ear. "And you did it? Just like that? Now you make pads Indian women can afford?"

"Not just like that, madam. Six years I work on it."

"Your wife must be so grateful and proud. Why isn't she here helping you?" Olivia looked around, half expecting to see the woman skulking somewhere in the shadows.

"Yeah," Melanie said. "She could approach the women and then maybe their husbands wouldn't threaten to beat you up."

The man's mouth twisted into a wry grin. "Now we see the gods' sense of humor. I started this project for my wife, and she has left me because of the project."

Olivia, thinking that Scott would never have devoted so much as six minutes to something designed only to improve her life and health, sucked in a breath. Surely not. Maybe she misunderstood or perhaps the language barrier caused confusion. "She left you?"

"She went back to her parents. My mother left too. I am alone now, both women I try to help abandoned me."

"But why?"

"I try to solve a problem I will never experience. When I made napkins, I needed someone to test them. I cannot do. I give to my wife. I think women bleed every day. She tells me, 'No. Not possible. You have to wait.' But if I have only one woman to test them, I would not be here today. I would still be trying to find the right material. I need more women to test. But of course in India, a man approaching women is not acceptable. In our village, tongues wagged with gossip. My interest in women as test subjects twisted into dishonorable intentions. My wife listened and believed and left me. A few months later my mother saw me examining used napkins, packed her things, and left me too. When the rest of the village saw me carry buckets of goats' blood to my home, they decide I need an exorcism. I had to move before they tied me upside down to a tree." He cracked a smile again.

This time, Olivia didn't laugh. Was that last bit a joke? She didn't understand how he could make light of the situation.

Perhaps he'd learned how to successfully lock away painful memories. Perhaps he could teach her something.

She didn't know. But she knew one thing, sure and crystal clear. From the moment she'd seen the announcement for an open teacher's position in the middle of nowhere, India, she'd known in her heart she was meant to come. The universe intended her to be here, even if no one else understood—even if she herself hadn't completely understood until this moment. And even if Scott's incessant disapproval glared at her from the depths of her memories. *Smart people don't make rash decisions. You won't be able to make this work. Why try?*

Olivia wearied of being criticized and doubted by men. Breathing heavily, she mentally crossed her arms and told Scott's memory he no longer got a say. This time, insisting on doing things her way would work, she knew it. It had to. As a spark of excitement licked into determination, she knew she needed this.

She handed the flyer back to Mukesh. "I want to buy one of your machines."

Chapter Twenty

Walking back to the car after exchanging information with Mukesh, Olivia walked on air, lost in thought, already imagining the women and girls of the village happily going about their much-improved lives. So what if the machine cost several thousand dollars? Where else in the world could an investment like that do so much good? The money from her house with Scott sat in the bank doing no good for anyone. Now she realized why she'd left it sitting there for six months, loathe to acknowledge, much less use, it. It was tainted money, blood money, money associated with Scott and her lost baby girl. She could never use that money to buy a house—a house that could never feel like a home. Not with the empty, echoing rooms reminding her every moment of every day that her new life had been built on the ashes and ruins of a previous disaster, on her failures. No, she couldn't do it. Ever. But now she had the opportunity to do something good with the money. Something incredibly good.

The other teachers remained quiet. No one said a word. They didn't need to. She could tell they all silently judged her and didn't approve. Once again, Olivia found herself facing well-intentioned skepticism from everyone around her. So be it. She'd been right before, and she knew to the deepest depths of herself that she was right this time too. They didn't understand. No one understood.

They reached the car and squeezed in amid much grumbling from the back seat. The women teased good-naturedly, but Olivia only half listened, biting her thumbnail and staring out the window at the sari-clad women walking toward the market, the loose fabric from their clothing fluttering in the wind, trailing behind them like whispered secrets. What did they deal with at home on a daily basis? Did any of them finish school? Had they as young girls dreamed of going to college, of traveling, of holding jobs?

She suspected Aditi's mother regularly dealt with abuse. Did Aditi? Was her father like Olivia's? Or, like Scott, did he simply bluster and demand his way, but never actually strike them? Each one of these women carried secrets, she realized, possibly harboring torments and deep pain. Had they been forced to abort children as Meena had?

Tisha struggled to close the door without smashing her hip. "Can someone please explain to me why Olivia's skinny butt is sitting up front in that lone seat when some of us smashed in the back could actually use the extra room?"

"I'll switch! I don't mind at all!" Olivia said, grabbing the door handle and preparing to hop out.

"Not now!" Delilah said. "We're in. The door is closed. Let's go, Chris."

Chris obliged and maneuvered into traffic, where the silence continued until Aubra broke it.

"Are we going to discuss the elephant in the room? Or in the car, as it were?"

Tisha clicked her tongue. "Okay, now. I am not as big as an elephant."

"I'm talking about Olivia. What in the world were you thinking?"

Olivia threw a glance over her shoulder and discovered four pairs of eyes staring back at her, all clearly wondering the same thing.

Chris tapped his thumb against the steering wheel. "I have to say, for someone who has seemed as concerned about money as you, it did seem like a rather rash decision."

Smart people don't make rash decisions. She'd thought Chris at least would understand. His concern, though mild, echoed Scott's constant criticism. She squirmed.

"It's thousands and thousands of dollars just for the machine," Tisha said. Her tone reminded Olivia of a parent trying to talk a toddler down from a tantrum. "Maybe you want to think this through. We don't know anything about this man at all."

"And I hate to be the one to say it," Aubra said, "but scamming foreigners is common practice here. My dad reminds me every time I hear from him."

The others murmured in agreement.

Chris glanced sideways at her. "I have to agree with them. He seemed nice enough, but what do we really know about him? You need to consider your safety."

"And not be gullible to scams," Aubra reiterated.

Got it, she thought, but bit the words back. "I know we just met him, but I did see something about pad machines online the other day."

"And it specifically mentioned him?" Aubra pressed.

"Well . . ."

"Where do you intend to install the machine once it arrives?"

"Well . . ."

"I mean, you'll surely need a pretty large space for manufacturing goods. How big is the machine? How much space does it require?"

"We didn't really discuss that . . ."

"And who's going to operate it?" Melanie asked. "We can't. We already teach."

"No, he said local women," Olivia reminded them. Hadn't

they been listening? "Local women who need jobs and their own income." At least she knew the answer to one of the questions they peppered her with.

"Who?" Aubra pressed. "Which women? How will you recruit them?"

"I'm sure plenty of women will want the work." But in fact, the point was valid. How would she get word out? Okay, so maybe she didn't have all the answers. Yet. She could figure this out.

Silence once again descended over the group, tacit disapproval hanging over them all like wisps of stale cigarette smoke. The stink of it seeped into Olivia's buoyant mood. When Chris parked, she gladly hopped from the vehicle, eager for fresh air and distance.

Clutching her strings of lights, she scurried across the courtyard to her room before anyone could dump more dire warnings on her. Thankfully, the electricity was on. She flipped the switch on her window unit and turned the dial to high before turning on her laptop and dialing into the internet. While the laptop buzzed and beeped, she stood directly in front of the air vents, trying to cool off in the sweltering heat. Her room turned into an oven when she was away. Though she slowly adapted to much warmer temperatures than she was accustomed to, sometimes she thought she might wilt. The constant heat wore on her, sapping energy and leaving her drained.

Once connected to the internet, she brought up her email and discovered her mother had responded to her previous message. Distracted with thoughts of her real purpose—how to get money from her bank back home to someplace she could access it here—she skimmed her mother's email. *Was work still going okay? She missed Olivia so much and hated not being able to talk with her regularly. Did she still enjoy teaching the children? Had she noticed the full-time English professor position hadn't ever filled at the community college?*

Her stomach sank. She hadn't noticed that. Of course she hadn't, because she wasn't watching for jobs back home. But she should be. She would eventually need a stable job. She couldn't keep hiding in India forever. And she couldn't keep living with her mother forever. That wasn't fair to her mom.

Thinking about home and trying to carve out a new life there upset her stomach. Tendrils of depression wound their way around her, dragging her down to a place she didn't want to be, didn't want to return to.

She shook her head, pushing those thoughts aside. Right now, she would focus only on the children in her classes, Mukesh's pad machine, and how to make that happen. The rest of it she could deal with later. Or continue ignoring. She liked that idea. Refocusing on her mother's email, the last bit grabbed her attention and jolted her with a shock.

Olivia, I struggled with this, I really did. I still don't know if it's better to keep this from you or let you know. But I decided the truth will reach you eventually. I saw Scott last week, with another woman. He had his arm around her, and they were giggling and cuddling, so I don't think this could be a platonic friend . . .

Her eyes glazed over. She couldn't read any more. Her ex-husband was already involved with another woman. In retrospect, she probably should have expected as much. Then again, she still found it hard to believe. How could he? Shattered and an emotional wreck, the idea of allowing a man close to her, ever again, turned her stomach. And yet, while she struggled to put one foot in front of the other, spent months barely able to get out of bed to eat, grappling with the hole in her heart their baby girl had left there, he had already moved on with his life. Already had another woman in his arms.

Morbid curiosity got the better of her. His graduate student? She wished her mother had described the young woman a bit.

What had she ever seen in him? Seriously. Her thoughts weren't clouded or inflamed by jealousy or fury. She truly struggled to remember what had drawn her to him in the beginning. And likewise, what had attracted him to her? If he'd ever said, ever reminded her why he liked her and had at one point decided he fervently and passionately wanted to spend the rest of his life with her, she'd forgotten. The memories had grown foggy after ten years of marriage, at least half of them pretty lackluster, as the two of them navigated life together, side by side, yet never quite on the same page. At least that's how she saw it now, with the benefit of hindsight. And of course, the final tragedy had completely derailed everything. Why didn't she care? She waited for some spark of something—anger, fury, jealousy, rage, something. Anything. A shred of disappointment even would assure her she was okay, normal.

She didn't know how long she sat there in a stupor before a quiet knock brought her back from her thoughts to the real world. She blinked a few times before full awareness resumed. Oh, right. India. She was in India. She moved to open the door and discovered Tisha standing there, her face arranged into a soft and gentle expression. And the woman greeted her with a soft and gentle tone.

"Hey. I thought maybe we could talk. Would that be okay?"

She nodded numbly and allowed her fellow teacher into her room.

"How are you feeling?" Tisha asked.

She rubbed her head. "I've had some news from my mother that didn't sit well, I guess. But I'm okay. It wasn't anything serious really." Or at least, if it was serious, it didn't seem to be slamming her in the gut like she thought it ought to.

"I just came to check in on you. I thought maybe you'd like to talk."

Talk? No, she needed to get back to work, figure out how to get her money to Mukesh, where to install the machine, start rounding up women to work it. "About what?"

"Anything you'd like to talk about."

Ah. This was counselor Tisha, worried about her and here to

intervene. "I'm okay, I promise. I don't need to talk about anything."

"Can we talk about your plan? The pad machine you're planning to buy?"

She gestured to her laptop. "That's why I found the email from my mom. I got online to look the guy up. I'll do my research."

"I only want to ensure you're not acting out of misplaced guilt. Or doing something you might someday regret. Believe me, I understand. I've been there. I once gave a man I was dating ten thousand dollars to pay off his loans. He was in trouble, and I decided to help. Except the man showed up at my house and threatened me with a knife, drunk, demanding more money. Smart women can do dumb things when we're under the influence of love. It took me, someone who works with victims of domestic abuse, a lot of time, distance, and counseling to realize I was a victim myself. Love, real love, isn't abusive."

Smart women can do dumb things. Interesting take.

"But I'm not doing this for a guy. It's not the same at all."

"I'm just saying, I've been there too. It's not you. Whatever you're feeling guilty about, you didn't cause it. You have nothing to atone for."

What was Tisha getting at? "I'm not trying to atone for anything. Really. I know it must seem impetuous, but I want to do this. And no, I'm not wealthy. But I have a little bit of money from my divorce, and this is what I want to do with it."

"You deserve to be happy. No matter what your husband said to you or how he hurt you, you deserve to be happy." Tisha's intense gaze made her squirm.

Who could be happy after the year she'd experienced? But that wasn't Scott's fault. Was it? She'd made the decision to fight for her baby's life. She set the events in motion. Scott had made that clear. *"If you had listened to me, this wouldn't have happened. You made that poor baby suffer for nothing."*

What an asshole. Chris's words interrupted her memories of

Scott blaming her for their baby girl's death, for the terrible pain she'd put them all through. Scott had been right though. Hadn't he?

She sat beside Tisha on the bed. "Scott wasn't like that. He wasn't abusive."

Tisha cocked her head to the side. "Are you sure? Abuse comes in different forms. He didn't have to beat you black and blue to be abusive. I have observed some tendencies that caused me concern. Most recently this morning with the yelling man. You appeared to be exhibiting signs of a panic attack."

"I don't know anyone who likes yelling," she said.

"Fair enough. But not everyone has trouble breathing or looks like they're about to run away when someone nearby them yells. That can be an indication someone has suffered abuse in their past."

She stared at her hands. This wasn't something she liked talking about with anyone. "My dad. He abused my mom. Not me as much. Usually he just yelled at me to draw her into a fight. Or locked me in a closet. Or put me up on a shelf. I am a little afraid of the dark. And heights for that matter." She laughed it off to show Tisha it was no big deal and she'd gotten over it long ago. "Mom got rid of him though. Years ago, when I was little."

"But somewhere inside you, that little girl still huddles in the dark closet, scared and confused. That wasn't your fault. Imagine how you would react if your ex-husband had locked your daughter in a closet."

She whipped her head around to face Tisha. "No one would touch my daughter. I would kill him before I'd—" She sucked in a breath.

"Exactly. We minimize and make excuses and tolerate things ourselves that we would never allow to happen to people we love. Especially when someone has told us we don't deserve better. Something to think about."

"No one ever told me that, though."

"Your dad did. He showed you, the way he treated you. And

as a child, you had no defense against that treatment. You internalized the message, recording it in your psyche. That's what happens to children who are victims of abuse. Then that recording flips on throughout our lives, replaying over and over, telling us we're not good enough, that we don't deserve better in life. Are you sure your ex-husband never triggered that recording? He wasn't abusive at all? He was a loving, nurturing man who made you feel like the sun that lit his life every day?"

She snorted a laugh, despite the feelings Tisha's words dredged up. Scott treat her like the sun and the moon? That was a joke. She couldn't stand chick-flicks or romances of any kind. Watching guys bring women flowers and bend over backwards to win their affection made her want to puke. Guys needed to feel important, superior, and in control. Praising their significant other only made them feel inferior. It didn't happen in the real world. "No, of course not. What guy ever treats a woman that way? That's just something invented to appeal to women and sell books and movies."

"A strong, confident man with a healthy sense of self, who truly cares about his significant other, that's who. Okay, so movies dramatize a bit, but it's not completely invented." Tisha gave her a moment. "You sure that ex of yours wasn't abusive?"

"He wasn't. He never hurt me. I mean, he might've yelled sometimes when he wanted his way." *Which was all the time,* a tiny voice in the back of her mind whispered. "He wasn't like my dad. Kind of the opposite really. It's like he had no inner strength and just crumpled in the face of crisis. He couldn't handle anything."

"That sounds about right. Someone with ego issues, someone who feels insecure all the time, will look for a relationship they can dominate, to help them compensate for their insecurities. Blustering at you, making you cower and give in, demanding his way, and blaming you for things outside your control—these are all a form of abuse."

Scott abusive? She'd been so careful not to repeat her mother's mistakes, been so sure she'd chosen someone exactly the oppo-site of her father. And her ex-husband had never laid a hand on her. But if she was completely honest with herself, he did often look pleased with himself after arguments when she broke down in tears. Why would anyone be happy that they'd made their wife cry? That was a form of victory for him, wasn't it? And how many times had her father strutted around the house once her mother collapsed into a heap on the floor, crying her eyes out, having given up and agreed with whatever toxic garbage spewed from her father's mouth?

Something shifted inside her, a tiny little cataclysm that rocked the foundation on which she'd built all her beliefs. The plate tectonics of her life butted against one another, the rumbling quake threatening to topple everything. The cracks that opened spilled memories of her father's red face as he raged at her mother, Scott's perma-scowl that clouded her days, then his dark face brooding as they returned home from the hospital with empty arms, accusation rolling off of him.

All the places she'd stuffed the difficult memories, the things she couldn't deal with, threatened to burst open. The carefully constructed brick walls and dark, secret closets of her psyche quiv-ered, ready to let loose a barrage of emotional devastation she couldn't face. She would not melt down again. She would not.

Her heart hammered in her chest as if she were running a marathon, her stomach churned, and she couldn't breathe.

Tisha rested a hand on her arm. "Breathe with me. Breathe in on a count of three. Hold for three. Exhale for three. You are okay. Nothing can hurt you. Here we go."

She followed Tisha's example, breathing evenly in, holding, then releasing the breath for another count of three. Between counting, while she held her breath, Tisha repeated again and again that she was okay and nothing could hurt her. Slowly, her heart resumed a normal pattern, her pulse slowed, and she could breathe normally.

Tisha smiled at her. "There we go. Much better. Yes?"

She nodded but didn't trust herself to speak.

"Good. Remember that breathing technique. You can do that any time you feel things getting away from you." Tisha stood. "Pretending everything is okay when it isn't exacts a huge toll. Holding in all those emotions takes so much energy. But that's a dam that will break. And when it does, it will all come pouring out. It's like a festering wound. You have to drain the poison out and deal with the infection so you can heal."

"I'm fine," she reassured Tisha, rising to see her out the door.

Tisha nodded again, her face smooth. Olivia appreciated the woman's ability to maintain such a comforting expression. "I'll leave you alone. But you know where to find me."

When the door clicked shut, she took a deep breath and went back to her laptop. That was enough of that. She shoved aside all thoughts of Scott and her father and abuse and everything else that caused her stomach to ache.

She pulled up a browser and searched for Mukesh. A little thrill of excitement pulsed through her when she discovered a story about him in a small Indian newspaper referencing his pad machine. She clicked on it and read about the machine that could make affordable pads beside a photo of Mukesh standing next to a machine installed in another tiny Indian town. The article explained the machine produced pads, intended as an inexpensive option for rural areas where women were embarrassed to buy from male shop owners. The machine could be operated by women, the pads sold by women to women, leaving men out of the process entirely. They were also a tiny fraction of the cost of pads purchased from vendors in markets. This wasn't meant as competition to the big-name manufacturers. This was an option for women who otherwise would not have access to pads.

The article confirmed everything Mukesh had told them in person. Spurred on by vindication, she emailed her mother, completely ignoring the information about Scott. Who the hell cared what he did? A pang in her heart tried to disagree with that thought, but she squashed it flat.

She searched for a reputable bank in Kochi and asked her mother to please inquire from her bank at home how to transfer funds across the Atlantic. Step one done. She would figure out how to get the money to Mukesh. She didn't care what anyone else thought or said. She was going to do this.

Chapter Twenty-One

Unable to believe what she thought she'd heard, Olivia simply blinked, dumbfounded. Surely, she'd misunderstood. She glanced at Chris, who shrugged, apparently as confused as she was.

"You're saying the building is for sale, but you won't sell it to *me*?" She half expected the man to burst out laughing, then joke about her inability to understand English, the latest joke circulating the town at her expense.

Since she'd undertaken the project to fund and install a pad machine, she'd faced roadblocks, ridicule, and scorn in town. She understood how Mukesh had been driven from his village by gossip and threats.

On top of everything else, a visiting professor who presented to the older classes at the school wanted to meet all the volunteer teachers. They'd gathered for tea in the dining hall. Ms. Vanya brewed up her spiciest concoction yet, and Mrs. Gupta introduced them all.

The other teachers seemed to understand the professor well enough, but his thick accent garbled the words in Olivia's ears and left her confused and shaking her head. "I'm sorry, what?" she asked again and again when he posed a question or comment to her. He grew weary of needing to repeat himself and still requiring Mrs. Gupta to "translate" for her and demanded, "Where are you from?" That question she clearly understood—the words at least, though not his intent.

"Where am I from?"

"Yes! Where?"

She'd looked around for help, but everyone else appeared equally baffled.

"America?" The word came out more question than statement. The answer seemed so obvious.

"No! Before America. Originally."

"Before . . . I'm American. Born and raised in America. I've never lived anywhere else."

"How can that be when you do not even properly understand English?"

The other teachers had snorted into their hands and Mrs. Gupta attempted to conceal a smile while Olivia's cheeks burned with embarrassment. Rather than believe his clipped, broken, and marginal English the source of the language barrier, the man instead blamed her inability to understand. The story somehow—everyone present swore they didn't tell a soul—spread through the little town like wildfire, turning her into the village idiot, basically. Everywhere she went, people pointed at her, huge smirks on their faces. At the market, vendors greeted her with smiles and eyes that danced with a joke. "The American who cannot speak English! Hello!"

She held a master's degree in English for God's sake. And now, with cash in hand, she sat before the property owner as The American Who Cannot Speak English, the village idiot, listening to this man, who most likely didn't even graduate from high school, turn down her offer.

"But why not?"

The man narrowed his eyes at her. "You teach Aditi?"

There. The lifeline she needed. Now he would understand and sell her the building. "I did! Yes. And maybe we can help her get back in school. This building will mean a different life to the girls and women—"

"No!" He scowled. An emphatic hand gesture dismissed her.

"But—"

"I think he didn't mean that in a good way, the way you took it." Chris stood and gripped her elbow, encouraging her up as well. "Thank you for your time. We will go."

On the street, she squinted, the vivid sun blinding her after the dismal darkness of the concrete building. They trudged back to the upscale shopping market where they'd left the other teachers browsing. She slumped with disappointment. "And now we're back to square one."

She'd sat at square zero for longer than she'd liked, trying to ensure that a non-Indian could in fact legally purchase Indian property. Someone at the bank had eventually quoted several laws and regulations, full of acronyms and lengthy numbers, assuring her that she could. But what could she do if everyone refused to sell to her?

"It's okay. We'll find another location," Chris assured her.

"But that one was perfect. Right here by the shopping center where women gather anyway."

"Maybe. Or maybe we looked at it all wrong. Maybe it's good to be someplace less conspicuous, since they prefer to be discreet about it here. Ya know?"

Good ol' Chris. Always eager to solve problems and find silver linings. He'd jumped at the opportunity to chauffeur her to a bank in Kochi to transfer funds to Mukesh for the machine and installation and take out cash to purchase a building in which to install it. She didn't like carrying so much cash and kept it hidden in her room. Frankly, she was grateful to Chris for all the support he continued to offer, always accompanying her anywhere she needed to go and acting happy to do it. He kept the conversation light as well, which appealed to her. They hadn't delved into personal information since he'd shared his mom's issues. Maybe she should invite him to share more, ask how he felt, that sort of thing. But that would open the door for him to ask questions in return. She preferred the easy friendship they'd settled into. Keeping it light worked just fine for her. She'd moved past her suspicious belief that he must want something from her and accepted that he did nice things without demanding anything in return. Letting down her guard felt good.

They discovered the other teachers window shopping at a jewelry store. She joined in, drooling over the show pieces, marveling at the intricate details and the incredible craftsmanship they must have required.

Tisha stared at her expectantly before prompting her, "Well? How'd it go? Are you in business?"

She shook her head. "He wouldn't sell."

"What?" Melanie sounded as disappointed as Olivia felt.

"That makes no sense," Delilah said. "Who turns down money?"

"Because you're a foreigner?" Aubra asked, grating on Olivia's nerves. The young woman's continued belief she knew so much more about India really got on her nerves.

"Maybe? I don't know."

"He did mention that she taught Aditi," Chris offered.

"What does that have to do with anything?" Delilah asked.

"Word is probably getting out that the American who can't even speak English is trying to open a business and employ women," Aubra said. "Combine trying to change their established traditions with an inherent mistrust of foreigners and no wonder you're meeting so much resistance."

She didn't trust herself not to bite the insufferable know-it-all's head off, so she simply shrugged.

"'Do I dare disturb the universe?'" Delilah said. "T.S. Eliot. Olivia dares disturb. Don't let them dissuade you, girl."

"I know what you need to help you feel better," Tisha said. "Jewelry shopping!"

"Yes!" Delilah agreed, looping an arm around Olivia's waist. "'Diamonds are a girl's best friend!'"

"Not a literary quote," Chris said. "I think you just like repeating other people. But you ladies should definitely treat yourselves. You won't find better deals anywhere."

"He's right," Aubra said. "We went inside when we—"

Olivia noted the obvious strain between them. They'd gone into a jewelry store as a couple? Had they looked at rings? Well, Chris had told her that Aubra had been pushing to get serious too hard and too fast. Maybe Aubra had dragged him in.

Diamonds weren't her best friend, but she shrugged and followed the group inside. Might as well, rather than stay out in the heat, even if she didn't want to buy anything. She wasn't much of a jewelry person. She caught her thumb rubbing absently against her bare ring finger, still searching for her wedding band after all this time. Frustrated, she shook her hands and clenched a fist. Enough of that. She would just have to get used to the bare finger. Unlikely she would ever let anyone put a ring on it again. She made a point of not going anywhere near the rings and stooped to admire a necklace.

Chris nudged her with an elbow. "You know, opal is the birthstone for October."

She stood and faced him, wrinkling her nose. "And?"

"How do you even know that?" Melanie asked.

"My birthday is in October."

What was he getting at? "And you want us to get you something? With your birthstone on it?"

He threw his head back and laughed. "No, Olivia. I do not want you to buy jewelry for me."

Was he suggesting she should wear his birthstone? He couldn't possibly mean that. Sure, he had been a lot of help, and he always had something nice to say to her, and made her laugh when she felt down . . . No. She did not have feelings for him, and he couldn't possibly be suggesting they were close enough to be discussing jewelry of any sort. She shook her head at him, still unclear what he was getting at.

Aubra apparently wasn't sure either, judging by her still

posture and determined gaze staring into a jewelry case but clearly not seeing anything.

He scrubbed the back of his neck. "Well, I was just thinking, I know my mom wears a ring with my birthstone on it. You know."

"A mother's ring! Of course. I think that's a really nice idea," Tisha said.

Were they honestly suggesting that she buy a ring to wear as a constant reminder that she had lost her daughter? What were they thinking? "I don't know."

But she allowed Chris to lead her to a display case where he pointed out a simple setting. "Opals come in all sorts of shades. You can ask to look at loose stones, and they will make a ring for you to mount it on. You could design your own any way you like." When she said nothing, he waved over the salesman. "You have other stones?"

The man wobbled his head and went to the back to fetch them.

"The word opal is derived from a Sanskrit word. How perfect is that? A nice reminder of India, yeah?" Chris said. "Well, a Sanskrit word meaning 'valuable stone' and a Greek word that means 'to see a change in color.' And no two are the same, just like people."

How perfect is that? She thought of the perfect name she'd chosen for her baby girl and the meaning behind it and could scarcely believe it. And now this birthstone? The two things seemed to align almost too perfectly, as though the universe had brought her to this point and clicked into place. The name, the birthstone, the sweet delight she knew in her heart her daughter would have brought into her life. But that couldn't be. Her baby girl died. Everything aligned . . . so she could lose a child? That made no sense.

The shopkeeper returned with the velvet bag and poured the contents onto a velvet-lined tray, separating the stones with tweezers and encouraging her to evaluate each of the milky stones.

Chris pointed at one, flecked with pink. "Look at that one. It has a pink cast to it. How perfect is that?"

She wished he would stop saying "How perfect is that." Nothing about this was perfect. She turned to him to say she had no interest in a ring to wear as a constant reminder of the baby she lost. But the gentle smile and the pure kindness she saw in his green eyes left her speechless.

What did he want from her? Why was he doing this? No man ever did anything for a woman unless he wanted something in return—to later be able to throw it back in her face how much he'd done for her, or to use it as leverage to demand she reciprocate, or to insist on getting his way. He must want something, no matter how nice he seemed to be, or how supportive or generous. She didn't know what, and she didn't like the offer of help when she didn't know what the eventual cost would be.

She turned and left the store without a word, standing on the cracked concrete in front of the building, the sun's rays baking her dry, browning skin as it baked the earth around her. She gulped deep, dusty breaths and fought the tears pooling in her eyes, refusing to let them fall.

She heard the door open and close behind her but refused to turn or make eye contact, determined to regain control of herself before interacting with anyone.

Tisha's voice beside her, soothing, non-demanding, washed over her. "You know, I think his idea of a ring with her birthstone would be a really nice way to honor her. I've seen some parents choose to tattoo a lost baby's name on their arms. People cope with grief in a lot of different ways. Most at least keep hand and footprints. What did you and your husband do?"

What had they done? They'd refused to discuss it, Scott's silent accusations seeping into every crack and crevice of the house, bitter and musty, the decaying marriage rotting away. After a week of averting her eyes and gritting her teeth every time she walked down the hall past the nursery, she had disassembled the crib and cradle, dragging every piece of baby furniture and all the baby accessories and baby clothes out of the house and off to Goodwill. Then she had repainted the room back to the color it had been before she foolishly prepared for a future that wasn't meant to be. She'd believed she could put it all behind her, out of her mind, go back to the way things had been before. What business did she have wearing a mother's ring? She'd been a mother for less than twenty-four hours and in that time frame she had subjected her baby girl to pain and suffering, selfishly determined not to lose her. And then, to add insult to injury, she'd gone home and swept away every reminder of her existence.

The sound of the baby's first cries still haunted her dreams. She couldn't brush the memory aside the way she had hauled everything off to Goodwill. It remained firmly lodged in her mind, reminding her, over and over again. Just as her arms remembered the tiny weight of the swaddled body, the tiny little fingers and toes. How the sweet little thing had turned her head and quieted at the sound of Olivia's voice—

She squeezed her eyes closed and her breath caught in her throat until she thought she might choke.

Tisha's hand rested lightly on her arm. "Olivia, sometimes we do everything right and things still don't go the way we want them to. We make the best choices we can with the information in front of us. Some things are out of our control. You didn't do anything wrong."

Through clenched teeth, she managed to whisper, "I made her suffer. It was my fault."

"No. You did not give her that birth defect. You had no control over that. A doctor told you she could live with a surgery to repair the defect, and you chose to pursue that option. You fought for your baby, with everything you had, trying to ensure your baby would have a life. Why can't you see that's exactly what a mother does?"

A sliver of a crack peeped open in her heart. She wanted to believe Tisha, wanted to believe she had done the right thing. "But I wasn't really her mother. I barely even got to hold her."

"I know a woman who lost her daughter at the age of four, to a medical condition diagnosed shortly after birth. The doctors warned her the condition would most likely be fatal, but she tried everything. Despite that, she only had four years with her daughter. And every year on the anniversary of her death, she and her husband take cupcakes to the grave and celebrate her birthday. Because she lived. She was their baby girl. Do you think caring for her daughter for only four years makes her less of a mother?"

"Of course not. But this is different."

"It really isn't. You are hanging on to misplaced guilt and refusing to grieve. Blaming yourself for things outside of your control. We don't determine someone is a mother based on how long they care for a child. You had a baby and tragically lost her. You are still a mother. She is still your baby."

Something painful burbled up out of the deep recesses of her soul, enveloping her in darkness. She couldn't cope with it. Clamping her eyes closed, she crossed her arms across her stomach and squeezed, struggling for breath.

Tisha's hand ran across her back. "It's okay. You're okay. Let's breathe. Breathe in, one, two, three. And hold. And out again. Good. You're okay. I promise."

She wanted to believe she was okay, as much as she wanted to believe she'd been a good mother, if only for the briefest time. But while she stood breathing with Tisha and longing to believe in something good about herself, a voice kept chastising her, reminding her of every mistake she'd made in her life, swallowing the flicker of hope in its shadow.

Chapter Twenty-Two

At dinner that night, the other teachers admired and complimented one another's jewelry purchases. Olivia hadn't bought anything but couldn't stop thinking about that little, pink-flecked opal and imagining it mounted on a little gold ring on her finger. Part of her really wanted that ring, but the voice in the back of her mind continued to criticize relentlessly, telling her she didn't deserve it. And she couldn't turn that voice off. *How could you put that baby through surgery? Why did you think you could save your baby girl?*

Worst of all, she couldn't stop asking why her baby. Why did her baby have to develop a defect? Were her genes defective? Was her marriage defective? Millions of women gave birth to millions of babies all over the world. And some of them didn't even want their babies. So why did she lose hers? Was she just not meant to be a mother?

Tisha's words came back to her: *You are still a mother.*

Deep breathing and words of affirmation had calmed her down at the shopping center. She appreciated Tisha's breathing exercises. Although, if everyone would leave her alone, she wouldn't keep having meltdowns in the first place. Thankfully, everyone had given her space and gone about their days as though nothing had happened, as though she hadn't fled the jewelry store without a word like a crazy woman.

"I know a ruby was a big expense," Melanie commented, holding her new ring in the light so that it shimmered and gleamed, "but the red reminds me of that crazy rain that falls here."

"Only a big expense compared to cheaper stones," Aubra assured her. "You won't find a ruby for that price anywhere else. You got a deal."

"Speaking of the red rain," Olivia said, "you were going to tell us something you'd heard from a friend at Kerala University at the market the other day. Before the yelling distracted us."

"Oh, right," Aubra said. "Seriously, you cannot share this with anyone else. He swore me to secrecy."

"And who will we tell?" Delilah asked.

"I mean don't email anyone back home. Especially not your conspiracy-theorist boyfriend."

"Okay, okay."

"Like I said, he has an internship in a lab at Kerala University. The lab received samples of red rainwater to analyze, to determine what caused the red color." She paused and looked at each of them. "So far they have been unable to identify it. It doesn't match anything."

"What are you saying?" Melanie asked.

"Wait a minute," Olivia said. "One of the newspaper articles I read claimed the material in the rain is extraterrestrial. I wrote it off as nonsense. Are you saying that could be true?"

"Extraterrestrial?" Chris said. "From space?"

Aubra lifted her eyebrows and shrugged. "I'm only reporting what he told me. But they can't identify it. It doesn't appear to be sedimentary. They've isolated cells they cannot match to anything on the planet."

"Cells?" Chris asked. "Don't you mean particles? The word cells indicates something alive."

"I mean cells." Aubra lifted an eyebrow. "They've cultured

them in various temperatures and substrates. But I wasn't supposed to share that so don't tell anyone else."

"So it's something from space?" Chris repeated.

"They cannot confirm anything at this moment." Aubra clearly enjoyed being in the know and sharing this bit of information with them. Her self-satisfied smile irritated Olivia.

"That is really bizarre," Delilah said.

"I'm sure someone will figure it out eventually," Tisha said. Olivia wished she felt as confident as Tisha sounded.

"Oh, hey!" Melanie said. "I had the best idea for a Diwali craft for the kids! We could get clay, and they can all make their own *diyas*."

"Oh my gosh, yes!" Delilah clapped her hands. "I love that!"

"What's a *diya*?" Olivia asked.

"It's a little clay lamp," Chris said. "Picture Aladdin's lamp, but with no top on it. During Diwali, everyone will fill their *diyas* with oil and light the wicks. It's really pretty."

Melanie nodded. "After Chris described them, I checked with the local brick kiln, and they said they'd be happy to fire some for our students."

"That's perfect!"

"And then I was thinking instead of filling them with oil and lighting them, we could use little flameless tealights. It will have the same effect but be much safer than open flames around the kids."

"Brilliant," Aubra said. "I found some patterns for paper flowers that could be a great craft and decoration as well."

"And then we can have them draw chalk *rangoli*, like Olivia thought of," Chris said.

"I've been thinking maybe I could have the kids paint superhero shirts. That would be a good craft, wouldn't it?"

The other teachers' foreheads wrinkled, eyebrows twisting in confusion.

Aubra scowled. "Superheroes? For Diwali?"

"Yeah. Chris said something about someone beating a monster. Right?"

"Lord Krishna defeated the demon Narakasura. Likening him to a comic-book hero is a little insulting. I wouldn't recommend that." Aubra tossed her hair over her shoulder and shook her head, as if she couldn't believe anyone could be so dense.

Chris attempted to defend her. "I mean, it's good triumphing over evil. In that regard, it's a nice similarity."

"The kids won't make that connection. She'd be seen as making fun of a major tradition instead of honoring local customs."

"Sorry," Olivia said. "I guess I've been so preoccupied with the pad machine and getting that installed I haven't thought much about Diwali."

"Well, it's a huge holiday and you don't want to disappoint your students by not adequately celebrating it. You might want to focus on that."

"Right. Right. I'll get chalk for the drawing decoration things and whatever else we need from the shop at the market."

Chris cleared his throat. "I love that we will be celebrating Diwali with the kids. It's perfect. A custom to celebrate knowledge winning over ignorance. What better place than a school to highlight that?"

"Does knowledge win out over ignorance, though?" Olivia asked. "I feel like that's just the stuff of myths. I mean, it's a great story, but that doesn't happen in real life. People don't ever suddenly realize they were wrong and change their ways."

Aubra pursed her lips as if biting back words then said, "And who decides the beliefs or customs are wrong? Maybe they shouldn't be changed."

The edge in Aubra's tone caught her off guard, but Ms. Vanya bustled from the kitchen to the table, shuttling bowls and platters of food before the conversation continued. Olivia hadn't been hungry all day, but her stomach growled as a medley of cumin, cilantro, and fresh *chapatis* enticed her senses.

Delilah scooped *dal* into a bowl. "I lost another girl in one of my classes today. It never ends."

The other teachers glanced at Olivia, as if afraid the information might prove too much for her and set her off again.

She accepted a platter of *biryani* and helped herself. "Maybe when I get this machine installed it will end."

"Don't set your sights too high," Tisha cautioned. "Established traditions don't change overnight. Although, maybe this will change things slowly, increase awareness and health of women eventually."

"I don't expect anything to change overnight," she said, sliding a hot *chapati* onto her plate. "Frankly at this point, just finding someone to sell property to me would be an improvement. I'm absolutely stuck and Mukesh is scheduled to arrive next week."

"Oh, wow," Tisha said. "You're already moving forward with this, aren't you? You've paid him and everything?"

"Yes, it's a done deal. I'm doing this."

"Have you thought about who will operate it?" Melanie asked.

"I can't stop thinking about it. But until it's here and installed, I'm pretty much stuck there too. I'm not sure how to explain what exactly we intend to do until I can demonstrate and show them the machine."

Everyone at the table stared at their plates, intently involved with food. She knew they were all thinking, *I told you so.* But she didn't care.

Ms. Vanya hovered over them rather than scuttling back to the kitchen as she usually did. She wrung her hands, bangles jangling, as she shifted from foot to foot.

Chris looked up. "It's all delicious as always, Ms. Vanya! Thank you!"

"Welcome." She wobbled her head and brushed aside the praise. She stared at Olivia. "You would buy building?"

She swallowed a bite, nodding. Had the woman heard something in town or merely overheard their discussion? "That's right. I plan to put in a machine that would give women jobs. I tried to buy a building today, but the man wouldn't sell it to me." She left out the specifics, well aware at this point that periods and pads were not discussed, particularly in mixed company. Chris wouldn't care, but poor Ms. Vanya would be mortified.

"Uncle of Aditi," Ms. Vanya said.

She didn't immediately follow. But then the family resemblance clicked into place. "That man is Aditi's uncle? That's why he wouldn't sell to me? Because her father doesn't like me?"

Great. In a small community like this, one important person developing a dislike for you meant the whole town would turn on you. Their influence was too great, particularly once rumors and gossip started flying.

"Ignorance holds people back," Tisha said. "Maybe the students we're teaching will eventually rise up above superstition and find the success we're hoping to prepare them for."

"And who are we to decide that they should change their ways?" Aubra insisted. "Teaching them English, educating them, fine, yes. Obviously, that is an improvement. But we can't drift back into imperialism and start deciding we know best."

Really? The young woman from England was lecturing them about the perils of imperialism?

"We're not trying to turn everyone into little Westerners, Aubra," Chris murmured. "We're only trying to improve their lives."

"If everyone sits around waiting for someone else to fix the world's problems, nothing ever changes," Olivia said. "Or if everyone looks the other way and pretends no problem exists. The uneducated are far more susceptible to believing in myths and superstitions. If we don't combat that ignorance, if we don't help them see there is a better way, nothing will ever change for the better."

"And you get to decide your way is better?" Aubra's eyes met hers directly.

The anger there shocked Olivia. "I didn't decide. It simply is better. You heard Mukesh describing the miserable plight these women face. If we only look at the improvements to personal hygiene and ignore the social ramifications, this is one hundred percent a good thing for this community. Why are the men so determined to keep their women miserable and stuck at home?"

"That's the problem here," Aubra said, her voice rising in volume. "You can't separate out the social ramifications. Not here. You are flying in the face of tradition to encourage the girls to stay in school and the women to work outside the home. You will be threatening the status quo. It's the only way they know. We came to teach, not rock the boat."

"Listen to what you're saying. Continuing on in this manner, in the only way they know, endangers the lives of their women, keeps their daughters uneducated, and continues the cycle of poverty. Once this machine is installed, a machine I will remind you that was designed by an Indian man to improve the lives of his wife and mother, it will offer so much to this community. If it takes off, imagine the income it can provide to destitute families, to women left on their own and struggling to raise children."

Aubra's jaw jutted to the side in an angry scowl, and she crossed her arms. "And even his wife and mother left him. He's completely alone, ostracized, shouted at, and threatened with violence. No one wants this. Why can't you see that?"

Why in the world was her fellow teacher getting so worked up? "I'm not asking for your help."

"No, but your actions impact all of us! They already meet foreigners with suspicion. Now this."

"Now what? What are you talking about?"

"Aubra," Tisha cautioned.

She looked back and forth between the two teachers. "What? Are you keeping something from me?"

"She should know!" Aubra said, dropping her fork with a clang. "Chris has been trying to approach people in town, urging them to get behind your venture and support selling property to you."

She spun to face him. "I didn't know you did that."

His cheeks pinked, and he shrugged. "Just trying to help. I thought since I'm a guy, they might listen to me. Ya know?"

Ms. Vanya spoke up again. "No. Friend of Miss Olivia."

"Friend of . . ." Her head swam as frustration bubbled from her stomach to her larynx, choking the words in her throat. She paused to breathe deeply as Tisha had taught her. "So anyone associated with me is being blacklisted? Is that what you're saying?"

Ms. Vanya looked confused.

"Not blacklisted," Aubra said. "We're basically untouchables now!"

Unfamiliar with the word, Olivia shook her head.

"Untouchables, the lowest of the low. The outcasts, who aren't even included in the caste system here. Dirty and gross, so disgusting no one will get close to them or do business with them."

Chris pressed fingers to his temples. "Aubra, let's not—"

"Stop encouraging her, Chris! And you!" She whirled on Olivia. "Girls disappearing from our classrooms upsets you? Wait and see what you've done. No parent will allow untouchables anywhere near their children, much less to teach them. Get ready to watch all the children disappear from the entire school."

"We don't know that will happen, Aubra," Tisha tried to intervene.

"It will! Wait and see. How will we buy things for Diwali? How will we buy anything? Shopkeepers won't let untouchables in their stores. They won't be seen doing business with us. She's even managed to ruin Diwali!"

"Aubra." Tisha's voice held a note of warning.

"No. We've tried it your way. We've all been gentle and patient at your urging, but enough is enough."

Gentle and patient . . . at Tisha's urging? What was happening? She looked at Tisha, but the woman only shook her head. None of the other teachers would make eye contact. Had all their friendships been orchestrated? Did they all talk about her behind her back? Oh, poor Olivia. Everyone be nice to her. Be her friend because she's so pathetic she couldn't possibly make any real ones. What about Chris? She couldn't look at him. She'd been so convinced his concern was genuine. This cut deep. Somehow, his fake friendship hurt most of all.

She lowered her fork, appetite gone. Cheeks flaming, she stood to leave.

Chris grabbed for her wrist, but she shook him off. "I only wanted to help. Help someone. Save lives. I thought I could do something good."

Tisha stood and intercepted her. "You are. Aubra is getting carried away. Sit down. Eat."

"No, it sounds like she's right. If the entire town is turning against me, I don't have any business trying to force this on them. I can't make any progress on my own, and no one will help." She dropped back into her seat. How typical. Aubra was right—who did she think she was? Why did she think she could move an anthill, much less a mountain?

Ms. Vanya moved to stand behind her and placed a hand on her arm. "I help, Miss Olivia. I help."

Chapter Twenty-Three

S weating, and not only from the relentless sun beating down on them, Olivia trudged along beside Ms. Vanya. Confused did not begin to describe her mindset. She liked Ms. Vanya—the woman had always been kind and friendly to her and all the teachers. But why did the woman seem so determined to help her find a suitable location for her business endeavor? Mildly suspicious of Ms. Vanya's motive and extremely skeptical of her ability to assist, Olivia nonetheless wasn't about to turn down an offer of help. She knew she needed it.

Still, as she plodded down the packed-dirt pathway, she wondered if Ms. Vanya had any idea why she wanted a building. Would the older woman be upset when she saw the product produced by Mukesh's machine? After Ms. Vanya's offer—no, insistence—that she would help, following the dinner fiasco where Aubra basically accused her of single-handedly destroying the school, Olivia had politely told her she didn't need to do that. She'd assumed the woman couldn't stand to see Olivia so discouraged and hoped to lift her spirits by promising help. But Ms. Vanya refused to be let off the hook and kept insisting she would help. The woman had a job cooking for the teachers at the English school. What incentive could she possibly have?

Flummoxed, she followed the older woman, unwilling to upset her. After all, if she pointed out the woman had no reason to help her, Ms. Vanya might realize she was absolutely right and walk away.

Ms. Vanya, who hadn't spoken a word as they walked, adjusted the veil on her head and used the edge to daub sweat from her face. "I am mad dog, you are Englishman."

Olivia laughed along with her at the reference to the old Indian saying: Only mad dogs and Englishmen went outside in the heat of the day. Or something along those lines.

Indeed, the empty streets proved the truth of the old adage that dated to British Imperialist days. Indians knew better how to navigate their environment despite the old Imperialist belief the British knew best for foreign people. How ironic that British Aubra had lectured her to stay out of their business.

Ms. Vanya led her through an opening between a cinder-block wall. A tiny, square concrete building with a corrugated metal roof stood on a square of bare earth. If the building had been painted, Olivia couldn't tell what color. The dismal, gray-streaked walls cried out for attention.

"Come. Come!" Ms. Vanya motioned her to follow.

Oh, they were going inside? Olivia glanced about, feeling like a trespasser, but even if they weren't allowed on the property, no one was around to catch them.

The unlocked door squeaked open when Ms. Vanya pushed it. Olivia followed her up a few steps and crossed into the building. If she thought outside was hot, it had nothing on the interior of the building. Rivulets of sweat turned into steady streams in the oven-like box. Her bra, already soaked with sweat, felt like she could wring it out.

The interior of the building was as plain and drab as the exterior, though inside she could tell had definitely been painted a grayish-white color, despite patches having chipped off and fallen to the bare concrete floor. Nothing much to look at, but it was clean enough, she noted. Ms. Vanya proudly pointed out it was equipped with electricity and water.

She looked around. Only a couple of windows, but they let in light and potentially could be opened to allow a breeze. This wasn't what she'd envisioned, but then again, her options were extremely limited and if the owner could truly be convinced to sell to her, well, beggars can't be choosers. They might be a bit cramped in the space, but it should be adequate to hold the machine and allow the women a little bit of elbow room as they worked.

She met Ms. Vanya's exuberant but questioning eyes and nodded. "I think you've found our place."

Ms. Vanya broke into a grin and appeared relieved, almost grateful. Strange.

"Of course, whoever owns it might not sell to me. That happened last time," she reminded Ms. Vanya.

"You will see," Ms. Vanya smiled. "We can see him."

"Right now?"

"We go now."

She fell in beside the woman for a second time and followed her to a series of small concrete dwellings. She'd never been inside the home of anyone in the town and hesitated before entering. Painted a lovely blue, this well-maintained home did not show signs of weathering or neglect. The corrugated metal roof even gleamed bright silver in the midday sun, rather than the crusty brown rust many roofs took on with time.

Ms. Vanya leaned back out and gestured her in. "Come, Miss Olivia. This is my home. You are welcome."

Her home? What was happening? She crept inside the darkened interior and into a small sitting room. As her eyes adjusted to the lower light, she saw the bare concrete floor was covered with a rug. To the side, she glimpsed an open door to a tiny space with a squat toilet in the floor and a bucket sitting beside it. The scent of heavy spices drifted from the kitchen area of the house, where a pot simmered on a simple stove, stirred by a woman who appeared to be about Ms. Vanya's age. Exposed pipes led from the wall to a sink, and a plain spigot perched above the basin. A hallway led away to what she assumed was the bedroom. But she also noticed a jumble of pillows and bedding off in the corner.

A silver-haired man pushed himself up from the couch and approached to greet her.

Ms. Vanya introduced the man. "Miss Olivia, my brother-in-law, Rahul."

She shook hands. "Hello. Nice to meet you."

"Olivia." The man nodded to the kitchen. "My wife."

She waited but that was it. The woman made eye contact from her place at the stove but didn't join them. She couldn't read the woman's expression either. Irritation? Curiosity?

"My husband is no more," Ms. Vanya told her, casting her eyes downward.

"I'm so sorry. I had no idea."

"Our parents are no more, but Rahul let me come live with him and his wife, since I have no more relatives."

Here was another example of how difficult things were for women who lost their husbands. Although Ms. Vanya had a job. But perhaps the job didn't pay enough for her to support herself. She would never be so rude as to ask. Mukesh had told her he'd been forced to drop out of school to contribute to the family income after his father passed away. The money his mother made as a cleaner had not been enough to keep them housed and fed. This was probably a similar situation. Without a working son, perhaps Ms. Vanya had been forced to accept Rahul's offer. Did Ms. Vanya think her new business might make more money? Is that what drew her to help?

"Sit! Sit!" Ms. Vanya directed, pulling her to the couch. A stick of incense burned on a small table, the smoke curling languidly toward the ceiling. So many scents assaulted her.

Rahul joined her. Facing the kitchen, he called something to his wife, who nodded and lifted a teapot, which she proceeded to fill from the spigot. Was the water okay to drink from the faucet here?

She held up her hands. "It's okay. I don't need tea."

They looked at her like she was crazy. Rahul gestured to his wife, who continued filling the pot. "Yes, tea."

Ms. Vanya sat on her other side, beaming. Rahul leaned back and laced his fingers across the paunch beneath his ample *shalwar*, quite obviously sizing up Olivia. What was happening? Though she didn't feel threatened or uncomfortable, she had absolutely no idea what was going on. She glanced around the room, her eyes landing on the bedding again. Did Ms. Vanya sleep on the floor? She hoped at least perhaps the couch. She never would have suspected this about the always cheerful, smiling woman. She also noted a sheet hung across one corner of the tiny room. Perhaps that was to allow their permanent guest some privacy?

Rahul seemed to arrive at some conclusion and Olivia got the feeling it wasn't good. His facial features scrunched into a dubious and disappointed expression. He scratched the back of his head. "You would buy building?"

"That's . . . your building? You own the building we just looked at?" His lack of enthusiasm further confounded her. If he owned it and wanted to sell, why was he so reluctant? She glanced at Ms. Vanya, beaming and nodding, clearly certain she'd found the solution.

He tipped his head to the side.

"Yes. I have money! I do want to buy it. It's for sale?"

He tipped his head again, this time so quickly and so slightly she worried it translated to, *Yes, it's for sale, but not to you.*

She'd been through that and had no intention of repeating the experience. She sat up straight and leaned forward. "How much?"

Rahul shrugged a shoulder noncommittally.

Ms. Vanya switched to another language, speaking rapidly, her tone and volume rising as she went. She gestured to Olivia several times. Whatever the woman said, her appeal seemed to fall on deaf ears. Rahul remained stoic, jerking his head slightly as if dismissing Ms. Vanya's argument. Olivia longed to know what was being said. Ms. Vanya nearly leaned across her lap by the time Rahul's wife carried a tray of teacups into the room, settling it on the table in front of them. Olivia caught her eyes and started to thank the woman, but she glanced away as if caught doing something she shouldn't be. The woman scurried back into the kitchen area.

Ms. Vanya appeared to be pleading. Rahul leaned forward to pluck a cup of tea from the tray. He sat back and slurped loudly, peering over the cup's edge at Olivia. He lowered the cup and called, "Navya!"

The curtain twitched and a young woman slid from behind it, toddler on her hip wrapped snuggly in her veil. The woman's veil partially obscured her face. Slightly shocked that another person had remained unannounced behind the curtain this entire time, Olivia struggled not to appear unnerved.

Ms. Vanya gestured emphatically toward Olivia but continued to speak in a language Olivia couldn't understand.

The young woman's gaze never left the floor. "Hello."

"Hi. I'm Olivia," she greeted the newcomer in her most encouraging, upbeat tone.

Ms. Vanya continued to speak, but the younger woman appeared next to tears and only jerked her head sideways. Olivia thought that gesture meant *no*, but she still struggled to differentiate between the head wobble that meant *yes* and the slight jerk that meant *no*. Not to be confused with the sideways jerk employed by rickshaw drivers and vendors that meant *go ahead*.

Ms. Vanya clucked her tongue in a manner easily understood as sheer frustration, then turned to Olivia. "My daughter."

"Oh! This is your daughter?" She freshly appraised the young woman and reevaluated her assessment of Ms. Vanya. She'd had no clue the older woman had a daughter. But how would she have known? They didn't know each other.

Ms. Vanya nodded. "Navya. And her daughter Jaanvi."

"You have a granddaughter?"

Navya pulled her veil away from the little one so she could see the baby clearly. Dark hair clung closely to the little girl's head. Dark eyes peered back at Olivia. The baby lifted one fist to her mouth and hiccuped before burying her face in Navya's shoulder.

Ms. Vanya laughed. "Shy!"

"That's okay," Olivia assured her. Her arms reached out, without any thought, longing to hold the child. "Can I . . . will she let me hold her?"

Navya looked to her mother for guidance. Ms. Vanya held out her own arms and gestured for her to hand over the baby. Jaanvi leaned into the more familiar arms, but Ms. Vanya settled her onto Olivia's lap. The little one squirmed but only glanced back and forth from her grandmother to Olivia, seeming to draw comfort from proximity.

"She is so beautiful," Olivia gushed, fighting tears as she thought about the baby girl she never got to hold on her lap this way—who never learned to sit up or crawl or toddle. "Her chubby little cheeks are so cute!"

Jaanvi fussed a bit, clearly unsure what to think of the stranger on whose lap she had been deposited. Olivia clutched the baby under the armpits and bounced her, hoping to entertain if not delight. One of the little girl's arms hung at a funny angle.

Ms. Vanya patted the arm. "Father hurt her."

Her head whipped to face the older woman. "What?"

The woman nodded and then gestured to Navya, who sighed deeply but obeyed the command her mother gave her. The young woman shifted her veil, revealing a disfiguring scar across one side of her face. Deep red and puckered, the skin seemed shriveled.

Olivia sucked in her breath but fought not to outright gasp. The poor girl had probably suffered enough shocked reactions to last a lifetime. "What happened?"

Ms. Vanya, her voice hard and cold, answered. "Her husband."

An abusive husband and father. And worse even than the man at whose hands Olivia herself had suffered. Though she'd been scarred on the inside, and she'd seen him hurt her mother, neither of them had been hurt physically so badly.

"What did he do?" she asked, drawing the baby against her chest in a tight hug, as if she could protect against the horrible events that had already marred her.

"He beat them both. He made little money. He spent it all to get drunk, then hurt them. I wanted her to leave, but she stayed. Until he threw hot oil in her face while she tried to cook his dinner."

The young woman's voice quavered as she finally spoke, barely above a whisper. "He wanted more money for alcohol. I had no money to give him." She dropped her head as if in shame.

"While Navya screamed in pain, her face burning from the oil, he picked up Jaanvi by one arm and shook her, then threw her against the wall."

"Oh my God." Olivia stopped trying to fight tears and allowed them to flow freely down her cheeks onto the top of Jaanvi's little head.

"She finally left him. But no man will take her now. She cannot go out. She is lower than untouchable. No one will hire her even to pick trash or clean toilets. What will happen to my daughter and my granddaughter when I am gone? When Rahul is gone?"

Olivia's head snapped up. This was why Ms. Vanya so desperately wanted her to succeed. She turned to Rahul, who had watched the entire scene unfold without saying a word.

He leaned forward and rested his arms on his knees, hands clasped. His gray hair shimmered in the dim light. "I went with Vanya and took Navya from her husband. We brought her here. They are all welcome to stay with me, and her husband will not come looking for her. I made sure of that."

When he clenched his fists, she wondered if Rahul had simply put the fear of God into the man or if he had perhaps strangled the abusive drunk. She herself would not blame him one bit if he had permanently put an end to the threat to his family.

"But Vanya is right. What will happen to them when we are gone?" He patted Jaanvi's head and looked directly at Olivia, piercing her with his intense dark eyes. "Will you let her work if I sell to you?"

This was the cause of his hesitation? Did he really question whether or not she would employ Navya? "Yes. Of course. Why wouldn't I?"

Rahul gestured to one side of his face.

A fire in her stomach burned, an angry fury that kindled from her very core. They may have gotten Navya out of her abusive situation, but the ex-husband still won, since the community ostracized and punished the victim of abuse. No more. "I don't care about that. At all. Not one bit. Why would I punish her because someone hurt her? And the baby. Has she seen a doctor for her arm?"

Heads shook. Was it access? Financial restrictions? Olivia swore she would get the baby to a doctor and do whatever she could to ensure the use of both arms in the future.

"Yes. Navya is welcome to work for me, as soon as the machine is installed."

Rahul nodded once and held out a hand. "It is yours."

She shook hands, and elation filled every fiber of her being. Let Aubra criticize her. Or anyone else. She would go to the mat for this young woman and her baby. And Meena. And Aditi. And every other woman in this town who needed help.

She had her building, and she had her first employee.

Chapter Twenty-Four

Olivia waited with Chris at the bus station, watching for Mukesh.

"This reminds me of when I came to pick you up," Chris said. "And if someone had told me that day what a firecracker you would turn out to be, I never would have believed them."

"Firecracker? Does that mean troublemaker?"

"No, not at all. You were so subdued and withdrawn at first though, I never would have believed you'd be so outspoken when something upset you."

She couldn't help but take that as a compliment. Chris always made her feel good about herself. "Hasn't exactly made me any friends."

"Hey. That's not true." He turned to look at her, a genuine pout on his face. "Are you saying we're not friends?"

"No, of course not. But everyone else is either upset with me or ostracizing me."

"Not everyone," he reminded her. "Just a few."

"Enough to cause problems and slow us down." Even knowing this, she couldn't ignore the little quiver of happiness in her stomach, knowing he had stuck by her and continued to advocate for her across town. Aditi's father and his brother were leaning on Rahul not to sell his property to her. She didn't think they even knew what she intended to do with it. Their negative attitude seemed based solely on spite and disapproval of her gifting books to Aditi.

Aubra's dire predictions that they would all be deemed untouchables had turned out to be false—an extreme exaggeration and nothing more. No one gave them a wide berth on the streets, no children had been abruptly yanked from the school, and shop owners and street vendors still gladly continued to accept payment for goods from all of them. Aubra seemed inclined to doom and gloom, a negative outlook, quick to believe the absolute worst. No wonder Chris had called it off. Why he had dated her in the first place was the real mystery. Then again, she was extremely attractive and smart. Never married, childless. It sounded like she came from money and her father was apparently well connected. In a lot of ways, she was far more desirable than Olivia.

"Hey!" Chris said.

She nearly jumped out of her skin. Had he been reading her thoughts? But no, he was leaning out of the window waving to Mukesh, who had just exited the bus station. She hopped out of the car and waved until he spotted them. Chris helped him stow his bag in the trunk. She insisted he take the front passenger seat and climbed into the back.

"How was the trip?" she asked. He seemed so relaxed and laid back, unlike her following a lengthy bus ride.

"Good. No problems. I am here, so it was a good trip." His infectious smile lit the car.

How long would his good mood last when she shared her bad news? "I'm afraid I have some bad news. I have found someone willing to sell me his property. The building has water and electricity, like you told me the machine will need. But he hasn't actually sold to me yet, so things aren't ready. I know the machine is about to be delivered and you need to train the women, but I only have one woman so far willing to work and I—"

He held up a hand, tossing his head to the side. "Madam, when I book my travel to install a machine, I only go one way. Never return trip. I never know how long these things will take. Please do not worry. It will all work out."

She sighed deeply. "Okay, good. Thank you." A weight lifted from her shoulders, and she relaxed into the back seat. She'd been so anxious he would be upset with her for not having everything ready, or at the very least clearly disappointed. She hadn't expected such a no-big-deal response.

Chris drove them back to the guest house at the school. The town was too small to offer a hotel or any guest accommodations. As always, Chris had come to the rescue and spoken with Mrs. Gupta about the possibility of Mukesh staying in the guest house with the other teachers. They had arrived at a deal so that Mukesh was officially "hired" on for a month, more consultant than teacher, and would speak to the children about personal hygiene as well as share his experiences and how he had invented a new machine. Since Mukesh had recently been invited to speak in a number of capacities around the country, it wasn't unprecedented to consider him a guest speaker and allow him to stay. And now Chris would have some company in the men's dorm. She was glad he would not be over there all alone for the next month.

When they arrived at the school, all the women came outside into the courtyard to meet him, even Aubra who she suspected let curiosity get the better of her. Although the younger teacher had mellowed out some since her terrible predictions fizzled out. Then again, it was nearly dinnertime, so perhaps she was simply hungry.

Chris blew through introductions, which Olivia knew from experience would not stick.

"Don't worry. You'll learn them all eventually," she said.

"We're a lot at once, I know," Tisha said, "but you'll learn all our names soon enough. Olivia managed just fine."

Mukesh threw back his head and laughed again, something she was starting to suspect he did a lot. "I am nomad. No home. New faces every time I go."

Chris led Mukesh to the men's side dorm. "Come on! I'll show you to your room. Finally, I'll have some company over here."

Olivia drifted into the dining room, finding comfort in knowing Ms. Vanya was on the other side of the swinging door, rattling dishes, bustling about. Her mouth watered as the scents of cooking dinner reached her. She doubted her ability to recreate the dishes at home and wondered what she'd do when she left. The thought left her with a sudden chill. No more Ms. Vanya cheerfully serving them scrumptious meals, no more Chris propping her up with his endless positive outlook as he shuttled her about, no more Tisha and her gentle words of wisdom, determined to mend her broken parts, no more girls' nights, sharing, laughing, goofing off. In such a short time, this place and these people had filled something empty in her and come to feel like home.

Home. She realized with a pang of guilt that she had never answered her mother's last email, and in fact hadn't even thought about Mom in several days. Wasn't home with her mother? She was supposed to get her crap together, go back a new woman, find a job, get a new house . . . Yet none of those things appealed to her now. What had happened? The idea of a full-time job teaching at the community college, which had once been her sole dream and expectation, curdled in her thoughts, leaving a sour taste in her mouth. But if she didn't do that, what would she do? What job could she get? Where was her home now? Where did she belong?

Thoughts raced through her mind, berating her, pummeling her. She didn't know the answer to anything anymore. Her eyes watered and she struggled to remain in control of what she had learned was a panic attack, brought on by anxiety. She was still worrying too much about things she couldn't control. She breathed deeply as Tisha had taught her, in and out.

She felt a hand on her arm. "Good," Tisha said, "just like we practiced. What set this off?"

"I just realized how much I'm going to miss all of you when I go home." Her voice cracked.

"That's a long time from now," Tisha reminded her. "We're here now, and we're not going anywhere."

"I know. It's just so much. It's all so much, and I don't know what's going to happen next."

"You don't need all the answers to everything right now. Let's just focus on today. Maybe start thinking about tomorrow."

She nodded, snuffled, and swiped away the lone tear that escaped down her cheek.

Chris led Mukesh into the dining room. "And here's where we eat. Breakfast and dinner. You already know where the market is—that's where we met you. But let me know if you ever need a ride anywhere."

They took seats, and Ms. Vanya began a long parade of food, platter after bowl after tray. When she finally deposited the giant stack of steaming *chapatis*, the indication she was finished, she folded her hands and bowed her head to Mukesh, almost reverently.

They marveled at the quantities of food. Ms. Vanya had outdone herself.

"What's with the feast?" Chris asked. "Is this all for Mukesh?"

"And Miss Olivia." The woman beamed at her and rushed back to the kitchen, eyes glistening.

Every face at the table turned toward her.

"What in the world was that about?" Delilah asked.

"Remember when I mentioned that Ms. Vanya helped me find the building?"

Heads bobbed, along with murmurs of *mmm-hmmm*.

"Well, I didn't tell you about her daughter and granddaughter."

"She has a daughter?" Melanie asked.

"And a granddaughter?" Delilah added.

"And you didn't mention that?" Aubra sounded personally slighted.

"It seemed so personal, like it's not mine to share. You know, like I don't necessarily want everyone I meet to know about my divorce or that I lost a baby. But in her daughter's case, she can't hide it." She looked directly at Mukesh. "And I understand now why you were so eager to give women something of their own. I can see the impact your machine will have."

She told them the entire story. No one took so much as a bite while she described the grisly treatment Navya and Jaanvi had suffered and how both of them were forced to rely on a male relative since Navya was considered unemployable. When she finished, Chris's hands were clenched, Tisha's hands covered her mouth, Delilah dabbed at her eyes, Melanie shook her head, and Aubra sat stock-still, staring at the table.

"I found a doctor willing to try to help baby Jaanvi. I just hope he can. And without surgery." She lost it at the thought of that baby girl being wheeled into an operating room, tiny, helpless, alone, and scared. The pad machine and the location to install it, once she actually purchased it, would nearly deplete her funds. She also intended to fund production for the first year to give the women time to get on their feet and start turning a profit. Purchasing a year's worth of supplies would take another bite out of her dwindling money. But somehow, if Jaanvi wound up requiring surgery, she would ensure she could have it. If she had to take on more tutoring and go without sleep to earn enough, so be it.

"Olivia, this is too much for you to handle alone," Tisha said. "How can I help?"

Startled, she gaped like a fish out of water. "Well, Mukesh will oversee installation. But I think we will need some more guys to help with the heavy lifting."

Chris curled his arms, showing off the muscular biceps he

didn't have. "I'm on it! Consider me and my guns in your service."

Delilah eyed him critically but with a gleam in her eye. "Those aren't more than twenty-twos, but we need all the firepower we can get."

The table erupted into laughter, breaking the tension.

"Wait till I can get to a gym and bulk back up!"

He had ample muscles, as far as Olivia was concerned. "Since we've got Hulk Hogan over here to help move equipment, my main concern is that Navya can't handle the entire operation herself. We have to find more women willing to work it. I didn't exactly expect to have hordes of women beating the door down, clamoring to work, but I did think I'd have slightly more interest than this."

"Who all have you asked?"

"Well, that is a problem. I can't just waltz up to someone and be like, hey, want a job? I don't even know how to approach anyone. I can't help but think Meena would be perfect for this, but I have no idea how to find her."

"Ms. Vanya?" Chris called.

The door swung open, and the woman appeared.

"Do you know how to reach Meena?"

"Yes!"

He turned to Olivia. "Done. What next?"

Olivia rubbed her temples and glanced at her watch. The night was slipping away but she had a few more assignments she had to complete before she called it quits and got a few hours of sleep. She stretched and went back to correcting an essay for her student.

When she first heard a tentative tap at her door, she shook her head, believing she'd imagined the sound. But when it repeated, louder and more emphatic, she knew someone stood at her door. She just couldn't imagine why. She glanced again at the clock to confirm the late hour.

Aubra stood at her door when she cracked it open. Her confusion deepened. "Yes?"

"I know it's late. I saw your light on."

"It's okay. I'm awake." And completely confused. What could she possibly want? If she'd come to apologize, Olivia wished she hadn't. The awkward and uncomfortable tension between them was bad enough without an awkward and uncomfortable apology she'd have to accept.

"I just spoke with some old friends of mine in England. People I went to school with."

Okay. Not seeing why Aubra felt the need to race over and tell her this.

"They're working toward a graduate degree in film. I had invited them to come to India to shoot a documentary on the English school. But I just told them I have a better idea than the school. Something far more important, that people need to hear about. I suggested they document you setting up your machine."

She sucked in a breath. This was so unexpected, she took a moment to comprehend what this could mean. "I . . . I don't . . ."

"And Mukesh. They can interview him and tell his story since he's here. I can't promise anyone will ever see it, but maybe this will bring attention to the problem you're trying to fix."

"I don't know what to say. I don't feel like I have a story to tell. Were they interested?"

"They got so excited." Aubra offered a watery smile.

This was clearly as close to an apology as Aubra would get. But that was okay. This was far better than a stumbling and half-hearted, muttered string of words that Olivia would have had trouble believing anyway. She had another ally, of sorts, one who was ready to take action to help the best she could. And perhaps something really good would come from this.

She forgot how late it was, forgot her headache, forgot even the nearly insurmountable tasks remaining before her plan could reach implementation. "When can they be here?"

Chapter Twenty-Five

The power had been out for five days. Olivia's frustration grew to the point she wanted to throw her head back and scream into the sky. She knew that would accomplish nothing, but the helplessness was infuriating. The warm temperatures coupled with thick humidity left a slick sheen of sweat on her skin. Her clothing clung to her, her armpits itched, and her hair hung limply, growing sadder and oilier by the day. No amount of brushing helped as that simply spread the oils around.

The first day, never anticipating the outage would last and last as no previous outage had, she had bucked up and taken a quick, lukewarm shower. Now her hot water heater hung on the wall, powerless and dark. And she couldn't stand the thought of a cold shower, however brief. At first, they'd all made an adventure of it, joking and teasing, making light of the situation. Today, no one could muster so much as a smile. Weary of cold water and complete darkness, they'd grown cranky and got on each other's nerves.

The one constant turned out to be Ms. Vanya's meals. Somehow she'd kept them all fed like normal. Breakfast wasn't too difficult, considering they had corn flakes and fruits most days. But she'd even managed toast for them. She must have a gas stove back in her kitchen, Olivia mused, watching her deliver their evening meal.

They heaped plates and "tucked in" as Aubra liked to say. Silence continued, other than clanking silverware and chewing, which Olivia realized kind of got on her nerves.

Chris swallowed a bite and finally spoke. "Guys, we have to get out of here. Let's walk down to the market after dinner. Or go see the building again. I'll bet we can move forward with plans to clean up and paint it. Right?"

Tisha nodded. "You know you're bored and stir crazy when cleaning and painting an old building sounds like a good idea."

"I'm in!" Aubra declared, helping herself to another *chapati*. "Although the film crew will be here this weekend. Shall we make sure they get a little 'before' footage? As much as I like the idea of having it ready to go, I think showing the entire process from beginning to end would be more dynamic."

"Mukesh," Olivia said, "it's your time we're wasting. What do you think? I feel so bad we lost power right after you arrived. Nothing has really moved forward, and you've been here nearly a week. I thought we would have the machine working by now." Frustration at the snail's pace grew by the day.

As always, Mukesh wobbled his head good-naturedly and seemed to pat the air in front of him. "We have the building. We have done good things."

Like Chris, he always found the bright side. And he was right—with a man at her side, Rahul had felt better about selling the property to her, less concerned about the pressure from local men, suspicious of the American woman and her motives. Good things had happened. But excruciatingly slowly.

"Maybe today is the day we track down Meena and talk to her about working for you," Delilah suggested.

She squirmed. "They won't really be working for me," she said for about the eight thousandth time. That's how it felt to her at least. "I'm not going to run the business. The women will. They'll be working for themselves."

Delilah waved away the stipulation. "You know what I mean."

"And maybe we can try to approach some other women while we're out at the market," Melanie suggested.

"Anything would be better than just sitting here, waiting and wondering when the electricity will come back on," she said, feeling better than she had in days. The others looked refreshed at the prospect of a project to tackle as well.

After making the decision, they devoted all their attention to devouring dinner. Ms. Vanya still refused help with clean up, no matter how they cajoled and pointed out they needed her help on their mission—Mukesh argued quite adamantly and gave up last —and shooed them all away to get ready to go visiting.

"She does have a point," Delilah said as they crossed the courtyard. "We want to look our best when we go calling."

"Agreed," Olivia said. "We want to look our most professional if we want to impress."

"And persuade them to take a chance," Melanie said.

Olivia lifted a lock of stringy hair. "I won't look my best when we have no power and can't clean up. My face is completely broken out. But I'll do what I can."

They ducked into their rooms. Olivia lit candles so she could see at least a bit in the bathroom, then peeled off the sticky, sweaty clothes she'd worn several days in a row now and stared at the lifeless water heater on the bathroom wall. No amount of wishing would change a thing, so she sucked in a breath, gritted her teeth, flipped on the cold water, and ducked under the showerhead. Her teeth chattered as she set an all-time record for shortest shower ever. She even marathon-washed her hair before quick-scrubbing her face, armpits, under the breasts, and crotch. She dove back in to power-rinse from top to bottom.

Shivering, but invigorated, she turned off the water and wrapped in a towel. Relieved to have rinsed away the grime, she actually felt much better, now that the painful part was over. She selected the least-worn *shalwar kameez* from the clothesline "closet" and pulled it on. After combing out her hair and donning her toe-loop sandals she loved so much, she was ready to present her plan and recruit new workers.

She went back to the dining room to wait for the others, who drifted in one by one.

Melanie took one look at her and shook her head. "Seriously? You washed your hair? Glutton for punishment."

Once everyone appeared and Ms. Vanya emerged from the kitchen, they set off on foot. The dry dirt scrunched, their feet sending up little puffs of dust with each step. Olivia thought of Pigpen from the old *Peanuts* cartoons, the character who walked around unwashed in a cloud of dirt. At least she'd managed to shower off.

"And we can simply show up unannounced?" she asked Ms. Vanya once they'd set off on their evening promenade.

"No problem, Miss Olivia. No power. Everyone walks and visits."

They discovered the truth of the woman's words soon enough. People wandered up and down the sidewalks, children darted through the streets, clusters of families gathered and chatted. Every house they passed, someone greeted them from the front door, waving and calling out. The market brimmed with meandering browsers, not like the Saturday market where people bustled from one destination to the next, intent on completing purchases.

"Where can we find single women who might want to work?"

"Not easy," Mukesh told her.

"The fathers will not let them out alone," Ms. Vanya said.

"At university," Mukesh said. "That is where I found medical students to help me develop my napkins. They tried out and told me if they worked."

"Is there a university around here?"

"Kerala Uni," Aubra said. "But that's hours away."

"That defeats the purpose. We want local women from the town to run the business."

"Let's stick with the plan and start by asking Meena," Delilah said.

"Would Navya come with us?" she asked Ms. Vanya. "She could encourage Meena to listen to us, maybe get her excited to work with other ladies."

Ms. Vanya shook her head and gestured to her face. "She will not come out."

"I hate that she's so upset by her scars," she said. "They're not her fault. And she's still beautiful."

Ms. Vanya made a dismissive gesture. Clearly only Navya could change her mind.

Tisha bumped her with an elbow. "Hmmm."

"What? What was that for?"

The woman lifted an eyebrow and shrugged.

Was she implying the same thing applied to her? But her case was completely different. Wasn't it?

"Auntie! Auntie! Ms. Montag!"

A small body darted across the street and launched itself at her, wrapping arms around her waist in a fierce hug. She knew who it was, even with the face buried in her abdomen. "Aditi! Hello! How are you?"

"Aditi!"

Oh, no. She knew that voice. Her stomach fell. Aditi's father stomped across the street, his pregnant wife and toddler daughter trailing in his wake.

"I do not wish for you to speak to my daughter," he said.

"I—uhhh . . ." The bizarre demand scrambled her thoughts so completely that she couldn't form a reply.

"You give her bad ideas."

"Bad ideas?" She gathered her wits. "Like what?"

"She can stay in school. She can do magic. She can be a doctor."

"Wait a minute, I never told her she can do magic. That book is only for fun, something to challenge her because she reads so well. She's very advanced."

He seemed startled by her reply. It was his turn to be rendered speechless.

"And she can be a doctor, but only if she stays in school."

"And what are you doing to our town?"

Oh, good. He'd recovered his voice. "I'm not doing anything to your town."

"You stir up trouble. You buy a building and try to steal women from their homes."

"Steal—" She took a deep breath. Getting worked up would not help the situation. "I am only trying to help women. I'm not stealing anyone."

"He"—he jabbed a finger toward Mukesh—"spoke to my wife. Showed her . . . private things."

She pursed her lips tightly, struggling not to guffaw and further inflame the situation. But seriously, private things? He made poor Mukesh sound like an exhibitionist. The idea caught her off guard and cracked her up. What would happen when she started showing "private things" in hopes the women of the town would purchase and use them? Oh, boy.

"He only wants to help women—"

Ms. Vanya stepped in, rattling off rapid-fire sentences she couldn't understand.

Aditi's father backed off, but only a little. "We do not want your help!"

"I respect your decision. And if you refuse to allow Aditi to come back to school, refuse to safeguard her health with sanitary products from our machine, that's your decision. But you don't get to decide for the other girls and women in town."

She hugged Aditi again before her father pulled her away. She kept her poise until they'd moved out of sight, then, legs quivering, she let out a huge breath. The incident left her shaken, feeling weak and out of her league.

"You okay?" Tisha asked.

"What a jerk!" Chris said.

"I'm fine. I'm just no good at confrontation."

"That was pretty mild, hon," Delilah said. "Don't let it get to you."

"I know, but that's easier said than done. Should we still go see Meena? Am I an idiot for thinking this will work?"

"Hell, no!" Chris said. "Don't let that guy discourage you. He's one crank. You have all of us on your side."

She smiled and took another breath. He so rarely cursed. He must really mean it.

Ms. Vanya led them to a house similar to her own in size and appearance. They let her greet Meena's mom, who appeared flustered by the flock of foreigners congregating on her stoop. But she allowed them inside. The interior of the home also resembled the one Ms. Vanya lived in—a simple sitting room, incense curling smoke toward the ceiling, a kitchen off to one side, a toilet room, and a hall leading, presumably, to a bedroom or two. The furnishings were a bit more worn, and Olivia had the impression Ms. Vanya's brother-in-law had a little more money than Meena's family. Which made sense, considering he'd had property for sale.

Meena's father sat on the couch. His eyes widened as they paraded in. Since the sitting room didn't offer enough seats for all of them, they stood—and even then barely fit. Meena also sat on the couch, pressed into the corner at the end, feet tucked up under her, stitching clothing. Unlike her father, whose face twisted in confusion, recognition dawned in Meena's eyes at the sight of her former fellow teachers. But her brow wrinkled when her gaze landed on Olivia.

When everyone stood awkwardly, no one speaking, Olivia decided this was her rodeo and started the conversation. "Hello. We would like to speak with Meena."

Her father shrugged and gestured to her. Meena set aside her sewing and stood. "Hello."

The other teachers greeted her with hugs and asked how she was. Quiet and shy, Meena demurred.

"I'm Olivia." She held out her hand. Meena shook it, still appearing completely confused.

Ms. Vanya spoke to Mukesh in their native language. He tipped his head, agreeing with whatever she said to him. "We will explain," she told them, much to Olivia's relief.

Mukesh presented their case for them. Olivia couldn't help but smile, watching his fervent, animated delivery. She almost believed she could understand him simply from his emphatic gestures, though she couldn't translate a single word. How could anyone not be swayed by his total conviction to this cause?

She turned to see Meena's father's reaction and was dismayed to discover a scowl hardening his face.

Meena's mother entered the room, bearing a tray of tea. Only six cups rested on the tray, probably every teacup she owned. Ms. Vanya and Mukesh accepted drinks and thanked their hosts. Meena's father gestured to the remaining cups. Chris insisted the women take the remaining four.

Again, Olivia led the way, since they were all here on her behalf and she didn't want to insult anyone. Delilah didn't mind joining Chris in not partaking. "I like sweet tea, but not with all that heavy spice in it."

Meena's father slurped loudly in the silence as they all awaited his response. He took his time before he answered. Even though she couldn't understand the words he spoke, Olivia could tell he was denying permission for Meena to come work. Why? Why would he do such a thing? What negative could he possibly see in his daughter earning money and being able to support herself? He was denying her a future. She stepped forward, ready to explain more clearly why this was so important and such a good thing for Meena. Chris held an arm out, discouraging her from proceeding.

Mukesh nodded toward the man and thanked him for the tea and his time. Ms. Vanya's head hung, but she also acknowledged the decision, though it wasn't to their liking.

Olivia had no choice but to allow them to lead her out of the house. She glanced over her shoulder as she walked out the door. Meena stared at the ground, hope once again shattered.

As disappointed as Olivia felt for herself—would she ever convince anyone to work?—she felt worse for having dangled possibility in front of Meena, only to have it snatched away.

Chapter Twenty-Six

The film students arrived the day after the disappointing meeting with Meena. Two men and a woman joined them. Bleary-eyed and semi-catatonic, the British newcomers showed Olivia what she must have looked like her first week. And the lack of power didn't exactly sit well with the exhausted group. Olivia missed their names, distracted by the mesmerizing blue eyes of one of the two guys. Tall and lanky, with a shock of dark and unruly hair and day-old stubble, he set her pulse racing. Startled and embarrassed, she mumbled a greeting and looked away.

"No shower? Oi!" the other guy muttered as he trudged behind Chris on the way to his room.

Aubra's friend, Emma, managed a weak smile during introductions but also seemed dismayed by the current state of affairs. "I won't lie. I was rather looking forward to washing off the trip in a hot shower."

"I'm so sorry!" Aubra said.

"What were the guys' names again?" Olivia asked Emma as they crossed the courtyard. "I didn't catch them."

"The taller one is Noah, and the other one is Jack," Emma told her.

She was glad Emma didn't refer to Noah as the one with the dreamy eyes. That was how she thought of him, although he was indeed taller than Jack.

The men's dorm had filled with the additions, and Aubra appeared delighted to share her room with her old college friend. Mrs. Gupta had no problem allowing them to use the guest house, particularly when they offered to pay for room and board. But the spotlight they would shine on her little school with their documentary didn't hurt either.

Once they settled Emma's luggage into Aubra's room, they congregated back in the dining room, chatting about the town and assuring Emma they'd take her to the market later that evening.

"Chin up," Aubra told her. "The power has to come back sometime. And it's been out for days, so surely any time now."

Chris brought Noah and Jack down to join them. "Hey, guys! Noah wants to go ahead and start recording."

"What, just like that? Right now?" Delilah asked.

Noah held a camera in each hand and passed one to Emma. "We're here to make a documentary, and it's not like we can do anything else right now. Chris here says dinner won't be for an hour. Let's get a look at the location. Get shots of the machine in the crates before it's installed. Where's the man? The guy who made the machine?"

"I'll get him!" Chris volunteered and ran back upstairs.

"Which one of you bought the machine and started this project?" Noah asked.

Olivia sat up straight, butterflies quivering in her stomach. "I did."

His gaze pierced her own, seeming to delve into her very core. "Awesome. We need to interview you. You'll be the star of this thing, along with the man."

"Mukesh," she told him. "His name is Mukesh."

"And here I am," he said, following Chris into the dining room and taking them in. "We have become quite a big group."

Chris surveyed them all. "Yeah, too many to all squeeze into the car."

"It's okay," Olivia said. "I've been there enough that I remember the way. I can walk."

"I'd love to come along and see the process," Tisha said. "I won't get in the way."

"Sure!" Seeing her friends get excited about the project added a new element. And she could use all the help she could get. "And anyone else who wants to come."

"We don't have anything else to do," Melanie said. "I wouldn't mind stretching my legs."

"I wouldn't miss seeing a documentary get started for anything," Delilah said.

"Okay, so should I drive the film people or . . ." Chris looked to her for guidance.

"If they want a ride." She glanced at Noah, trying not to notice how freaking hot he was.

"If . . . I'm sorry, what was your name?" Noah asked.

"Olivia."

He grinned at her. "Really? My mom once told me she almost named me Oliver. Wouldn't that have been something?"

The grin and the warmth in his eyes sent her insides squirming. What was she supposed to do with this? Okay, so she wasn't married and wasn't doing anything wrong, but she couldn't seem to convince herself of that. Her thumb drifted to her empty ring finger again. According to her mom, Scott had moved on and was seeing someone else, so why did she feel like she flirted with cheating? Everyone stared at her while she gaped at Noah like a fool. She forced a laugh. "Yes. That's so funny." Funny? It wasn't funny. What was wrong with her?

"Anyway, that will be easy to remember. If Olivia is walking, we should walk with her. We can interview her while we walk. Jack, get some shots of the town. We can set the background and then open with Olivia telling her story and what prompted her to do this."

"Got it," Jack said through a huge yawn.

Mukesh stuck his head into the kitchen, alerted Ms. Vanya of their intended destination, and assured her they'd be back for dinner. Then the entire group headed off on foot. Noah directed Emma and Jack where to point their cameras, describing his vision for the beginning, even down to the type of background music he planned to accompany the opening shots.

"We need to set the mood as well as the lay of the land before we dive into the project itself," he said. "Establish the significance right away. Then people will see why this will make such a huge difference."

Olivia's cheeks warmed at the sound of the praise. "I genuinely hope you're right, that this eventually makes a difference in the women's lives."

Noah pointed his camera lens at her. "Meet Olivia, the woman who started this entire project. The one whose soul stirred at the plight of the women and girls of this community. So much so that she stood up and said, 'Enough is enough,' and decided to do something about it."

Too much. Way too much. His words caused her face to warm for an entirely different reason. "I wouldn't really describe myself that way—"

"And how would you describe yourself?"

She thought for a moment. "I'm just a regular person. Nothing special. But trying to do something good."

"Nothing special?" Noah repeated. "I doubt anyone else sees you that way, Olivia."

She started to offer to make a list of names for him, beginning with her ex-husband, but Chris jostled through the conglomeration to get to her side. "I've been telling her that."

"And you are?" Noah asked, clearly for the benefit of the documentary, since he already knew him.

"Another of the teachers. But I recognized how amazing Olivia is the day I met her. And she's been proving it to me ever since. None of us ever considered doing something like this. We teachers came to make a difference, to help the children and perhaps open the door to a better future. But she's taking it a step further, and I believe the impact will be even greater thanks to her."

Completely taken aback, Olivia couldn't say another word. This was too much. Suddenly, the documentary seemed like a terrible idea. She expected Mukesh to do most of the talking. He was the main story here. She tried to correct the mistake. "Mukesh is the one you want to focus on. He invented the machine, spent years of his life developing it, and sacrificed a lot to do it. You should ask him his story."

Noah swung his camera to Mukesh and introduced him while they walked. Good. Mukesh was funnier and much better at this sort of thing. She would gladly remain in the background, a side note, but nothing more.

At the location, all the cameras took in the little building and the many crates of unopened equipment sitting outside it. She unlocked the door and let them in. "We're working on freshening it up," she assured them, "and we will eventually paint it. I know it's small, but it'll look nice when we're done. We've just been working around our teaching schedules, which limits the time we can do it."

"You could pay someone," Noah suggested. "Labor is cheap here. But the money would be a lot to someone local, wouldn't it?"

"Actually, that's a good idea. Why didn't I think of that?" She beamed at Noah.

He returned her smile with his own. "I took some international business classes. I know a thing or two."

"I was going to help paint," Chris reminded her. "We all were." He seemed a little off, and she couldn't figure out why.

"Noah's right, though. Hiring someone local to do it means it will be finished much faster. I think that's the way to go."

Chris's brow furrowed.

"Don't sweat it, mate," Jack said. "Painting's not as fun as it's cracked up to be. Let someone else do it."

"But that will cost her even more money. We were trying to keep costs low."

"If it turns out to be too much, we won't hire someone," she assured Chris. "But I can at least check into it."

"You're not someone wealthy looking for a cause, then?" Noah asked.

"She's not. She's working extra jobs and drawing from her own limited funds," Chris said.

Noah brought the camera back to her. "Still believe you're nothing special?"

The power outage resolved the next day. Olivia wasn't sure which she was more excited about: finally being able to take a hot shower again or that Mukesh could install the pad machine. He'd found several local men willing to help with the heavy lifting. Mukesh would assemble the pieces himself. Not thinking, she'd asked if he was sure he didn't need an electrician or something to hook it up.

"Madam, I made machine. I know how to put the pieces together."

"Oh, my gosh! I'm so dumb!" She shook her head and laughed with the others at her goof.

"It's difficult for us to comprehend that," Aubra said. "Back home I struggle to operate the microwave sometimes. I definitely couldn't design and build a whole machine."

"And I can't even boil water," Delilah drawled.

Everyone laughed again.

"We think you're amazing, Mukesh," Melanie said, in case their jokes got lost in translation. "Really. To just think up an idea to fix a problem and then gather parts and put it together."

"It's pretty awesome," Chris agreed. "But I'm super disappointed I won't be there to help. I planned to set it up with you."

Olivia felt exactly the same way. "Me too. But classes must go on. Especially after losing power for a week. I'm so far behind, my anxiety is through the roof."

"And Diwali is creeping closer," Melanie reminded them. "We definitely want to make those clay *diyas*. What if we lose power on Diwali? None of our string lights would work."

"That would be awful. Okay, to the market for clay and battery-operated tea lights as soon as we can."

Noah, Jack, and Emma, with no teaching responsibilities, had joined them in the courtyard, ready to accompany Mukesh and capture the entire process.

"Don't worry," Noah said. "We'll get it. You'll be able to watch over and over again. And so will the rest of the world if our documentary wins attention on the awards circuit and gets picked up for distribution."

"It's not the same," Chris muttered under his breath.

"No, it's not," she agreed quietly.

He glanced up, startled maybe that someone had heard him. Or perhaps that she agreed.

A taxi honked from the street, Mukesh and the film crew piled in, and the teachers waved them away.

"Don't forget to ask Mukesh why he built the machine to begin with," she called after them.

The world? Noah's last line sunk into her brain, where she slowly digested it. "Aubra, you said this documentary is a final project for film school."

"Yes."

"Then why is he talking about awards circuits and distribution?"

"Noah's good. Really good. He submitted last year but his subject matter wasn't deemed far-reaching or powerful enough. At least that's what he told me. When I told him about your machine, he flipped out. Said it's just what he's been waiting for. He planned to turn down my idea of focusing on the school and trying to break the poverty cycle. Too similar to his homeless crisis theme last year. That's why I blew up at you over dinner. I took it personally. First Chris liked you better, now Noah."

Olivia spluttered as her misfiring brain attempted to form a cohesive reply. "I don't . . . they don't . . ."

Aubra held up a hand. "I know."

"Besides, I'm hoping to break the poverty cycle too."

"But women's issues, the millions of women around the world who could benefit from this machine, that's sure to garner far more attention."

"See? It isn't me Noah likes. It's the machine Mukesh designed and how it will help Noah."

Aubra seemed to miss the point she was making and nodded emphatically. "And shining a light on the idea will only help Mukesh in return. Imagine if this documentary does get picked up for distribution. People all over the world will see what you did and how many lives you improved. It could very well inspire others to do the same."

Olivia fell silent. She didn't want attention, didn't want to be seen by people all over the world. She had reached out to Mukesh to help the girls in her classes and the women of this town, not to "garner attention." But, if Aubra was correct, and Noah's documentary project truly brought worldwide attention to the plight of these rural women, and millions more like them, that wouldn't be a bad thing.

They'd arrived at the school building and hurried inside so they wouldn't be late for the first class session of the day. Her mind wandered incessantly all day, imagining Aditi and Surithra and all the other girls back in their empty chairs—and wondering how much longer the remaining girls had before they, too, were yanked from school.

Finally, the day ended. She hurried to drop her teaching materials in her room, wondering if Chris might agree to drive her or if she would have to walk. She couldn't wait to see if Mukesh managed to set everything up.

She headed to the courtyard, hoping Chris would hear her if she called up the stairs to him, since she couldn't go inside the men's dorm. But she didn't have to go inside at all. He waited for her in the courtyard and jangled keys when he saw her. "We'll get there faster if we drive."

Of course he was there. Somehow, he always managed to anticipate her intentions and know exactly the best way to help. Relief and gratitude suffused her, a warm flush that lifted her spirits and lifted her lips in a wide smile. "Yes, please. I was hoping you would."

His eyes glowed with delight. "Happy to help."

The other teachers spilled from the dorm, arms emptied of classroom materials.

"We want to go!" Melanie called.

"Don't you dare go without us," Delilah said.

"Come on, girl," Tisha said. "We're invested in this now. Maybe we can help."

"And I want to see Noah," Aubra said.

Olivia shook her head at how radically Aubra's mercurial emotions swung from one end of the spectrum to another. The young woman had been friendlier while anticipating Noah's arrival. Now that he was here, she seemed to have completely forgotten her initial jealousy over Chris. And forgotten Chris. Which Olivia found she didn't mind at all.

They piled in and pulled up to the cinderblock wall in no time. Olivia led the way to the gap-in-the-wall entrance but stopped in her tracks, so suddenly the others bumped into her.

"What's wrong?" Chris asked.

She recovered her wits but remained confused as she continued through to the building. "Nothing is wrong. It's just . . . the building is painted. I wasn't expecting that."

In fact, as they approached she saw several men still running brushes up and down the final exterior wall. They stared at her but didn't say a thing as she went inside.

Mukesh squatted in front of a metal machine, his head and shoulders twisted underneath.

"Hey, hey!" Noah greeted them. "Just in time. We're about to flip the switch and fire it up."

We're? The only equipment he and his crew appeared to care about were their cameras. She would bet money he hadn't lifted a finger all day. She looked around, noting the interior had been painted flat white and the floors were freshly swept.

"The building . . ."

His mouth quirked into a lopsided grin. He appeared quite pleased with himself. "Yeah?"

"It's cleaned and painted."

He finally dragged his attention away from the view screen of his camera. And winked at her. "You're welcome, love."

Love? Who did this guy—

Aubra stepped in front of her. "But how, Noah?"

"After they uncrated these things and put them where the big guy told them to, I offered to pay them to paint. I wanted blue—"

"Pink or red would have been more appropriate," Tisha said.

"—but the big guy insisted you told him you wanted yellow."

"Yes. Yellow. A bright, happy color. You paid them?"

"From my budget. It's cool. You don't owe me anything. Helps speed things along, but also gives the appearance of time passing. We have funds but not unlimited, so we can't dally. Our time here isn't open-ended."

"Good," Chris muttered.

She agreed but kept her mouth shut. A piece of her—a big piece—didn't appreciate Noah hijacking her plans. And frankly, he was starting to irritate her. But she set aside her bruised feelings and frustrations in light of the bigger picture—the building looked great, the machine was installed, and they were nearly ready to begin.

Mukesh extricated himself, stood and brushed off. He lifted a hand and nodded to her. "Ready?"

"Ready."

He flipped a switch. The machine whirred and hummed. It worked. Now she needed women to work it.

Chapter Twenty-Seven

The sun shone brightly Saturday morning. The rays streamed in through the window of Olivia's little building and brightened the space, which she decided was absolutely perfect. Why had she ever considered it small and dank? Now that it was clean and painted, she found it downright cozy, not cramped, even with the four machines installed and the raw materials stacked nearly to the ceiling, waiting for someone to turn them into salable product. One corner sat empty, and that was where eventually her team would store packages of pads. Mukesh told her each independent group of women designed their own packaging and even chose the name for their product line. She didn't know any words in the local language, so she couldn't begin to imagine what the ladies who eventually worked the equipment would select.

A timid knock at the door announced Navya's arrival. She balanced Jaanvi on her hip and kept her eyes cast downward, even as Ms. Vanya coaxed her inside. The way the young woman draped her veil over the lower portion of her face, only her eyes visible, reminded Olivia of Scheherazade and the Arabian Nights. But the downward cast of the eyes, defeated slump of her shoulders, and withdrawn attitude surrounding her was not alluring and mysterious but dejected and forlorn. Navya clearly didn't want to be there. This wasn't the exciting, bubbly beginning she had imagined.

Disappointed her one recruit appeared hesitant at best, Olivia forced a broad smile on her face, deeply aware of the film crew on hand to record this dismal beginning. "Hello! Come in!"

Mukesh also welcomed them enthusiastically and set about demonstrating how to operate the machinery. He opened a box of raw cellulose material they would break down and gestured for Navya to join him.

Noah swooped in for a close up. "Now what is this?"

Mukesh held up a handful of the material. "Many years I could not figure out what was inside. I thought, it is cotton. But the napkin I make from cotton leaked. No good. I called American companies to ask, 'What is the material? What do you put in?' My phone bill hundreds of dollars! They asked me what machine I used. Their machine cost millions of dollars. They did not understand, I am not competition. I am one man in India. Finally, they sent a sample. Finally, I knew what to put in my napkin."

He led them to the first machine in his line. "I did not have millions of dollars to buy industrial machine. So I designed a simple set of four machines to accomplish same tasks as the big machine. First, the grinder."

He dropped the material into the mechanism and switched it on. The blades tore up the packed raw material, producing a light fluffy result. He cut a piece of thin fabric from a roll and laid it across a rectangular metal mold on the next machine.

"Next, we put the material into the press. First, we put the covering. You see?" This he directed at Navya, who stared, transfixed, watching his every move. "The cover material will pull the fluid away and keep the skin dry. Special material." Once he'd adjusted the covering to his liking, he transferred the fluffy material into the mold and pulled a lever, lowering a heavy press.

He sealed the ends, showed her how to apply the adhesive

backing, then moved to the next machine. "This UV, to make sanitary. Put inside and turn on like this."

"Fascinating," Noah said. "You irradiate them with ultraviolet light to ensure the product is completely sterile."

"Yes. Like women who use cloth could lay out in the sun to make more sanitary. But they will not." While they waited for the machine to complete its cycle, Mukesh told them, "I wore napkin when I could not get women to volunteer. I made a bladder from a ball, added tube, and filled with goat blood from the butcher. That pad did not work at all. My genitals were wet all day. I do not know how women survive this every month. Cold, wet genitals for a week. They should all be sick all the time. I knew I had to perfect this, even though my friends disowned me and thought me possessed by demons."

The film crew laughed at his telling. She marveled at his devotion and dedication. And then nearly burst out laughing at the thought of Scott wearing a homemade pad and fashioning a bladder of goat blood. Mukesh's empathy and concern astounded her. Everything he did for this project was for other people, for women. He did not benefit from his years of work. In fact, he suffered ridicule and ostracism for years. Even now, he sold the machines virtually at cost. When had Scott done something for her without expecting something in return? *After everything I've done for you?* How many times had she heard that as he demanded his way about one thing or another? Come to think of it, what exactly did he even mean? What *had* he done for her? Everything he did was designed to make him look good or advance his career. *Charity is for chumps.*

What an asshole. She'd felt compelled to rush to Scott's defense when Chris first uttered those words and explain that it was her fault, that she'd brought it on them and deserved Scott's contempt. But a tiny tremor shimmered through her as her image of Scott cracked. Chris was right. Scott was a jerk. Why couldn't she see that before? If Scott hadn't left her, she'd still be with him.

Once Mukesh finished showing Navya the final steps and how

to package them, he went back to the grinder and encouraged her to try for herself.

Olivia held out her hands to Jaanvi to free up Navya's hands. The toddler pulled gooey fingers from her mouth and leaned toward her with her good arm. The arm hanging at an odd angle tore at her heart, and she fought tears. The doctor could not come soon enough as far as she was concerned. She snuggled the little girl close, overwhelmed by so many emotions when Jaanvi laid her head on her shoulder. For so long, she had not been able to look at a baby without choking up, without a burst of jealousy and resentment pulsing through her, no matter how much the caustic emotions shocked her. She knew other mothers were not to blame, knew that she had no rational basis for these horrible feelings she tried so hard to push aside and ignore.

In this moment, with soft baby hair snuggled against her neck and sweet baby smell permeating the air, the weight of the little one warming her arms tripped a scale. She recognized a deep and lingering sadness that her own little girl wasn't here in her arms to play with Jaanvi and perhaps be passed around to the other mothers. But she also felt a twinge of happiness, a twinkle of joy peeking out from the darker, harsh emotions that had consumed her for nearly a year. She rested her cheek against Jaanvi's soft little head and simply enjoyed the moment, relieved to find she could.

Navya thrust her hand into the box of cellulose material and repeated Mukesh's actions, remembering every step with no reminders or additional instructions. When she finished, Mukesh examined her work. Jack and Noah moved in close to examine as well.

"Yes! Perfect, first try!" He turned to her. "Very good. Good quality."

She bounced Jaanvi and beamed at Navya. "You're amazing! I just need a few more exactly like you, and you'll be ready to launch your line."

Navya pressed her fists together and stared at the ground. Behind her veil, the woman appeared to flush—with embarrassment or discomfort or pleasure, Olivia couldn't tell. But she felt certain the young woman was unaccustomed to praise of any type.

Mukesh bobbed his head and gestured toward the machines. "Okay. Go. Make more."

Within an hour, Navya had a decent-sized stack of pads. Her production time decreased with each repetition as she became more familiar with the steps. Though she hid behind a veil, sheltered in her uncle's home, Navya was a smart and talented young woman. And now the young woman would be able to use that to build a business and contribute to the local economy rather than sitting at home doing nothing.

Olivia's chest seemed ready to burst with happiness at the thought. She bounced Jaanvi and made faces until a wide smile broke across the little girl's face and she giggled. That big baby-belly giggle sparked a giggle of her own, lighting the kindling of general happiness into a flame of excitement she didn't know what to do with. She tickled Jaanvi, each laugh prompting one in return. Soon, her restless feet danced around the room, both of them laughing, and Olivia couldn't remember a time she'd felt so good.

She'd forgotten what happiness felt like, it had been absent from her life for so long. Even before the terrible tragedy ripped her life apart and tore the stuffing out of it, she had simply been existing. She hadn't been miserable, hadn't really even been unhappy, but her life had lacked joy, something to fill her with happiness. On some level, she must have expected her baby girl to fill that empty space. And instead, the loss had created a bigger pit, darker and emptier than anything she'd ever known.

As she danced around the small space laughing with baby Jaanvi, their happiness seemed to spread. Ms. Vanya clapped along to her aimless steps and began to sing in a language that she couldn't translate yet understood on a primal level. That dark empty place didn't have to be where she stayed forever. She had the capacity to feel good again, even if she continued to mourn the loss of her daughter. The two could exist within her together. What would her daughter look like if she'd survived? She'd be nearing her first birthday—younger than Jaanvi, but she imagined balancing her daughter on her hip, laughter erupting from a gummy mouth. And somehow, through the pain, the thought made her smile and tear up. And next thing she knew, she laughed and cried, the emotional storm exacerbated by the realization that, had she not lost her baby, she never would have come to India and met these people, nor would she be dancing around with Jaanvi while Mukesh taught Navya a skill to build a new life on—while a film crew captured the entire thing for a documentary. She laughed and cried harder.

Ms. Vanya stopped clapping. Navya left the UV machine and moved to her side. "What is wrong?"

They didn't know. They couldn't. She must look like a crazy woman standing there laughing and crying all at once.

"I'm okay," she reassured them, wishing the statement true. "I had a baby girl. But she . . . is no more." She liked the phrase that Ms. Vanya had employed to describe her late husband. Her baby was. But now she was no more. Somehow it didn't hurt as badly as saying her baby died.

Ms. Vanya and Navya each placed a hand on her and lowered their heads. They didn't say anything, and they didn't need to. What could they say in the face of such horrific grief? There were no words, and their silent sympathy expressed an inherent under-standing.

"What is her name?" Navya asked.

She didn't know if the verb tense was a mistake but didn't care. She liked that better too. What *is* her name? Not what *was* her name.

You are still a mother.

And her baby girl was still her baby girl. She hadn't been able to bring herself to share the name with anyone, not even her own mother. She hadn't been able to name her on the birth certificate either or the death certificate that immediately followed.

The look in Navya's eyes above the veil that hid her face, told her the young woman understood. They had both experienced horrific, life-shattering pain. They would both have to work hard to overcome it.

"Lucy. Her name is Lucy." The name had come to her suddenly one night just before she fell asleep and from that moment, she'd thought of the baby by her name.

"Beautiful," Navya said.

"It's Greek for light. I looked up the meaning. She would have been the light of my life." She glanced around the room, Mukesh and Ms. Vanya watching with sympathy in their eyes, cameras with blinking red lights recording her most intimate and raw emotions on display for the entire world. She scrubbed at her cheeks, erasing the tear lines. "Enough of that. We're here to launch a business. What do we do next?"

Mukesh looked at the stack of pads Navya had made. "Take to women. Convince them they want to buy, and they want to make."

Olivia nodded. "Recruit and sell. Got it."

Chapter Twenty-Eight

The film crew followed Olivia and her entourage as they moved through town. Navya carried a basket with the pads wrapped inside. Olivia carried Jaanvi, delighted the little girl continued to allow it.

Ms. Vanya took the lead. Everyone seemed to know and like Ms. Vanya, and Olivia completely understood why. She felt a strong connection to the older woman, deepened by their working together on getting this new business off the ground. Her gratitude for the support only grew as they made their way through town. The film crew and the presence of foreigners in general raised some concern and made a few women downright skittish. But mostly the women were willing to hear them out, and she knew that was entirely due to Ms. Vanya's presence. Doors opened to them that would have remained firmly shut thanks to the woman's intervention and everyone's trust in her.

As they passed Meena's house, Olivia shook her head and clicked her tongue, disappointment, frustration, and anger at the situation swirling into an ugly emotional cocktail that rolled around in her stomach and made her queasy. She wanted to march up to the door, take Meena by the hand, and lead her away. But she couldn't. That was Meena's home and at the end of the day, she had to be able to return to it and live in peace. She could offer Meena a job, income, financial security. But in this culture, no woman could cut all ties to her family. Meena would need their approval, especially the male members, before she could agree. Olivia hated that but understood it.

And suddenly she also understood why her mother had not immediately acted to throw out her abusive father. The hard anger slowly calcifying inside her softened a bit, as she recognized the issue was not as black and white as she thought. Women who came to depend on men for support, whether it be emotional or financial, needed that element in their lives. Her mother must have grappled with the ugly truth that she'd married an abusive man and struggled with what to do about that. Olivia wondered what their lives would have been like if Mom had chosen a generous and loving man who doted on his wife and daughter instead of one who beat on them. But they would never know. That wasn't what happened. She also wished her mother had found the strength sooner to get rid of him. But she hadn't. Though her mother's situation hadn't been exactly the same as the women she was trying to help, Olivia could see that, without family to help her, her mother had no one else. She'd had to maintain a peace of sorts until prepared to throw her father out and make a life without him.

And if she hadn't been raised in that toxic environment, would she have married Scott? Would she have been blind to the insidious control he exerted over her, as Tisha had pointed out? She didn't want to believe she'd married an abuser, as determined as she'd been to find a loving man and enjoy a happy marriage. Over and over, she'd told herself she would not repeat her mother's mistakes. Scott didn't hurt her physically, but he'd squashed everything that was her. And she'd let him.

Ms. Vanya called out to a cluster of women on the street, possibly en route to the market. "Hello, sisters! We have something to show you."

Curiosity drew them in, but at the sight of pads they drew

back. Every one of them averted her eyes while Olivia explained Navya had made these by hand. She used important-sounding business phrases like "locally produced" and "completely sanitary" and "support your hometown's economy" and yet didn't seem to impress any of them as she expected. In fact, they stared at the ground or the sky, much as Mukesh had predicted. They also stole furtive glances at the cameras, clearly discomfited by their presence. And perhaps by the men who operated them.

She gestured to Navya to pick up the conversation and make a sales pitch, but the young woman looked as if she wished a hole would open up in the ground and swallow her. At a loss, Olivia reached into the basket and held out pads to each of them. If she couldn't sell them, perhaps at least she could convince the women to examine them. But no, the horrified women leaned away and were clearly done with the conversation.

"We're also looking for more women to work the machine, making and selling pads. It pays well," she ended lamely as the women sidled away.

This wouldn't do. What good was a pad machine that sat idle with no one to work it and no one to buy the pads? Mukesh successfully set up machines in other small towns, resulting in thriving businesses, employment opportunities, and improved female health. His model worked. But not for her. What was she doing wrong? Was every pursuit she undertook doomed to failure? Mukesh probably regretted working with her. After all, he'd assured her clearly and repeatedly that he stayed at each site until an entire cadre of women had been successfully trained, not only in production operations but also care and maintenance of the machinery.

"Madam," he'd told her, "no more difficult than a sewing machine. All parts on the outside. Easy to repair."

Sure. Easy. If you could find women interested in learning. But with her at the helm, they might as well all be on the Titanic, blissfully unaware she steered them toward disaster. Her heartbeat kicked up a notch. What would she do if no one ever came to work? Navya simply could not operate the entire process alone. Ms. Vanya depended on her to make this happen for her daughter. Every eye looked to her for their next direction. She couldn't let all these people down, but she didn't know what to do. She blew out a deep breath. Ms. Vanya patted her.

She sighed. "We're getting nowhere. Let's go back and rethink our strategy."

Noah lowered his camera. "Bummer."

The single word got under her skin more than any lengthy criticism he could have mustered. Flippant and self-centered, he somehow managed to make this all about him and his documentary. He didn't care about her investment, how much she stood to lose, or the women and girls whose lives she hoped to improve. He was bummed he didn't get any good footage. She could hear it in his tone. She squeezed her eyes shut and bit back the harsh words she longed to hurl at him.

The guy was starting to remind her of Scott, self-centered and completely assured of his amazingness. She'd spent so much time wondering what Scott had seen in her and questioning if she was good enough for him or could measure up to him and his accomplishments. Now as she saw him reflected in Noah, she wondered instead what she had ever seen in him.

She turned on her heel and headed back to the school and housing compound, utterly discouraged.

But one young woman from the last group they'd spoken with dashed back and snatched a pad from the basket. Startled, Olivia blinked as the woman hurried away with it, tucking it out of sight.

Well, okay. Not what she intended or expected, but she couldn't suppress the smile that spread over her face.

She stayed up into the early morning hours catching up on tutoring and brainstorming. Somewhere around midnight she decided the first change she would make when approaching the women in town was to bar Noah and Jack from accompanying them. Emma could record, and as surreptitiously as possible. The more she thought about it, the more she realized no men could accompany them, not even Chris and Mukesh, even though they weren't offensive in any way. Local women simply could not discuss such intimate and personal matters in mixed company.

Around one in the morning, as she stretched and rubbed her eyes, finally finished with the last essay she needed to proof, she decided to host a group presentation. Door to door, approaching the women individually seemed to catch them off guard. The large group of them could certainly be misinterpreted as ganging up on and pressuring local women. If she brought everyone together, so that the local women could find solidarity in numbers and familiarity, then have Ms. Vanya and Navya present the innovative product and the reason it would improve their lives, then perhaps no one would feel threatened. After all, the closest thing they'd had to success resulted from the cluster of three women, when one felt emboldened enough to take a pad.

And that led her to the third idea: free samples. She had a plan, finally—a presentation, followed by a side-by-side demonstration comparing their far superior product to local options, then distribution of free samples to every woman in town (or at least whoever would come listen) to try for herself. Yes, she would rather the women pay for the pads than hand them out free, but she needed to convince women to take a chance. Besides, she remembered as a child the thrill of receiving a free sample when she accompanied her mother to the store. A free thing of her very own had always made the day exciting.

In for a penny, in for a pound, as Delilah would say. Chris was right. Delilah spouted cliches at least as often as literary quotes.

The next day, she caught Mrs. Gupta between classes and explained about the meeting she hoped to host. The school headmistress already had Mukesh and a British film crew staying on site for the project. She seemed to deliberate a bit.

"It will be educational," she reminded the woman. Unclear who exactly Mrs. Gupta was accountable to, she hoped none of her activities could be deemed a dubious use of the facility.

"Yes. Okay. Meena can help. She has taught here. She can speak to the children. Give them personal hygiene lectures."

She hadn't considered that. But a health presentation to the female students would be beneficial as well. Perhaps if they planted the idea early, it would not feel so strange to the girls when they started their cycles. They could present the pads and introduce them to the idea and explain why they were a better option. Maybe someday, the general attitude would shift. She beamed at Mrs. Gupta. "That's a great idea! Thank you!"

She worked every minute she could spare with Navya in the little building. She learned to make pads and soon could produce them almost as efficiently as Navya. Quality control would not be an issue—Navya, a perfectionist, crafted perfect pads every time, and even scrutinized Olivia's to ensure they met the required standard. Mukesh laughed and clapped the first time she carefully turned over a pad Olivia produced, eyeing it for defects. She laughed along. The young woman taking such a strong stake and caring so much was the best possible outcome she could hope for. Mukesh continued to praise Navya, about her work ethic and her excellent craftsmanship, and even with a veil hiding half of her face, Olivia could tell she smiled, glowing from the praise.

One afternoon after classes, a particularly warm and humid day, she hurried into the building and discovered Navya had removed her veil, presumably to breathe more easily, and worked bare faced.

At the sound of her footsteps, Navya spun and gasped, then fumbled to replace her covering with trembling hands.

She stopped but held out her hand to the younger woman. "No, please. Please don't cover up. Not for me."

"But I am ugly." Navya slumped forward, her shoulders shaking.

She crossed the room and hugged the woman. "You are not ugly! You are talented and brilliant and you have the sweetest daughter in the world. You are beautiful. Anyone who can't see that is blind. And anyone who tells you you're ugly is a jerk and completely wrong."

The woman's hand drifted to her scarred cheek. "People stare. They whisper."

"Let them stare. Who cares?" Fury fired her once again. Her hands balled into fists. "Your husband, the person who hurt you, *he* is ugly. He is ugly inside and out, and I wish I could punch him in the face for what he did to you."

Navya cracked a smile. "You would hit him?"

"I would hit him!" She held up her fists and scowled.

Navya giggled, but tears coursed down her cheeks. Olivia threw her arms around the woman again. It was her turn to laugh and cry. Nothing she could say would take the pain away. But she could hold Navya and let her know she cared.

Navya swiped the tears off her cheeks. "I am sorry."

"Don't be sorry." She looked her directly in the eye. "From now on, don't wear the veil in here. I like to see your face and your smile. Don't cover up, okay?"

Navya nodded.

Chris walked in. Navya jumped but Olivia squeezed her arm. "It's okay. You don't need the veil."

She stared intently at Chris, who looked momentarily confused, but then the pieces seemed to click together. "Hey, Navya. How's it going?" He lifted his chin at her in greeting and remained completely chill like, *no big deal.* Exactly as she'd hoped. His emotional intelligence rated through the roof. Somehow, he always knew exactly what to do and say. "Olivia, I came by to make sure you're about ready for the big presentation."

"Are you gonna help us make pads, Chris?" She grinned at him, moved by his unflagging support.

"Heck, yeah. If you need help, I'm your man. I told you this stuff doesn't bother me."

But it bothered Navya, who flushed and turned away, hurrying back to her machine.

"We're on track to be ready. And we're just packaging them in plain wrappers. Navya and her team will name their product line and design a wrapper once we have a few more people. Unless you just want to choose, Navya."

The younger woman shook her head, refusing to look up from her work. But she hadn't replaced her veil, which Olivia counted as a win.

"Later then. And thank you for the offer of help!"

"I'll bring the car when you're ready to move the samples to the school. Anything you need, just let me know."

If only he could produce another six to eight women eager to work with Navya. Alas, that was not going to happen. But maybe the meeting would help. She could only hope.

Chapter Twenty-Nine

Olivia wrung her hands as she checked for the fifth time that everything was ready for the presentation. She needed this to work. She didn't know what else to do if it didn't. She glanced at the door yet again. At this rate, she'd be speaking to an empty room. Well, Navya would do most of the talking. They'd decided that would be best and rehearsed and rehearsed what she would say. The information would be better received from another local woman, she knew.

The other teachers clustered at a table with Mukesh, on hand in case she needed anything, mostly there for moral support. Chris, Noah, and Jack had agreed to leave as soon as the presentation began, to ensure the women would be as comfortable as possible discussing the completely taboo subject.

The minute hand drew closer to the hour, and her stomach sank. She'd worried attendance would be low but assumed a few women would come, even if only out of sheer curiosity. Apparently, she had gotten even that wrong. Noah and Jack leaned against a wall, chatting, cameras in hand, ready to record for their documentary until they left. Emma would handle recording the presentation.

Noah glanced at his watch and shrugged at her. "Sorry, love."

Chris blanched. Startled? Disappointed no one showed up? Ready to throttle Noah for his insistence on calling her "love"? She could understand any of those responses.

She turned to apologize to Navya and Mukesh, when soft voices and the shuffling of feet sounded from the courtyard. She crossed to the door and peered outside. Ms. Vanya and Mrs. Gupta led a mob of women, many carrying babies or holding toddlers' hands or both. They streamed toward the door, the serpentine group stretching all the way out to the street.

Emma walked backward, recording the progress as they made their way.

"I'll be blowed," Jack said.

"Bloody hell!" Noah swung his camera to his face and began to record. "They did it."

"Remember, you're supposed to be invisible," she reminded him.

"Right, love." He backed into a corner out of sight just as the first of the women reached the door and peered in tentatively.

"Come in! Come in!" Olivia encouraged.

Ms. Vanya slithered through the hesitant bodies and popped into the space, her smile and enthusiasm filling the room with new energy. Olivia swore the room got brighter while the woman guided and encouraged them all to come inside.

She nudged Navya. "Go ahead."

How had they managed it? The women continued to stream in, and she gladly slunk into the background, happy to let the Indian women take command. They sat at small tables, in chairs they dwarfed, until all the seats were filled, and then they sat on the floor.

Only when everyone had settled and no more bodies squeezed inside did Olivia move to the front to begin. "Thank you all so much for coming. I've spoken with a lot of you in town. I teach here at the school. Probably teach some of your children. We invited you here so Navya can talk to you about an opportunity. We're working with this gentleman, Mukesh, who invented a machine designed to help his wife and mother." She left out the parts about his town believing he'd been possessed by demons and his wife and mother leaving him.

Mrs. Gupta jumped in during the pause and spoke in another language, presumably translating her words into something they could understand. Good grief, she hadn't even considered how many of these women might not speak English. Thank goodness the older woman had and could interpret for her.

Mukesh addressed the crowd in their native tongue as well. She couldn't understand but didn't need to. She had all the information she needed already. Besides, she could enjoy Mukesh speaking without understanding his words. He gestured a few times and mimed wrapping something up. Hesitant giggles erupted from the group, which broke the ice and relieved some of the tension vibrating through the space. He always set her at ease and made her laugh with his quick wit and humor. She was not surprised he'd cracked a joke so much as she was to see the stoic, standoffish women break into laughter.

After Mukesh excused himself and disappeared out the door, taking the other guys with him, Olivia nodded to Navya. The young woman moved to the center of the room where she could address everyone. She unfastened the edges of her veil and lowered it, exposing her scarred face. Olivia sucked in a breath along with many others present. She had not suggested or encouraged Navya to do this. It wasn't part of their practiced speech. But she couldn't deny the young woman had captured her audience's attention.

Navya took a deep breath. "My husband did this to me. And he hurt my baby. My baby sees a doctor now because Olivia arranged. Maybe she will use her arm again. My baby and I are safe now, but how can I take care of us? My uncle and my mother take care of us, but when they are no more, what will I do? I could not get a job, but now I have a job. Mukesh brought his machine to help us all."

Olivia watched the rapt expressions, saw sympathy and understanding, and knew she'd been correct to have Navya lead the presentation. They could identify on a level and connect in a way a foreigner could not. Once she had grabbed their attention, Navya shifted into the material Olivia had prepared with her, driving home the health statistics and the risks to all of them that the pad machine would eradicate.

"Sisters," Navya said, "we deserve better. Let me show you."

On cue, Olivia brought forward a plastic tub, cloth strips, two pads, and a pitcher of water. She placed everything in the center of the room and encouraged all the participants to gather in close.

"When we use cloth," Navya said, "we must stay home because the bleeding can go everywhere. It is messy and the cloth stains and we must clean the best we can. But sometimes we cannot clean well."

Olivia held a wad of cloth strips in her hand and poured water over them, which of course rushed off into the plastic tub, splattering everywhere. The water saturated the fabric almost immediately. She squeezed the cloth and water pressed out between her fingers, dripping into the tub.

"But most women have no choice. Napkins are expensive. And even if we can buy napkins at the market, they can be messy."

Olivia repeated the demonstration but using a pad from her purchase at the pharmacy. Water spilled from the sides of the thick, bulky thing. And when she squeezed, water leaked from it. "Better, but still not great if it leaks all over your clothes."

"With the new machine, we make our own pads. They will be much cheaper, they are easy to wear, and you can move in them without leaks. They are made here, by your neighbors and sisters. When you buy, you get good napkins, and your neighbors and sisters get good jobs."

She poured water over a pad made by the new machine. The top layer grabbed the liquid and pulled it to the absorbent core. When it was fully soaked, she squeezed, and no water escaped. The gasps that escaped the women watching her were exactly what they'd hoped for. Murmurs followed. For the first time in weeks, Olivia allowed herself a glimmer of hope. Maybe they could pull this off after all.

Navya raised her voice to be heard over the hubbub. "Sisters, I will tell you, it is my time, and I cannot tell. I use the napkins I make and I can go to the market, I can get water, I can work." She turned around and showed her clean britches with no evidence of her time of the month. "With these napkins, I cannot tell. You cannot tell. No one can tell when it is your time." She took the veil off her head. "I do not have to hide."

That last bit they had not practiced. Navya turned around and looked to her. She smiled and nodded. The young woman had exceeded her hopes. Completely nailed it. A moment of utter silence worried her though. What were they all thinking?

The women nearest Navya reached toward her, hand open to accept a sample pad, ready to try. The other teachers joined them and helped distribute sample pads to every woman present.

In the midst of the excitement, the thrill of finally making progress and seeing light at the end of the tunnel, she glanced at the door. Aditi's father stood there, scowl on his face. Every time she saw him, he scowled, so at this point she couldn't be sure if a permanent scowl chiseled his features or if he reacted that way specifically to her. She found it difficult to imagine a smile on his face though. Now what did he want? This was for women only, and they'd made that abundantly clear. Why had he intruded and how much had he heard? And why did whatever he'd overheard appear to anger him?

Aditi's mother reached for a pad. Olivia tore her gaze away from the door and pressed a second pad into her hands. "For Aditi." The woman hesitated a moment before closing her fingers around it and nodding vigorously. The pads disappeared some-where inside the folds of her clothing. Though the need to hide pads infuriated her, Olivia knew her fury would change nothing. These women would adapt to change the way circumstances required and that was the best she could hope for. If it meant surreptitious use of their product, so be it.

Meena and her mother hovered nearby, remaining close even after accepting pads. They seemed reluctant to approach her directly, so Olivia invited them. "Yes?"

Meena's mother pushed her forward. "She will work."

Startled, and not certain she understood correctly, she looked to Meena. The woman's face fought to suppress a smile, but her eyes danced with delight. Though that told her everything she needed to know, she asked for clarification. Just to be sure. "You can work? You can come work with us?"

Meena nodded.

"But your dad?"

Meena's mother wobbled her head. "She can work."

Apparently Meena's mother had made the impossible happen. Olivia had her second employee.

The sound of a man's raised voice cut through the noisy banter of many excited children. Olivia and the other teachers attempted to separate the middle- and high-school-age children from the younger group, the girls from the boys, and those with permission slips from those without. You'd think they were heading out on an exciting fieldtrip from the cacophony and general carnival atmosphere. Apparently, any deviation from an established schedule could rile up children. Diwali crept closer and closer, and the impending holiday probably didn't help.

The children were in for a shock, she feared, as today was the day of the personal hygiene presentations for the students old enough to attend and who'd received permission—not only for the talk itself but also to be recorded and potentially appear in a documentary. Noah went crazy at the thought of including the children's reactions. Mrs. Gupta had agreed, with the one stipulation that the parents must agree in writing. Olivia remembered her own awkward experience in elementary school, sitting completely still with her fellow classmates, uncomfortably listening as the school nurse had them all make a fist and explained their uteruses were all approximately the size of their fist. Not their neighbor's fist. Their own fist.

What a perfect analogy, she thought, that illustrated every woman was unique with her own set of issues and talents and shouldn't compare herself to her neighbor.

But now in the midst of this craziness, an angry male voice grabbed her attention and startled her. Though the sound quickened her heartbeat and soured her stomach, she negotiated a path through the children, following the heated exchange to Mrs. Gupta's office. She saw a man in the office, and every instinct in her body told her to go hide in her classroom. Frustrated that an angry man could still affect her on such a physiological level, she took a deep breath and refused to turn away.

Mrs. Gupta sat at her desk, arms crossed, as Aditi's father railed at her. Mrs. Gupta caught sight of her, drawing his attention to the newcomer in the doorway.

He spun and turned his ire on her. "You have done this! You confuse our women and now you will corrupt our children."

"Confuse them? How have I confused anyone?"

"They talk of things we do not speak of. You wish to share our private things with foreigners and strangers."

"Private things? Menstruation is as normal as using the toilet. Why should women be ostracized from society for a normal function of our bodies? We only want to keep your women healthy."

"You tell them to work. Teach them to leave the husbands and take control."

"I haven't told anyone to leave their husband. Navya left hers before I arrived in India, and with the help of her uncle who feared for her life. Meena never had a husband. How do you expect women with no husbands to provide for themselves? Do you wish them to starve to death?"

"They have fathers and uncles."

Her blood began to boil. Who did this man think he was? "For now. They won't always. And what happens to women who have no male relatives? You would see them starve to death? And their children? How should Navya support her daughter?"

"I won't let you corrupt the children! I forbid it!"

He forbid it? Could he do that? She glanced at Mrs. Gupta, silently asking the question. The woman responded with a slight sideways jerk of her head, which Olivia could not interpret, but she didn't appear the least bit alarmed or upset.

"You can't forbid us from doing anything. You don't even have children at this school. If you did, you could refuse for your children, and your children only, to attend this presentation but no one else's. We have segregated the children who did not return a permission slip for whatever reason, but you do not get to stop us from teaching the other children."

She had never talked back to a man, but this seemed like a good time to start. Adrenaline coursed through her, prompting a panic that spiked her heartrate and told her to run. But she stood her ground. She cut a glance to Mrs. Gupta again, afraid she had perhaps said too much. The school mistress's countenance hadn't changed. If anything, she seemed to be trying to suppress amusement.

"I will stop you!" the man insisted. "I will not allow you to change anything."

She crossed her arms and frowned at him. "Why would you want things to stay the same? Is that what you want for your daughters? For Aditi? Do you want to risk her health? Watch her develop a terrible infection that could take her life or leave her unable to have children? Why would you want that?"

"I will stop you. You will see. The other men in the town are with me."

She didn't think he listened to her. "You should hope nothing ever happens to you. Your wife and daughters would be left with no way to survive other than begging. You better hope they never need to support themselves in the world you're determined to maintain." She felt a glimmer of victory at the shocked look on his face. "Aditi could be a doctor someday if you would allow her to return to school. And then you'd never have to worry about her. But have it your way. Leave her at home, uneducated, at the whim of a husband who may beat and disfigure her. You're right, that's much better."

She nodded to Mrs. Gupta, turned, and left the office before he could see how badly her hands trembled. How dare he? Who did he think he was? And now she had images of a cowering Aditi, helpless to defend herself against an abusive husband, playing through her thoughts. Great. Tears pooled in her eyes. She wanted to shake some sense into that man but knew she had already overstepped her bounds, just by talking back to him.

She stalked down the hallway, breathing deeply and focusing on slowing her racing pulse, to the room where the other teachers had wrangled all the girls. This would not do. She could not get upset every time she became embroiled in a disagreement with a man.

She bumped into Meena in the hallway, a secret they'd kept under wraps for the children—their former teacher would present to them today. Mukesh and Navya had trained Meena completely at their tiny shop. Not surprising to anyone, the young woman picked it right up and mastered the tasks in no time. Olivia could see a marked change in Meena's countenance too. Finally, the young woman had something productive to think about and focus on instead of the endless years ahead of her without the man she loved and their baby. Olivia still secretly and fervently hoped that Meena would one day make enough money to run off with the man and be able to live her own life.

"Are you ready?" she asked.

Meena nodded. Olivia situated her out of sight, went inside the room, and nodded to Tisha, who stood at the front.

"Okay, ladies, everyone calm down. Quiet, please. We have a surprise for you today. A guest teacher is here to talk with you."

Everyone had agreed that this information needed to come from a trusted source, someone familiar to the children, an Indian woman from their own town. Meena was the best choice, hands down. Thank goodness her mother had managed to convince her father to allow her to work.

The class quieted and Tisha gestured to the door. Emma swung the camera to capture the entrance, and then panned over the desks to record the girls' reactions. Most of them gasped as their faces broke into wide smiles. A few of the youngest in the group jumped from their chairs and ran to hug their former teacher. Olivia shared a look with Tisha and the other teachers. Yes, Meena had been the perfect choice for this.

Once everyone settled again, Meena began. "Today we are going to talk about something we do not normally talk about. But it is okay for us to talk about it. How many of you have heard of periods or your menstrual cycle?"

The older, high-school age girls broke into embarrassed grimaces, then pulled their lips in to stop smiling. They stared up at the ceiling or down at their desks. No one would look at the teacher anymore. Some of the younger girls reacted in much the same way, but a large number of them appeared baffled and looked to their older counterparts, observing their responses.

Those younger girls would be right on the cusp of starting their periods and were completely clueless. As uncomfortable as her own personal hygiene experience had been in elementary school, at least she had some instruction. And her mother had made sure to speak with her prior to "the talk" at school. She could only imagine how shocked and mortified these little girls must be when they started bleeding for no apparent reason, at least in their minds. What a horrible introduction to their cycle. They must suspect they were sick or dying. She was glad Meena would prepare them today, glad Mrs. Gupta had agreed, and glad for the parents who had given permission. Perhaps things could slowly start to change.

Chapter Thirty

The email from her mother struck Olivia with guilt.

I haven't heard from you in quite some time. Please let me know you're okay.

Every time she sat at her computer, she intended to send an email detailing everything keeping her busy. But between preparing for class, staying caught up with tutoring, checking on Navya and Meena at the building, and continuing to make the rounds through town, reaching out to women they still hadn't spoken with, spreading the word and encouraging women to seek better options for their health, the email always seemed to get pushed to the backburner.

She clicked REPLY and began sharing all the things she did every day, plus how her little project was the subject of a documentary that could very well be seen all over the world. She described how Noah had shared a few clips of recorded footage with news outlets back home, no doubt hoping to create some buzz for his documentary before he even finished filming it. His efforts paid off at least a little. He'd mentioned a few news sources picked it up and ran stories. The film students wouldn't stay much longer, but had decided to remain at least through Diwali, since the beautiful festival would add gorgeous images to their short film.

Noah periodically dropped not-too-subtle hints that he really wanted to close on a happy ending and be able to share this as a success story. Did he honestly think she wasn't already doing everything she possibly could? The man's ego and completely self-absorbed nature rubbed her so far the wrong way, she was embarrassed she'd ever considered him attractive. Exactly the way she was starting to feel about Scott.

Noah also had heard about the mysterious red rain and frequently voiced the opinion that he would really like to capture that phenomenon while he was here. "What a great addition to the documentary that would be," he mused.

Olivia disagreed and had no interest in experiencing that ever again, despite Aubra's assurances that her lab intern friend had let her know the rain was harmless. Though still not able to identify the compound or explain why the rain was red, Aubra insisted that if he said it was harmless, then it was. Olivia didn't mention the bizarre rainstorm to her mother, not sure she believed the "unknown but harmless" rationale.

Trying to describe Diwali to her mother when she hadn't even experienced it yet herself left her staring at the screen, searching for the right words. Someone knocked on her door.

She opened it to reveal not someone but several someones—all the teachers plus Emma congregated in the hallway.

"Code red," Melanie said. "We are so far behind in Diwali preparations, we've declared a state of emergency."

"Emergency shopping trip!" Delilah said.

"We need Diwali craft supplies," Tisha said. "If we don't have the kids make their *diyas* soon, we won't have time to have them fired at the kiln."

Olivia glanced back at her computer. "I have so much work still waiting for me. I don't think I can go. I'll send some rupees with you and you can pick up—"

"All work and no play makes Jane a dull girl," Delilah said.

"But I need to—"

"Nope," Tisha said. "We insist. Delilah is right. You stay cooped up in here working far too much lately. Even when you're out and about, it's for work. Come shop. It's technically also work-related, but we will force you to have fun too."

She could see they wouldn't take no for an answer. "I'll get my shoes." She saved the email draft and made a mental note to be sure to finish and send it tonight. Mom would be asleep right now anyway, since it was the middle of the night on the other side of the globe.

Chris met them in the courtyard.

"No other guys today?" She stared past him to see if Noah and Jack followed him from the dorm.

Emma held up empty hands. "No, they're reviewing what we've recorded so far. Noah wants to ensure we have a solid arc. We don't need more random market footage. I just want to go shop."

"Good. We can all relax." Olivia had discovered the constant presence of cameras made her anxious and guarded, constantly re-evaluating any words before she spoke and acutely aware of her physical presence. In the footage of herself she'd seen, she fidgeted, shuffled back and forth, crossed and uncrossed her arms. And Noah seemed to find any possible excuse to turn the camera on her and zoom in on her face. It struck her as a little creepy.

Emma squeezed into the already-crowded back seat of their little car, nearly perching on Aubra's lap, and reassured Chris she was fine. "It's a short drive. Just go."

"How did the personal hygiene presentation go with the girls?" Chris asked after he pulled into the street.

"Eye opening to say the least," she answered. "Meena kept things factual and straightforward. She mentioned babies but not sex. The girls still wouldn't answer her questions, though. Just stared in their laps."

"Mukesh handled the boys the same way," Chris said. "He told them why education is so important. He shared he didn't learn about menstruation until his thirties. Some of the boys did attempt to answer questions. Hesitant and embarrassed, but they tried to guess. One of my upper-level boys said he'd heard menstruation is a sickness that only women can catch. That really shocked me. The lack of education is appalling." He glanced at her. "I supported you at every step, even when I doubted you could pull it off. But we have to pull it off. If you change only one life, it will be worth it."

Sure her face pinked with pleasure, she smiled at him but said nothing. What could she say? She hoped the look in her eyes sufficiently conveyed the eruption of gratitude she felt. No way could she form words to adequately express what his support and encouragement meant to her. Had any man ever treated her this way? His gentle but steely kindness trickled over her aching soul like water soothing parched ground.

"The children were shocked, no doubt," Tisha said, "but imagine how much greater the shock to start bleeding and have no idea why."

"Or the shock when someone hands you the *Kama Sutra* on your wedding night without a word, just leaves you to figure it out for yourselves."

"No way," Melanie said. "Get out of here."

"Happened to Mukesh and his wife," Chris said, shaking his head.

Aubra leaned forward. "It's less likely to happen in big cities, of course, and Mukesh is a bit older than us. Attitudes are slowly changing. Still, it happens, particularly in the most remote areas."

"Maybe eventually we could attempt some sex education," Tisha said. "Though not in front of cameras and only for the eldest students."

"Parents will argue we will be instructing them and encouraging it," Aubra said.

"To be expected," Tisha said. "That's true back home in the States, too, particularly when birth control methods are included."

"Meena and her beau figured it out, even with no talk and no instruction," Delilah said. "Look how that turned out."

They rode in silence the rest of the way. Olivia didn't know what to do with this new bit of information and tried to imagine the shock on a wedding night if this wholly new expectation got sprung on you.

At the market, they were delighted to find prolific Diwali decorations and supplies everywhere. They bought bags and bags of vividly colored sand for *rangoli*, plus chalk so the children could make their own. They loaded up on bright paper the children could fold into flowers. They picked up pounds and pounds of clay for the *diyas* they would make. Battery-operated tea lights proved a bit more challenging but eventually they found enough of them that each student would be able to light their *diya*.

Olivia noticed some glances as they shopped but thought nothing of it. She'd become accustomed to the attention and odd looks foreigners attracted. But when they walked past the news-stand—the place where she'd attempted to stay abreast of the mysterious red rain—her own face stared back at her from the front page of some of the papers. A photo of Mukesh ran alongside.

"What in the world?" She lifted a copy and read the accompanying article.

NAPKIN DESIGNED BY INDIAN MAN REVOLU-TIONIZING INDIA

She bought one of each paper and stood reading the article. The article highlighted the documentary and her struggle to bring the pad machine to and win acceptance from the small town, but also discussed Mukesh and his inventions, both the affordable pad as well as the machine to make them.

Aubra took a paper and skimmed the article. "This is similar to the articles Noah ran back home. He issued a press release and it got picked up by several outlets. In fact, this is so similar I'd say it was more or less lifted from British papers."

"Like this? With my photo?"

"Oh, yes. It's promotional. Noah received some donations, too. That will help complete his project once he gets back home."

"Funny. He didn't mention donations to me." Olivia pressed her lips together to refrain from speaking the choice words she'd love to say about Noah. It was all about him. Everything. He didn't come to India to help anyone but himself. He only supported her project as a means to an end for his documentary. And he used her image to help market and promote himself, to gain accolades for being a great guy focused on women's issues when he hadn't contributed to the project in any way.

"The publicity helps you too," Aubra said.

"It hasn't yet. I won't make a penny from this project. Nothing. Noah is literally profiting off Mukesh's work."

She closed her mouth before she said anything more. Aubra constantly vied for Noah's attention. She had no trouble imagining Aubra racing off to tell Noah what she'd said about him.

Chris rubbed at the back of his neck. "I was thinking maybe we could go by the jewelry store again."

"Do you need something to make you feel pretty?" Delilah teased him.

"Actually, I think Olivia should look at that pink opal again. I can't stop thinking about it. Seems like it's here in this little town just for her."

They all turned to look at her. She didn't feel the same shock at the suggestion that she'd felt before. "Well, if everyone wants to go . . ."

"I will always look at jewelry," Melanie said.

"Maybe Chris needs something for his birthday," Aubra suggested. "That's next week."

"Next week? You didn't tell us!" Delilah said. "I wonder if Ms. Vanya can bake a cake."

"No, I don't need anything," he insisted. "But maybe Olivia can size her ring finger."

Her thumb ran over the empty finger at the mention of it. The last time she'd been sized for a ring, Scott had just proposed, and the ring slid all over her finger, threatening to fall off. "I suppose it doesn't hurt to look."

Remembering Scott's proposal sent her down the rabbit hole again, wandering back through her memories, gathering pieces, attempting to puzzle together what had happened. Why had he even proposed? They'd met at a faculty function, when she'd been adjuncting at the university where he'd landed a coveted full-time, tenure-track position. He was older than her and held a PhD to her master's. She knew a community college would offer a more likely chance of permanent employment for her. Still, that first meeting, they'd been the only two singles in the room and naturally gravitated to each other. He'd been charming on top of attractive, his blue eyes nearly electric as he leaned close and spoke in her ear to be heard over the general din. She swore a spark had crackled the air around them, the chemistry so immediate and intense. They'd been convinced it was kismet, meant to be.

Only after they'd married, probably much too quickly, and cohabitated did he begin picking at her incessantly, criticizing her in the most insidious ways. Thinking back, she saw that it started slowly, chipping away at her confidence and her sense of self, but then snowballed until he took control of everything. Always he had a rationalization for his behavior, and always he couched it as for the best. He was "helping" her or "protecting" her. He isolated her to keep others from hearing about and commenting on the situation. She heard Tisha's voice asking her again if she was sure her husband wasn't abusive. And it took coming all the way to India and spending time with a gentle soul like Chris for her to recognize it.

She'd been married to an abusive, controlling, emotionally manipulative man who had made himself feel better by tearing her down.

As she shook her thoughts from the past, not sure what to do with this revelation, she noticed three young women followed them through the market as they continued to shop. When they crept closer, Olivia recognized them from speaking to them before. One of them was the young woman who had dashed back and grabbed a pad. They continued to follow and watch the group of teachers but seemed unwilling to speak.

Olivia smiled and invited conversation. "Hi. Did you need something?"

The women threw furtive glances around the street. "We . . . we buy napkin?"

Her jaw fell. "You want to buy some?"

All three nodded, not only the woman who had spoken. Judging by their surreptitious demeanors, you'd think they were attempting to initiate a drug deal.

"Okay! Yes. The girls haven't designed official packaging yet, but—yes!" No way would she turn down paying customers. Customers had eluded them for so long, she had all but given up on the idea. Why hadn't they made sales routes and distribution a higher priority? And why hadn't Navya chosen a name for the product line? Of course, she knew the answer to that—Navya wanted it to be a group decision, not hers alone. And they still lacked an entire team of workers. "Can you go by the building to buy them? Anytime during the week."

The young women nodded and went their own way.

"Chris, you were right. Judging by how awkward and uncomfortable those women were, having the shop set up away from the main market is way better. I need to have the girls start thinking about sales routes though. How can things move so quickly and so slowly at the same time?"

Tisha smiled and hugged her. "Relax. It will all come together. This is a major turning point. You just got your first customers. Let's go celebrate by looking at jewelry."

Olivia could not wait for classes to end. She wanted to go by and check in with Navya and Meena. A few more women had approached them about purchasing pads, and she wanted to make sure they didn't have any trouble with the sales. They planned to map out door-to-door sales routes to make buying pads as easy as possible. That way, women wouldn't have to come to them.

The newspaper articles seemed to legitimize the business somewhat. She grudgingly had to admit Aubra had been correct. The publicity was helping indirectly. Noah had sent an interview of Mukesh to news stations and reported it had made it onto the news. That would benefit Mukesh. In fact, they needed to finish up here and let him move on. The attention had sparked interest in additional interviews and additional sales. She would miss Mukesh horribly, but she'd known he wouldn't stay forever. Knowing more small towns needed him to install machines made her feel a bit better about him leaving. After all, that was the point. This was a good thing. If only she could convince more women to work.

Ms. Vanya and the other teachers went with her to the building to check on Navya and Meena. This time the film crew followed them, documenting the slow acceptance as women opted to use the pads. The two young women met them on foot, headed to the school to find them, faces stricken. Navya spoke to her mother in their native language, Jaanvi balanced on one hip. Olivia didn't understand a word, but Ms. Vanya gathered her skirt and hurried after her daughter. She quickened her pace, heart thumping. What had happened?

The moment she reached the gap in the wall, her stomach dropped. She stepped back, as if punched in the gut, and sucked in a breath.

Her beautiful little building had been vandalized, words and symbols she couldn't read spray-painted all over the exterior walls. She was afraid to look inside. Had the machine been torn up? What if all the work had been for nothing?

Chris's hands drifted to his head. They all stood speechless, while Noah and his crew recorded every moment of their complete shock and devastation.

Then she thought about the two women. "Are you two okay? Were you here? Did someone threaten you? What happened?"

Navya tossed her head. "We went home to lunch. When we came back . . ."

They moved closer to the building, jagged, dripping letters scarring the once-pristine yellow walls.

Mukesh attempted to comfort her. "The door is locked. No windows broken. We can paint over harsh words. Inside is still okay."

"Is it?" She wouldn't believe it until she saw with her own eyes.

Navya unlocked the door. Sure enough, the interior was unharmed, the machine untouched. She breathed deeply. The hateful gesture hurt, but it could have been so much worse.

"What does the writing say?" she asked.

"Madam, be glad you cannot read."

"That bad, huh?"

Ms. Vanya wrung her hands. Navya and Meena were clearly shaken. She looked around for some way to hearten them but fell short. She didn't know what to do or say to encourage them in the face of such ugliness.

Chris picked up a can of paint left over after the men had finished painting as well as a brush. Olivia had intended to do something with the supplies but could never figure out what to do with them, so they still sat where they'd been left. Silently, Chris carried the can and brush outside, popped the top, dipped in the brush, and dragged the bristles over the graffiti.

They had a total of four brushes, but everyone joined in, taking turns to repaint the building yet again. Her stomach still churned, but at least this way she had something to keep her hands busy.

Mukesh stood by her after they finished one wall and moved to another. "It is nearly Diwali. And to prepare we clean.

We will start fresh again. Knowledge will triumph over ignorance."

He meant well and she appreciated his positive spin and attempt to calm nerves. But she couldn't bring herself to believe him.

The sound of a scooter stopping outside the cinder-block wall startled them all to stillness. Had the perpetrators returned? Back to wreak more damage? At least they could face them down as a large group this time, though she worried what they would do if things turned violent.

Aditi's father appeared in the gap in the wall and stopped suddenly. He appeared startled by the large group clustered around the building. Of course. Of course it had been him. And now that he was outnumbered, he didn't know what to do. Fury, the likes of which she'd never felt before, churned in her stomach. Heat infused her, and it had nothing to do with the sun beating down on them.

She fisted her hands and went to meet him face to face.

"Olivia," Chris cautioned.

But she didn't listen. Men who skulked around in secret, tearing down the good others tried to accomplish, holding women down, strangling the life out of them—she couldn't take it anymore. She may be a guest in this country, but Navya and Meena and Ms. Vanya and countless others like them cried out for help. Enough was enough.

"Did you do this?" she yelled before she even reached him, pointing behind her at the building.

He held up his hands, as if in surrender. "Please."

Please? Not the reaction she expected. She stood directly in front of him and realized he looked different. Shaken. Upset. But for once not angry.

"I . . . need your help."

Totally baffled, unsure what to do with her mounting rage in the face of this bizarre turn, she simply stood and waited for an explanation.

Aditi's father gestured behind him. A woman joined him, her lip bleeding and swollen, her eye a sickening green-black color. She gasped and brought her hands to her mouth. "What happened?"

"My sister." He placed an arm around the woman's waist and guided her into Olivia's arms, which stretched out to receive the battered woman without a conscious thought to do so. "Her husband—"

Aditi's father appeared ready to break down. He couldn't finish the sentence, but Olivia had no problem discerning what had happened. She hugged the woman fiercely. "Let's get you cleaned up and find some ice for your lip."

The woman, Aditi's aunt, shuddered against her.

He met her gaze. "You will help?"

No hesitation. "We will help."

His mouth pursed, and he seemed to struggle, grappling silently with something. "She can work for you?"

Olivia nearly cried. "Yes, yes, of course she can work with us. Of course."

He pulled a wad of rupees from his pocket and urged them into her hand.

"No. I don't need your money."

"You will take." He glanced at the building. He had not denied involvement but hadn't admitted to it either. "For my sister. You will keep her safe?"

"We've got her."

"I will speak with the other men. And then I will go see her husband." The man's jaw set, and the black look in his eyes left no doubt his brother-in-law would deeply regret lashing out and hurting his wife.

The scooter fired up, and he left for his errand. She led the woman back to the others, who all welcomed her with open arms and comforted her.

Mukesh stood beside her while Ms. Vanya took their newest addition inside to clean her up. "You see? When you shed a light on a problem, people can learn. Someday I hope all India napkin using. But we can only take one step at a time. This was a good step."

She never would have believed Aditi's father could turn such an about-face. When she'd challenged him to imagine his wife or daughter in this predicament, he'd been unable to fathom it. Now he didn't have to imagine. His sister's abuse at the hands of her husband drove the point home as Olivia never could have.

Chapter Thirty-One

M s. Vanya, Navya, and Meena explained the celebration of Diwali to Olivia as best they could to someone who had never experienced it. The Festival of Lights spanned five days, not just one. Christian Americans didn't celebrate a comparable holiday, though as they described the customs of cleaning on the first day, purification and prayers, visiting family and friends, giving gifts, strengthening family bonds, sharing sweets, and setting off fireworks, she thought it sounded rather like Christmas, Halloween, and the Fourth of July all rolled into one holiday.

The day before the holiday arrived and brought with it giggling, rambunctious classes of students. The teachers distributed cleaner and cloth rags and put all the excess energy to good use.

"Clean out your desks," Olivia instructed, knowing almost nothing was stored in the desks from one class to another. "When we finish, we will light the *diyas*!"

Squeals preceded a new burst of rigorous scrubbing. Once finished, she returned each student's clay *diya*, which she agreed did rather resemble a tiny genie's lantern with no top on it. She passed out tea lights and allowed them to flip the lights on and enjoy the flickering glow while writing about their favorite Diwali tradition or memory or food or whatever. The assignment was meant to keep them busy, so she didn't care what they wrote about. After today, they would be home on holiday with their families.

At recess, each student drew a chalk *rangoli*, truly impressing her with their creativity and artistic talent. Each round work of art was filled with swooping swirls and delicate flower petal designs. She would miss these kids when she left.

After dinner that night, the teachers adjourned into the courtyard and switched on the strands of lights they'd strung. In the dusky haze of the setting sun, they twinkled, absolutely beautiful.

Chris had not exaggerated Ms. Vanya's ability to create breathtakingly ornate *rangoli*. Gorgeous red and orange swirls intertwined in her circular patterns. Ms. Vanya stepped outside with oil-filled *diyas*, placed them around the *rangoli*, and lit them. Magical. Olivia felt transported to a fairy realm.

"Want to make one?" Chris asked. "It's fun."

"I'm no good at art. I hate to spoil the effect."

"Don't be silly. We're all making one and who cares if they're not the best *rangoli* ever? Come on." He retrieved the bags of sand.

Everyone spread out, choosing a spot in the courtyard to draw. She knelt down and breathed deeply, clearing her mind, then reached for a bag of yellow sand. She formed a circle, the base of the other *rangoli* she'd seen. Ms. Vanya and the children had filled theirs with flower and leaf motifs, swirls and curlicues. But as she stared at her yellow disc, she could think of only one thing she wanted on top of hers.

Tears pricking her eyes, she selected a bag of pastel pink sand and wrote in her best script *Lucy*. She reached for bag after bag, adding purple curlicues, orange polka dots, and green swirls, giving tribute to the lost life, swiping at the tears she couldn't control, lest they drip onto her artwork and ruin it.

When she finished, she stared at her handiwork and remembered her sweet little one. A soft moan escaped her lips, rising in pitch until she sobbed, breath rasping in huge, uneven gasps.

Chris knelt beside her and placed a hand on her back, rubbing gently. "Lucy. Your daughter's name?"

Unable to speak, she sucked in another ragged breath and nodded.

"You're right. It *is* beautiful."

He sat, silent witness to her raw grief, gut-wrenching pain she didn't know possible. When she doubled over, collapsing under the weight of it, he pulled her into his arms and propped her up. She stayed there, helpless to control her grief while he stroked her back.

"I'm so sorry," he crooned over and over. "It just isn't fair."

She didn't have enough strength to apologize for the unadulterated anguish, and for once she did not feel compelled to.

Tisha joined them, kneeling and holding her hand. "There you go. Let it all out. Finally."

Melanie, Delilah, and Aubra left their *rangoli* and surrounded her in a group hug.

When another set of feet joined them, she recognized Noah's stupid, red-splattered shoes he must have thought made him look artistic and cool. Great. She didn't look up but knew her emotional meltdown and personal trauma would be recorded and on display for the entire world to see.

Aubra leapt to her feet. "Get that camera out of here, Noah, before I smash it to the ground! This is personal and has nothing to do with the project. Show some decency." Then the young woman knelt directly in front of her, shielding her from view.

"Thank you," she managed, before choking on a fresh wave of sobs. She'd never felt so drained in her life.

Aubra squeezed her hand.

"We've got you," Chris murmured. "We've got you."

The third day of Diwali, the biggest day of celebration, stores closed and schools were not in session. Ms. Vanya had the day off, but the woman came to the school and cooked for her "kids" regardless, treating them to *samosas, gulab jamun,* and other new and exotic dishes she didn't know the names of. Olivia ate entirely too much, knowing she'd be eating all day as they walked through town visiting people and exchanging small gifts of food and sweets.

She practiced her deep breathing exercises, hoping to keep control of her emotions. October twenty-eighth. One year ago, she'd labored through childbirth and suffered the most devastating loss imaginable. She remembered how only a few months ago she had expected not to be able to function today. But she didn't want to miss this holiday. And she didn't want to push her friends away. Isolating herself, pushing the grief away, and trying to run from the pain turned out not to work. Still, even if things had taken a different turn than expected, she was glad she ran. Looking at all the smiling faces around her, thinking of all the people they'd call on and visit today, she was happy her path led her here. Her heart hurt. She would give anything to change the past and be able to have her daughter live. But nothing could change that. Her daughter was no more, her marriage had crumbled, and she would never be the same. She knew that. She could, however, reassemble the shattered pieces and move on. She could make the best of life. She could feel happy and shouldn't feel guilty about it. And she knew that if her daughter had lived, that's exactly what she would have wanted—her mother to be happy. She knew because she wanted her own mother to be happy. She wanted her mother to have the chance to be loved and cherished by someone who valued her. One tear slid down her cheek, but she swiped it away.

Ms. Vanya came through the swinging door again.

"I thought you went home to be with Navya and Jaanvi!" Olivia said.

Then she saw what Ms. Vanya carried in her hands: a little cake, decorated pink, a single candle glowing on top. She looked around the table again, at all the knowing faces. They were all in on it.

"Happy birthday to Lucy," Tisha said, her voice catching in her throat.

Chris sniffed and seemed a little misty-eyed too. "We couldn't let today go by without celebrating her life, even if it was far too short."

Tears blurred her vision, but she smiled through them. "You guys . . ."

"We know it's a sad day," Melanie said. "But we couldn't ignore it. It's too important."

"'I will not say do not weep, for not all tears are evil,'" Delilah said.

"*Return of the King*," Chris said. "Finally, a literary quote I recognize."

Delilah nodded. "It's true, though. Sometimes you have to cry. And now for my favorite three words—let's eat cake!"

While they ate yet more sugar, knowing full well there was much more to come, they asked her about the pregnancy, how she'd decorated the nursery, how long she'd been in labor. She described the first time she felt Lucy kick and how active she'd been. She threw wide the door to the secret closet in her mind and allowed everything she'd stuffed inside to come spilling out. She laughed. She cried. She shared it all. And she felt better. Not great. But better.

Chris slid a wrapped package toward her. "It's from all of us. Not just me. A birthday present for Lucy. And you."

"You guys shouldn't have done this!"

"We disagree," Tisha said.

"In all honesty, it was Chris's idea," Aubra said. "But we thought it brilliant."

She lifted each piece of tape gently, trying not to tear the paper one bit. She would keep it forever. A birthday cake and a birthday gift for Lucy—she never would have considered it. But perhaps every October twenty-eighth she would have a cupcake and remember the brief happy moment of watching her daughter suck in her first breath. She would remember the window of life, when she still believed with her whole heart that her little girl had a chance. And she would remember how these friends came together and helped her through her first October eighth. She would celebrate the day instead of dread it.

She pulled the wrapping paper away, revealing a wooden box decorated with a peacock and a little girl. "I love it. Thank you so much. It will match my peacock lamp."

"I thought so too," Chris said. "But the real gift is inside."

"Real gift? This is wonderful!" She rocked back the hinged lid and discovered a ring—a gold band set with the pink opal.

"Gold for the sun," Melanie said.

"And the pink opal for Lucy." She broke down, tears flowing freely. "Thank you. Thank you, really. It's the most beautiful mother's ring ever."

At the sound of footsteps clomping down the stairs, Olivia wiped away her tears and composed her features. She didn't want Noah to walk in on her crying again.

Mukesh joined them, though, not Noah. The always-cheerful man seemed even happier today. At their urging, he accepted a slice of cake. "Today is best Diwali ever."

"It's my first Diwali, but I agree with you," she said, unable to take her eyes off the ring.

"I have message from my wife. She saw me on TV and in newspaper. She asked if I have girlfriend."

"A girlfriend? You still call her your wife," Tisha said.

He placed a hand over his heart. "She is my only girl. I told her

I never had another girlfriend, and I never will. She asked to come home."

They erupted in cheers as her eyes pooled with tears yet again. Too much emotion today. She expected to be an emotional wreck, but this was proving to be too much. At least some of her tears were happy.

They cleared the dishes with Ms. Vanya, met up with the film crew, and started for town. But Ms. Vanya redirected them to the shop.

"But it's holiday," Aubra said.

"The girls cannot work today," she insisted.

"No work. Surprise," Ms. Vanya told them, eyes shining with the secret.

Five women waited for them—Navya, Mena, Aditi's aunt Rajana, and two women she didn't recognize.

"New recruits?"

Meena nodded. "We are halfway there."

"This is a wonderful surprise! You'll be fully staffed in no time."

"Surprise inside," Navya said. Jaanvi pitched forward, reaching for Olivia—with both arms.

"Her arm! She can use it? The doctor fixed it?"

Navya passed the toddler to her. "He fixed it."

"All better!" Ms. Vanya cried and hugged her.

"This is wonderful! Still not the surprise?"

Navya led her into the building and held out a blue package.

"Did you . . . design your wrapper?" She took in the sky-blue plastic with puffy white clouds. She turned it around so she could see the front panel. A yellow sun shone from one corner. The name Lucy shimmered across the sky in script, as if taking flight in a bid for freedom.

She pressed her empty hand to her eyes, fighting to stay in control and not have a meltdown. Not again. Not with Noah and Jack pointing cameras at her face. "This is beautiful."

The other teachers admired it as well and praised the women for their resourcefulness.

"Now even after you leave, your footprint will be here," Mukesh said.

"Just like Lucy's," Tisha added.

Finally, they headed into town, waving, chatting, stopping by homes for cups of *chai* and *gulab jamun*. Along the way, throughout the afternoon, young women met her gaze and gave her a knowing smile. The customer base was growing. One woman mimicked Navya from her presentation, spinning in a circle and declaring, "It is my time." Noah caught it all. He would get his happy ending.

At dusk, lights emerged all over town. *Diyas* flickered, light strands twinkled. And then the fireworks began. Children twirled sparklers as larger displays exploded in the air, shimmering cascades of vivid sparks above them.

In the center of town, near the edge of the market where she first met Mukesh, a crowd gathered, releasing sky lanterns. The thin paper lanterns, once lit, filled like miniature hot-air balloons, glowed softly yellow-orange, and floated into the sky. One after another, people lit them and sent them gliding into the air until a cluster of them lit the sky like a glowing cloud. Each light shone forth, dotting the sky with extra stars as they drifted away.

Chris opened a bag he'd been carrying and passed a lantern to each of them to light and release, to join the growing cluster of glowing yellow orbs already filling the sky above them. He saved Olivia for last.

"I made a slight modification to yours." He lifted it from the bag, and she saw that he had colored "Lucy" onto the lantern in pastel, along with beautiful scrolls and flowers—all shades of pink. Her eyes brimmed with tears.

"It's beautiful."

Someone tugged at her hand and she turned to discover Aditi at her side.

"Hello, Ms. Montag!"

She squatted and hugged the girl. Her father stood off to the side, staring at the growing cloud of lights hovering above them. He nodded to her. She beamed in return and waved to his wife and to Rajani, both holding Aditi's sisters.

He came closer. "You think Aditi can be doctor?"

"Absolutely. Your daughter is incredibly smart. If you would let her go to school, her future could be . . ." She turned and gestured to the sky. "Her future could be as bright as the sky. As infinite as the stars. She can do anything."

He nodded once more and seemed to consider her words, before he tipped his head and returned to his family. Aditi waved and skipped to rejoin them.

Tisha moved closer to her and admired her Lucy lamp. "Seems a shame to let it go when it's so beautiful. But I think maybe you ought to take your own advice."

Chris retrieved a lighter from the bag and each teacher sent a glowing lantern rising into the air. She watched them go, one after another, then sparked the lighter Chris handed her, lit the fuse, and watched the Lucy lamp fill with air and take flight, soaring into the sky.

Goodbye, little girl. I love you forever.

Chapter Thirty-Two

Olivia held her breath as one class shuffled out and she waited for the next class to come in. She opened a drawer in her desk and withdrew *The Chamber of Secrets*. Her thumb drifted to her ring finger, running over the opal ring where once she wore a wedding band. The familiar presence comforted her and reminded her not only of loss and pain but also hope and potential. And when she went home, it would be a constant reminder of everyone she met in India—Ms. Vanya, Navya, little Jaanvi, Meena, her co-teachers, plus all the women who used the pads her machine made. Not her machine anymore —their machine.

More women had taken jobs for her little company. Fully staffed, the machine now operated all day, every day, making pads for area women. Sales of the affordable product had increased to the point they could barely keep up with demand. As long as electricity stayed on, the machine ran. And once they had enough profit, Meena and Navya would consider a generator for days when power went out. Meena would also soon begin making trips to neighboring small communities, sharing their product and, hopefully, expanding sales even further.

Aditi came through the classroom door, and Olivia struggled

not to rush to hug her. She couldn't show favoritism, but each time one of her little girls returned to class, she fought the urge to turn cartwheels. And now here was Aditi. Her classes had slowly returned to normal, plus a few new girls had been enrolled in the past few weeks as well.

Some of the other students squealed with delight when they spotted Aditi. Once hugs and welcomes subsided, she described the class project for the day. Everyone would decorate a T-shirt with a superhero symbol, because they were all super and all heroes. Even the girls. She distributed supplies and oversaw the busy hum of happy painting.

She squatted in front of Aditi's desk and handed her the book. "Your father said it is okay."

"Thank you, Auntie." The beaming girl lit a warmth in her chest.

She stood and oversaw her studious class. Part of her didn't want to leave. She would carry all of them home with her in her heart. Maybe she would apply for an extension and stay. Then again, her mom sounded so lonely in the last email exchange. Whenever she returned, whether soon or after another six months teaching, she would encourage Mom to get involved with social groups. Maybe the two of them could continue to help with Mukesh's pad machine project from a distance. But Mom needed her own pursuits and interests too.

A loud booming crack shook the building and startled her from her thoughts. A shadow crept across the room as an odd reddish hue permeated the atmosphere. Loud droplets spattered the window, beating faster and faster until a downpour soaked the school. She ran to the window.

The red rain had returned.

The children, moments ago engrossed in their projects, jumped from their seats and dashed into the hallway. She followed after them, caught up in the excited crush. Children spilled from the doorway into the courtyard, bodies pouring out the door in two rivulets.

Her students clustered at the door, peering out, pressed close against her side. They looked to her, gauging her response.

Aditi grabbed her hand and squeezed. "It is my time, Ms. Montag."

Olivia looked into her wide worried eyes, smiled, and squeezed the girl's hand in return. "It is my time, too."

She looked down at Aishwarya, Lakshmi, Surithra, and all the other upturned faces, looking to her for guidance. She grabbed another hand and led the children out the doors, into the courtyard. Rain pelted down, drenching them in moments. The children all raised their hands in the air and laughed, and she followed along, twirling with them as her sandals squished in the mud and her *shalwar* soaked rust red. Chris caught her eye and gave her a thumbs up.

She didn't know what her future held. She didn't know how long she would be in India or what would happen when she returned home. She had no idea if she would marry again or if she would ever have children of her own or what job she would eventually settle into. All she knew was this moment, right now, surrounded by her students and the other teachers, with Chris's smile sending butterflies through her stomach, she was happy.

She grabbed her students' hands and danced in the red rain.

A note from the author

From July 25 through September 23, 2001, the state of Kerala in India experienced several instances of bizarre red rain. While several theories have been suggested to explain the phenomenon, scientists do not agree on an explanation despite years of testing and research. Initially, the particles were blamed on an exploding meteor, which would explain the loud boom heard by residents. Researchers later changed the theory when electron microscopy determined the particulates resembled spores, possibly produced by algae and/or fungi. A later theory suggested the strange event was due to dust from sandstorms. Another study cast doubt on the connection between the loud (possibly sonic) boom reported to have preceded the rainstorm while others determined the red particles as "extraterrestrial in origin." To this day, the rainstorms have not been definitively and satisfactorily explained.

Acknowledgments

Thank you to my sister, Elizabeth, for sharing her experiences teaching English overseas, which helped bring authenticity to my characters.

Thank you to my beta readers and early reviewers. Everyone who contributed to the development of this story made an impact. I appreciate the support more than I can ever tell you.

And of course thank you to my readers. As John Cheever said, "I can't write without a reader. It's precisely like a kiss—you can't do it alone." My story lives because you opened this book and went on an adventure with me. I hope we can travel together again soon.

Make a difference

Red Rain is a work of fiction, but based on real issues faced by women all over the world. We can all make a difference and support women in need. Through the hard work of volunteers and ambassadors for period poverty and menstrual justice, The Pad Project oversees drives and donations for women in need everywhere and places pad machines around the world to empower women in remote areas. If you're interested in learning more, visit:

https://thepadproject.org

About the Author

Lara Bernhardt is a Pushcart-nominated writer and editor. Twice a finalist for the Oklahoma Book Award for Best Fiction, she writes supernatural suspense and women's fiction. You can follow her on all the socials @larawells1 on Twitter and @larabern10 on Facebook, BookBub, and Instagram.

Sign up for more

Did you enjoy *Red Rain*? If so, please leave a review wherever you purchase books.

Sign up for Lara's newsletter to be the first to know of upcoming releases, chances for contests, and to receive previews and insider information http://larabernhardt.com/contact

Also by Lara Bernhardt

Women's fiction

Shadow of the Taj

Wantland Files series

The Wantland Files
The Haunting of Crescent Hotel
Ghosts of Guthrie
Halloween in Hannibal
Christmas Spirit

More by Admission Press

Looking for your next great read?
Visit www.admissionpress.com